# IRISH

## *Goodbye*

### IRISH WOLVES LEGACY

## ANNE GREGOR

## HUGH O'FAOLAIN

HUGH WAS on his way to a small airport with several personal hangars that housed planes and helicopters, a few miles outside Dublin. He kept his own plane there, but today he needed a helicopter. He knew the man who owned the helicopter charter business on site and arranged the ride and the pilot.

He and the boys were interested in a large tract of land they believed was a good investment for possible development in the future. Daniel, Jonathan, or even his daughter, Bébhinn, might use it one day to expand on one of their current businesses or to create something new. Regardless, Hugh wanted an aerial view before he made an offer.

He massaged his neck at a stoplight, cursing when he felt the tension threading into his shoulders and upper back.

"Damn it," he cursed. He knew why he was out of sorts. He and Rowan argued that morning, and they never argued—or rarely since he became prudent enough to choose his words more wisely.

Rowan was his second wife, the mother of his youngest child, and his entire world. He still couldn't believe he'd let her talk him into a relationship with a woman twenty-nine years his junior. But that was Row, the most stubborn human being to ever exist.

She told him she loved him, and he loved her, and that was the end of it. They'd been married for twenty years, and her stubbornness was still her best quality in his opinion.

He'd dreaded his sixties, and the thought of entering his seventies was paralyzing. When they both happened, as time stopped for no man, his wife never looked at him differently. He wouldn't have believed it possible had he not witnessed the devotion shining from her eyes every day that they were together.

His dark hair was white now, much to the amusement of his two white-headed boys. He was no longer flush with the muscles of a man in his prime, even though exercising was still a part of his everyday routine. Still, she worshipped his body no matter the changes.

They'd worshipped each other's bodies that morning. Watching Rowan come apart in his arms was his favorite way to start the day.

Only after, she had become pensive. He asked, but she said nothing was wrong. Hugh had never been the type of man to let something go, and never with his wife.

"Tell me, Row," he demanded.

Sighing, she turned on her side and snuggled her naked body against his own. "You're exasperating, you know that, right?"

"Yes. Now tell me."

"You'll think I'm foolish," she hedged.

"You've never been foolish a day in your life," he countered.

"Last night I dreamed that you had an accident. In a helicopter."

He felt a hot tear touch his chest and pulled her closer. "It was only a dream, Rowan. Everyone dreams of tragic things from time to time. You've been overloaded at work, and I've made you more stressed by asking you to work less. Your brain was anxious."

"No, Hugh. It was like I was there. Like I was a ghost at your shoulder, watching the helicopter malfunction, seeing the terror on your face when you realized you probably wouldn't make it.

"I saw you texting me, damn it! Don't go today," she begged. "Any day but today."

Hugh took off slowly when the light turned green. Frustrated with himself. He should have handled her fears better. He should have stayed home until she was past the shadow of her dream. Instead, he told her that today was one of the last chances he would have for the aerial. The property was going up for sale in only a handful of days.

He needed the intel.

She wiped her tears and finally nodded her agreement, but her eyes were sad when he left, and he fucking hated that.

He promised to take her out for a night on the town later, with all the bells and whistles. Her response was to kiss his cheek and tell him, "I love you. Be safe."

Now, he was waffling his choices and basically kicking his own ass for upsetting his wife. Exhaling another disgusted huff, he picked up his speed, deciding to get the charter over with as quickly as possible. There was nothing to worry about except how he planned on making his wife smile again.

A shrill whistle screamed through the helicopter's cab as the pilot frantically told emergency services that their tail rotor had failed. Their location was given before the pilot yelled, "Fuck!" while he frantically tried to correct the helicopter's jerking spin.

Hugh's immediate thought as he saw the ground rushing toward them was despair at how his death would hurt his family.

"Rowan," he moaned. "Oh, God."

They had seconds until impact. The pilot was trying his damnedest, but it wasn't enough. Nothing would be enough.

Hugh felt tears pricking his eyes as he tried to steady his hands enough to type.

Hugh: Forgive me. I love you. Tell my chil

A fireball seemed to hold his body in stasis...and then nothing.

*Rowan. Rowan. Rowan.*

# *one*

SIX MONTHS AFTER—THE FUNERAL

## BÉBHINN

DEATH HAPPENS EVERY DAY, *every hour, every minute, every second. Death affects mothers, fathers, sisters, brothers, husbands, wives, and children...everyone. It certainly affected me.*

*Is it harder for the loved ones left behind to lose someone unexpectedly or to know their expiration date?*

*It doesn't matter, really. When they're gone, they're gone.*

*No more hugs.*

*No more smiles.*

*No more texts or calls when something amazing happens and the first person you want to tell isn't there anymore.*

*They aren't just gone, like on vacation, but gone forever. It hardly seems fair.*

*I don't speak much anymore. I do cry when I'm alone. A lot. My family is worried about me. I suppose I would be worried too. I'm being selfish in my grief. The whole family is wrecked. I don't own the majority of stock in our heartache.*

*My mother... Well, what can I say? I'm worried I'm going to lose both of my parents.*

*I ache with grief. God, how I ache. Every day, I wait for purple and black bruises to appear on my arms and legs...over my heart. Alas, they don't show. They're phantoms, like so many other things in my life now.*

*His voice. His hugs. His smiles, when he rarely smiled at anyone. My father had been my truest safe place. A mighty oak in a storm. When rain pelted me, or thunder and lightning tore up the sky, Dad's arms were my hedge of protection.*

*Oh Christ, how I miss him.*

*The loneliness has become white noise. It dulls my senses and allows me to sit for hours scrolling through memories. Contemplating shadow designs that the sun makes through the living room shades. Considering how many years stretch before me without him there.*

*He will never see me graduate. He will never chase off a boyfriend, walk me down the aisle, or hold my child in his arms.*

*Gone. Gone. Gone.*

*I have begun to manage a parody of normalcy, but only because Mom needs me. I get dressed in the mornings. I go to my classes. I eat dinner with my friends. I even tried laughing at one of Mags' jokes. Once. Once, I tried, and it felt terrible. My heart squeezed so painfully, I thought it would explode. I haven't tried again.*

*I rarely eat, and sleep still eludes me. I've only been to Mom and Dad's top floor apartment once since the funeral. Too many memories. Mom shouldn't live there, but she cried for hours when I suggested she move, even temporarily. I haven't brought it up since. I won't, but I can't go in there. Not yet.*

*My Aunt River always told me to practice the old adage, "Fake it till you make it," if I found myself in a shitty place.*

*I'm faking it, but far from making it. I will, though. Eventually, I will think of Dad without crying. Eventually, the family will speak of Hugh Darcy O'Faolain instead of remembering silently.*

*I look at the crisp, white, unopened envelope lying next to my phone charger on the whiskey barrel nightstand that Dad had made for me last year for my birthday. It featured the Three Wolves label burned into the wood. I loved it.*

*The envelope staring back at me—not so much.*

*The planner that he'd been, Dad had written letters to his three children and wife to be delivered after his death.*

*Mom refused the letter. She backed away from her white envelope, shaking her head in denial. Bran said he would keep it in case she changed her mind. To my knowledge, Mom hasn't asked for it.*

*Not that I had been any better. I accepted my envelope from the family solicitor but hadn't managed to open the damn thing all these months later. Dad didn't raise me to be a coward, though, so I made a promise to myself. I was going on a solo, several-day hike, something Dad and I had planned to do together, and I'd open it then.*

*He would like that I was going ahead with the plan.*

*He would not like me going by myself.*

*"Shouldn't have gotten on that damn helicopter, then, Dad. I'm not replacing you, and you aren't here to argue your point," I spoke to the empty bedroom.*

*So, alone it would be.*

*I wasn't naïve, or not too naïve. I totally knew my family would try to bully me into changing my plans, but I'd grown up with a master teacher in how to work around overprotective men. Mom had run circles around Dad's grumbles and growls for years.*

*Mom already tried to talk me out of the hike, but my face must have shown my determination. In the end, she'd sighed and softly said, "You may look like me, Bébhinn, but you are every bit your father's daughter."*

*It was the greatest compliment I'd ever received.*

## two

THE O'FAOLAIN RESIDENCE—DUBLIN,<br>IRELAND

## BÉBHINN

"HAPPY BIRTHDAY, BROTHER-UNCLE," Bébhinn said softly before giving Bran a hug and kiss on the cheek. She loved her brothers, Bran and Patrick, who were married to her mother's sisters. As family trees went, theirs tended to confuse the hell out of people. She avoided the explanation when she could.

Her dad's cheeks and the tops of his ears used to turn pink when someone insisted on the whole story. Mom's two sisters married two O'Faolain brothers. What caused most of them to have two familial designations was Bébhinn's mom marrying the brothers' dad. Her mom became Bran and Patrick's sister-in-law and stepmom. The waters became muddier as the three couples had children.

Bran didn't allow her to keep the embrace brief, which she had absolutely planned on doing. Too much love and tender moments brought an instant lump in her throat, but if Bran needed it, she would give it.

He cupped the back of her head and brought it to his chest.

She felt, as well as heard, the thumping of his heart and the heavy breath of emotion he released ghost over the top of her head, and felt her eyes prick with tears. Like she knew they would. *Nope. Nope. Nope.* She wouldn't cry and make the occasion any sadder than it already was. She counted to ten before wiggling from his embrace.

Bran gave her a look that made her squirm. He knew she was hiding her feelings and didn't like it. He relented, though, and with a small smile, said, "Thank you, Sister-Niece."

She'd always been close to her brothers. The passing of their father had brought another level of closeness. She liked that the family had closed ranks, so to speak, keeping anyone but their closest friends out, but it also meant that the men in their family were getting too used to herding their women into protective bubbles.

Bébhinn's nephew-cousin, Jonathan, groaned. "Jesus, Uncle Bran. Remember your promise never to speak of our convoluted family ties? I begged you and Dad both. It would ruin my chances with women. They'd run away screaming, thinking we're all a pack of inbreds!"

Jon was shaking his head and chuckling. He was always good at reading a room and knew that everyone present was valiantly trying to keep their shit together. She smiled at Jon, acknowledging his attempt to lighten the mood.

"I don't think it's our family tree but your personality that would send them running, dumbass," Daniel deadpanned.

Daniel, Bran's son and Bébhinn's other nephew-cousin, just leaned against the downstairs bar, shaking his head at his cousin's theatrics. Daniel, Jonathan, and she were as close as siblings, having grown up together. Daniel had just turned twenty-two and was working on his MBA at Trinity. He and his parents all shared February birthdays. Jonathan was twenty-one. His birthday wasn't until the fall. Bébhinn would be twenty-one in a couple of months.

It always amused her to see Bran, Pat, Daniel, and Jon together. The four were striking but also freakishly similar. Their height and white-blond hair turned heads wherever they went.

She didn't bother giving Daniel a birthday hug, since he was as good at sensing her moods as his father and probably wouldn't let her go. Instead, she smiled his way, hoping no one could see that the smile didn't reach her eyes. "Happy birthday to you, too, dickhead." He smirked and flipped her off. He smiled but his eyes remained serious.

Bébhinn glanced toward her mother, Rowan, standing just outside the family circle, to see if she found her nephew's antics amusing. She was pale and dabbing her eyes. *Damnit...* She hated seeing her mom so...so brittle. Moments like this one sent a shock of panic flooding her system because it felt like she was losing her mother too.

She was a literal carbon copy of her mother. With Native American and Irish heritage, both women, and Bébhinn's aunts, Raven and River, were pale-skinned, short, petite, hazel-eyed, and sported thick, long black hair.

The Byrne women married into a family that was as polar opposite as couples could manage. The O'Faolains were all tall and muscular. Her uncles' white hair was a shocking complement to her aunts' dark-headed loveliness. Bébhinn's father, Hugh, was—had been—a big, bold, dark-haired, Oklahoman oil tycoon and entrepreneur. He loved his three children fiercely and loved his wife with an unapologetic intensity.

Mom had been his whole world. *Do not go there, Bébhinn,* she chided herself. Thoughts of her parents, and what had been, equaled leaking eyes and wobbly lips.

Turning to her Aunt Raven, Bébhinn gave her a kiss and a

hug too. "And happy birthday to you, as well, Auntie Rav." Raven had recently cut her hair to just above her shoulders. It was chic and lovely. Despite all the family upheaval, Bébhinn knew it was only a matter of weeks before her mother and Aunt River followed suit. She and her cousins had always believed that the Byrne sisters, their mothers, shared a hive mind.

"Thank you, sweet girl. I'm glad you could make it," Raven said while brushing her finger down her niece's cheek.

Raven bit her lip and looked away for a brief moment. Long enough to control her emotions. It seemed that's all this family managed anymore. Managing.

"Daniel told me that you plan on taking your spring break next month to hike your way across the Welsh mountains. Alone." Raven was the oldest of the sisters and Bébhinn's most protective aunt.

"Daniel has a giant mouth, as usual." Bébhinn glanced around Raven and found her oldest cousin—technically her oldest nephew—lounging against the bar, sipping their family's Three Wolves whiskey, his perma-smirk in place. *Asshole.* Bastard must have been talking to Blair. Those two were as thick as prison cellmates.

Nothing for it but to put on a show while reminding herself to tell Blair, a roommate and one of her best friends, that oversharing with a male O'Faolain was never a good idea. Bébhinn widened her smile. She noted that Daniel and Jonathan's serious stares were drilling her. *Ignore them.*

"Yes! I'm so excited. My teachers are allowing me to be absent from classes for an extra five days if I complete my work before the break, which I will, of course. That means I have two weeks to hike and explore. Limited showers and intermittent phone service. Just me and nature. Now that so many Welsh trails interconnect, the routes are limitless. Though many of Wales's hiking trails prohibit tent camping, Snowdonia has a few campsites, bunkhouses, and a sprinkling of villages with B&Bs if you stay on track."

Walking up, her Aunt River asked, "Where will you sleep then?"

"Oh, they've plenty of bunkhouses and B&Bs. I'm choosing not to use the campsites, so I won't have the weight of a tent to contend with. I mapped out where I'll end up each evening. Mom insisted that she wants me to stay in the villages when possible. Hardly a compromise since I like showers and beds. I have bookings in several."

River and Raven looked in their sister's direction until her mother eventually joined the group. The four men in the group pretended to be interested in the telly, understanding that it was a huge moment when her mother joined in a family conversation.

"I wouldn't want to lug a tent on my back either, but aren't bunkhouses open to anyone? Men and women?" Raven asked, her tone indicating she wasn't pleased, but too kind to come out and say it outright.

"I think it's total bullshit you're allowing this, Row. How will we know if Bébhinn is in trouble?" River protested. At her mother's rapidly blinking eyes, River quickly changed course. "I'm being foolish, sis. Ignore me. Your daughter grew up roughing it in the woods. She and Hugh loved living off the land. Eating animal turds, boiling water, and crapping behind bushes was a holiday. She'll be fine."

"Her dad taught her well. I should have remembered that," Raven added softly.

Bébhinn wrapped her arm around her mother's back, pulling her close when she noticed how near she was to tears. Thankfully, Patrick announced, "No one needs to worry, Bran and I ordered a badass sat phone. We'll track her every move."

She was about to bite her much older brother's head off for

overstepping, when Bran double-downed, adding, "We can call her all the time, and she can call us. She'll be able to call you every night, Row."

*Jesus Christ.* The look Bran gave her imparted a "don't argue" vibe without words. *Noted, but ridiculous.* He could send whatever tech he wanted, but that didn't mean she had to lug it up a mountain. "I appreciate the," she paused before forcing herself to say, "gift, but I already have my Garmin SOS satellite communicator. I can be tracked, texted, and signaled in an emergency. Dad and I didn't really want the distraction of calls."

"You're still taking the phone, Bébhinn. We won't call—" Patrick started before his brother interrupted.

"Much," Bran finished.

"And I won't call at all unless I don't see a text from you," Mom started, before softly finishing with, "because your dad was an excellent teacher.

"I only wish... No, never mind," she flapped her hand before her face, brushing off the thought.

Bébhinn knew what it was. She wanted her only daughter to stay in Dublin and never leave her side. It was reasonable. Completely. But it was an ask that she couldn't honor. If she hadn't had the plan to leave Dublin and the memories of her father, just for a moment, she would have gone crazy.

Bébhinn wrapped her arm around her mother's tiny waist. They'd both lost weight. "You know, Mom, you told me you'd consider letting me teach you about hiking. I think you'd love it. Dad always wanted you to go with us."

Mom looked startled, her eyes rounding. "He did? I never wanted to interrupt your father-daughter time. It was something special for the two of you."

"Well, yeah, it was, but you're crazy if you ever thought it wouldn't have been just as special with the three of us." Mom dabbed her eyes. Her fists were never free of tissues. Her struggle to find her way as a widow was painful.

"I wish I—"

Bébhinn interrupted. "No, Mom. No more 'what if' wishes. We will start with small hikes and build up to the rest. You know Dad's still stalking us from Heaven. He'd be pleased to see our special thing become *our* special thing."

Bébhinn glanced at her aunts, who listened quietly while subtly blotting their eyes. Their expressions were one hundred percent hopeful. Hopeful that their sister would show some sign of life. The men were all still at the bar, but no one was speaking. Every ear was waiting to hear what Mom would say.

Mom nodded a few times before wrapping her arm around her daughter's waist. "I think I would like to do that. With you."

She leaned her head on her mom's shoulder and whispered for her alone, "This will be good for us, Mom. We need this."

"We do. Thank you, sweetheart. And..." Mom paused. "I'm sorry I've been so distant."

"Never apologize for loving Dad. I understand."

"No, you don't," Mom snapped back, showing more spark than Bébhinn had seen in six months. "Losing your dad almost killed me. If I lost you, it would have. I'm not saying there aren't many tough days ahead for both of us, for all of us, but I promise to commit to living again."

River and Raven wrapped their arms around the two of them, creating a circle of love and support.

"Thank God," River gustily sighed. "Think of all the fun hiking gear we get to buy for you, Row."

"She won't need much in the beginning, Aunt River. Slow your roll." Everyone chuckled at River's enthusiasm. The men joined them, discussing whether Mom needed her own sat phone.

Overstepping O'Faolain business as usual.

It would look silly to outsiders that everyone was so excited that her mom agreed to start hiking. It could have been anything, like country and western dance classes. It was simply that since the loss of her father, their family had been suffering, especially her mom.

No one had admitted just how concerned they were that her mom wouldn't or couldn't snap out of her depression. Choosing to do a new activity was the best sign that she hadn't given up on life yet.

"First things first," Mom started, getting everyone's attention. "I would like Raven to take me to cut my hair like hers. I love it, and I want something different too."

"Well, I want to cut mine, then. You guys aren't leaving me out," River pouted.

Bébhinn could only smile. She'd called that one. And after this evening, maybe she wouldn't have to worry about her brothers and cousins trying to run her life now that her mom was coming around... She was embracing bits of her feisty personality, which was a huge step in the right direction.

Daniel walked up behind her shoulder just as she let out a satisfied breath and said, "I still think it's bullshit that you're letting Bébhinn go on a solo hike."

Clearly, she'd counted her blessings too fast.

# *three*

BÉBHINN

"I SERIOUSLY CAN *NOT* BELIEVE you're spending the entirety of your break shitting in the woods. It'll be like Naked and Afraid but without dicks to break the monotony of foraging and walking," Mags complained, while lounging on their sectional couch.

Margaret Morrow, or Mags to family and friends, daughter of Aileen and Charles, was gorgeous with layered waves of brunette hair, petite frame, a bullshit policy set at zero, and a cutting wit that left many a person dazed.

Mags was one of Bébhinn's best friends, along with Gray MacGregor and Blair Barr. Gray was leggy, blonde, and gorgeous like her mother Josephine, with an air of stoicism like her father, Thomas MacGregor. Blair was the image of her mother, Catriona, tiny with long, bright red curls and a fiery temper to match. Her father, Coll Barr, had his hands full with those two.

It was inevitable that they'd become best friends since their mothers were. She and her friends made a pact that they would all go to Trinity so they could live together. The four lived in the historic Merrion Square, a short walk to the famous St. Stephen's Green and only a few minutes from Trinity.

Their historic brick townhouse was a stunner and just so happened to be attached to Daniel, Jonathan, and Ciar Murphy's townhouse. Her dad spent an ungodly amount of money to snag the properties, unwilling to consider any other arrangement. Hugh O'Faolain wanted his daughter and grandsons close, and their friends could like it or love it. Turns out, they loved it. Who wouldn't?

The three Sasquatches living next door should be sauntering in any minute, with girls on their arms fawning over every word their dates uttered. Bébhinn learned years ago to ignore her cousin's revolving door of randos. Her roommates were never short on comments, though.

Blair Barr, the youngest of her friends—and the smartest—rolled her eyes and simulated gagging at Mags's comment about shitting in the woods. They all burst into laughter. The friends did, anyway. Bébhinn was getting better, but she couldn't bring herself to outright hilarity.

Not yet. Not when she still picked her phone up multiple times a day to text her dad. It was getting better. *She* was getting better, which was how she found herself finally agreeing to a house party before she left for Wales.

While Bébhinn and her friends lazed in the living room, sipping everything from margaritas to wine to her own shot of Three Wolves neat, several of their school friends were milling about. The kitchen's center island boasted trays of hors d'oeuvres, with the sideboard holding a full bar.

She and Blair would have been satisfied ordering pizza, but Gray was obsessed with all things hospitality—she already had a few clients, thanks to her talent and her mother's contacts from O'Connor Hospitality—and Mags was too artistic to allow pizza boxes to mar the design flow.

Like her mother and aunts, Bébhinn loved all things interior design and worked part-time at their business, Triskelion Territory Designs. One would think her passion would also make her cringe over throwing a party with a kitchen full of cardboard pizza boxes covering every inch of space. Maybe it was that her mom and dad grew up in Oklahoma in the States that made her more laid back.

Blair only cared about plants. Décor didn't mean shit to her unless she was finding the perfect spot for her hundreds of green babies.

There was an excited vibe tonight, and it had nothing to do with the bougie spread. Spring break meant they were only two months away from summer break.

Gray gave her a contemplative look. "I know you're dead set on this Welsh hike, and that Snowdonia Park is less than five hours away, but still, Bébhinn... I don't know. I feel like it's still too soon to go off on your own." Gray sat forward, long, silky, honey-colored waves sliding over her shoulders to touch the top of her thighs.

Bébhinn glanced at her other friends, who had also sat forward with identical serious looks on their faces. She at least thought these three had finally let go of trying to talk her out of it. Clearly not.

"Go, Bé, for hell's sake, but hire a guide. Have them stay well out of your way but be there in case of an emergency," Mags said sans any snark.

"That sounds exactly like something Coll Barr would say," Bébhinn shot back through her teeth, looking directly at Blair, Coll's daughter.

Blair pursed her lips and stood, her body tight and angry. Signing, because she was born deaf, she said, "None of us are over your father's passing, so we know damn good and well that you aren't. It isn't a time to be alone."

She took a deep breath and said Bébhinn's name out loud. Blair normally would have never taken the chance of someone outside her family and friends overhearing her speak, even though it was a testament to her determination to communicate verbally and BSL.

It was only her name, "Bébhinn," but it showed how anxious Blair was about her friend going off on a hike alone.

She knew they were worried, and more, had every right to be. She was about to tell them that she planned on reading her dad's letter while she was gone and wanted the privacy of the hike to do that, when Daniel's voice butted in. She and her friends hadn't even heard the lumbering know-it-alls arrive. Daniel, Jonathan, Ciar, and their three scantily-dressed "dates."

"Jon and I think the whole trip is ridiculous, but at least our dads plan on tracking her through a sat phone," Daniel grinned.

"Mind your own business, O'Faolain," Mags demanded, standing, putting her at Blair's side.

Blair quickly signed, because they all learned BSL for her when they were little, "We only worry, but we trust our friend one hundred percent."

"I was being a whiner that she was going to miss the whole break, but I know she'll kick that Welsh mountain's ass," Gray said as she stood as well.

Unfortunately, Jonathan's little lady, a heavily made-up Barbie wannabe with fried blonde hair, chose to join the conversation. "Oh wow, the little redheaded girl is deaf, Brit. That's why her voice sounds so weird." The other two ladies giggled.

She even covered her stupid mouth with three fingers to "hide" her tittering at Blair's expense. Bébhinn stood along with Gray, and the four of them turned to stare at the newcomers. Jonathan's face was bright red, and bless his sweet heart, her youngest cousin looked ready to strangle his date. If Ciar's jaw were any more clenched, he would surely break teeth, and Daniel... Well, Daniel was all blank-faced fury.

For Blair's part, she kept her face devoid of emotion, though her fair, freckled skin couldn't hide the red flush of emotion that swept across every surface not covered by clothes. Blair had been teased as a child and had run into her share of ignorant people as an adult, but this moron was Bébhinn's first taste of how disgustingly insensitive people could be. It had to hurt Blair. No one was that robotic.

Mags looked ready to commit murder, while Bébhinn was as frozen as Blair. Thank God Gray was still functioning.

Gray cleared her throat, drawing attention away from Blair, and addressed their neighbors' dates. "If you three ladies," she stuttered over giving them the moniker of "lady," but continued, "would like a snack or drink, there's a full spread just through that door." She pointed to the doorway that would take them to the magazine-worthy display of snacks and liquor.

Bébhinn, Gray, and Mags forced tight smiles, performing pageant waves indicating the path the women should take.

In her head, Bébhinn referred to the women as #1, #2, and #3. They were all clones and not worth the time of individual introductions. The original Brit, #1, clapped her hands, and squealed in excitement at Gray's announcement saying, "I hope there's a bartender. I could use a Cosmo and despise making my own drinks."

The three idiots all giggled before rushing out of the living room. Thank Christ. Her cousins and Ciar stood frozen, looking at the four friends, probably wishing they'd never made the short trek to come to the girls' townhouse.

Blair looked Bébhinn's way, ignoring the men altogether,

and signed, "I noticed a section of my misters in the rose garden are down. I'll be back."

She was partway to escaping when Jonathan touched her arm and blurted, "Blair." He sounded as anguished over the encounter with his date as they all felt. Blair didn't slow or acknowledge her cousin's entreaty.

Once Blair was clear and there was no sign of the Brits returning, Bébhinn rounded on the three men. "None of us care who you choose to screw, but for fuck's sake, at least don't subject us to their disgusting ignorance. The three of us will go help Blair fix the nonexistent problem in her garden while you and your...your dates enjoy yourselves. Text me when you've left." Their flinches were satisfying but not nearly enough.

She felt her body prickle with sweat. Her emotions were riding her hard. "You're lucky I don't call Dad and tell him how your dates hurt Blair." It wasn't until the words left her mouth that Bébhinn realized what she'd said. There was no calling her dad. Not anymore. She slammed her knuckles against her lips to hold in the agonized whimper that wanted to escape.

Before she could spin on her heel and escape with Blair, Mags hissed, "Get the fuck out," to the men and at the same time, Gray growled, "Leave."

*four*

## BÉBHINN

BÉBHINN HAD a four-hour ferry ride to Wales to comb through the gazillion texts and calls from Daniel and Jonathan and several from Ciar Murphy. She ignored the calls. Their texts were harder to disregard.

She got it. The three men and she and her friends were all tight. They'd grown up together, even though her three besties were Scottish. Their families were so close that special events and birthdays were always spent together. So, she hated being at odds with any of them.

Getting into her messages, her eyes widened at the ridiculous overload of texts.

Daniel: I allowed people into your home who hurt you and your friends, Bébhinn. Please, talk to me.

Daniel: I'll come after you and make you say you forgive me. If you think that's an idle threat, then you need to remember who my father and grandfather are.

Jonathan: You're killing me with your silence, Auntie. I'm gutted that I brought someone into your home who hurt Blair.

Jonathan: Call me.

Daniel: Fucking call me, Bébhinn.

Ciar: I won't speak for Daniel and Jon, but I will never bring another person into your home that might do something, anything, to hurt you four.

Ciar: Tell me you forgive me.

Ciar was the oldest of the guys and absolutely covered in tattoos. He looked more Irish gangster than businessman. He worked for an uber-wealthy real estate shark from London. He was a closer, whatever that meant. He could have lived anywhere but refused to leave his best friends. He also happened to be one of the sweetest of men.

Daniel: You're my aunt and cousin, but you feel like my sister. Talk to me.

Daniel: Jon and I have an important Three Wolves board meeting this afternoon, and I won't be able to concentrate if I haven't heard from you.

Jonathan: Don't you fucking dare go on this two-week fucking hike without forgiving me.

> Ciar: We ruined your night. I KNOW THAT! Why won't you or the other girls text me back?

> Daniel: If you don't respond, I will admit to Dad that I hurt you and your friends' feelings. And you know what that would mean?

She groaned at the threat. And it *was* a threat. If Bran knew she was upset and alone, he would bombard her with texts and calls. Not only that, but he would also tell everyone, and then they would be relentless.

> Jonathan: I'm sorry I made you bring up Grandpa. I'm sorry you cried.

> Daniel: You cried over Grandpa last night. It killed mo. I miss him desperately, but he was your dad. Damnit, Bébhinn, fucking text back.

She had to press her fingers tightly to her eyes to head off the building tears.

She wanted to text them back that all was forgiven, but after witnessing Blair's hurt and then forgetting herself and acting as though her father was a phone call away... Well, her feelings were raw.

She wanted to call and tattle on the boys to her dad so bad it was physically painful to stop her fingers from pressing his contact.

The truth was, the boys made poor choices with their dates, but they would never, not ever, do something to hurt her or her friends. Blair said last night that she wasn't mad at the boys at all. The only wrong they committed was having poor taste in women.

They all agreed on that.

Blair said she was embarrassed that she'd used her voice in

front of strangers. They didn't bother to coddle Blair or try to tell her she was wrong to ever be embarrassed. It was her truth. It was how she felt, and only her opinion mattered on the subject. They'd learned that lesson years ago.

She knew the boys had gathered up the clone Brits immediately because they texted. The girls had already ditched the party to congregate in Blair's garden. The mood for partying was past rallying. As soon as they found Blair, Mags tattled about Bébhinn forgetting that her dad had passed and the nightmare that ensued, where she burst into tears, and Mags and Gray yelled at the boys to get out.

Bébhinn would have gotten pissed at Mags sharing something so devastating, but one, they didn't keep secrets from each other, and two, Mags and Gray were sniffling, which meant they were just as affected by her memory slip as she was. If one of them was hurt, they all hurt.

Still, she hated any discord in the family, including Ciar Murphy. So, instead of texting the guys back individually, she texted their group chat—Devils & Angels.

> Bébhinn: You didn't hurt me. I hurt myself. Let it go.

She would not comment on Blair's situation. Her friend could join the chat or not. Instant bubbles appeared.

> Mags: Fuck up like that again and see what happens.

Mags' vicious streak always made Bébhinn chuckle. Her friend could always be counted on to make dire situations appear less harsh than her tongue.

> Ciar: Jesus, Mags.

Gray: Your taste in women offends.

Daniel: Not always, Gray, but after last night…

She watched as bubbles started and stopped from Blair.

Jonathan: I'm not letting shit go. Try again.

Bébhinn was about to text again when Blair showed back up—and again didn't leave a response.

Bébhinn: See everyone in two weeks.

# *five*

## BÉBHINN

BÉBHINN TRIED to relax into the curve of an ultra-hard plastic chair in one of the ferry's lounges, having already left her white 2-door Jeep Wrangler on the parking deck. She exhaled a deep breath, relieved that her friends had, if not quite smoothed things over, at least begun communicating again.

Well, not Blair. That girl would internalize her feelings until she exploded. Bébhinn and her friends called each other on their crap, but they also knew when to pull back. They all went to Trinity and lived together—moods could get volatile quickly, which was why she didn't message Blair, and was the reason her best friends finally relented and stopped trying to talk her out of this trip.

Smiling, she knew that Mags would only last a day, two at the most, before she nosed into Blair's feelings. By the time Bébhinn got home, all would be squared away.

She'd wanted to say goodbye to her family last night and avoid doing so this morning, arguing that it would be too early to make everyone see her off. Her suggestion was ignored. It wrung her out emotionally to walk into the O'Faolain Building, as the family called the gorgeous, remodeled, four-story monster in downtown Dublin that Dad and her brothers had remodeled for the six of them to live in and raise their children. It sat next door to Triskelion Territory Designs, where all three of their wives happened to work.

Bébhinn tried to hide her flinch when she walked through the front door, still expecting to see her father leaning against the bar, waiting with his typical stern expression. He'd always had a smile for Mom and her, though.

That missing smile felt like a phantom limb. Painful.

Mom, her aunts, Bran, and Patrick were waiting inside the door. Bébhinn should have known it wouldn't be only her mother seeing her off. One would think she was leaving the continent for a year, not a nine-to-ten-day hike in Wales.

Bran and Pat explained how to message Mom on the sat phone, ending the class with bear hugs.

"I'll miss you, sister," Patrick admitted, while smashing her face into his chest and patting her back hard enough to rattle her teeth.

Bébhinn didn't complain, all too aware how lucky she was. Bran pulled her into his arms next, performing an almost identical smash and pat.

"See you soon." Bran cleared his throat but didn't say another word, fighting his emotions.

Patrick announced, "We'll leave you ladies to it. Bran and I have a conference call with our financial team in thirty."

As soon as the men started jogging up the stairs, Raven gave her a quick kiss on the cheek. "I won't maul you like your brothers," she laughed. "Have so much fun, Bébhinn. Take pictures so we can enjoy them once you're home."

"I have a great waist pack to hold my phone for easy access.

There should be some spectacular views on the mountain trail I'm taking."

River bussed her cheek loudly and gave a quick squeeze. "Have fun. Love you. Remember to bury your poop."

Raven gagged. "You're disgusting, Riv. It's way too early for that...crap."

Her aunts and even Mom snickered at Raven's joke. Bébhinn shook her head at their antics, turning to her mom. One last goodbye, and she could finally hit the road.

"Alright, Mom, I'd best get going." Bébhinn tried to ignore how quiet her mom was since Dad passed. Normally, she would have been ribbing her family and telling jokes. Dirty jokes used to be Rowan O'Faolain's forte.

She was getting better but hadn't quite found her footing, where she stood, without her husband. Before Bébhinn had lost her father, she couldn't have imagined how the death of a loved one impacted the ones left behind.

She didn't have to imagine anything now. It was a cruel lesson.

Mom wrapped her arms around Bébhinn's waist and held tight for several seconds before leaning back. The smallest of smiles lifted her lips.

"Have fun, sweet girl. Since you're so brave, I've decided that it's time I was again, too. Raven and River are going to help me pack up Dad's things while you're gone. I might even redecorate. Perhaps you might consider," Mom hesitated once more, "visiting the fourth floor again once you're back."

Bébhinn was sufficiently stunned to make her momentarily speechless. Mom's news was huge. It also made her feel like a selfish brat that her mom knew she had been avoiding their flat since her dad's death.

Rolling her lips in, she took a moment to compose herself

before nodding. "I'm proud of you, Mom. Of course, I'll come over. It'll be my first stop when I get back."

"I should have already packed some things away," Mom whispered.

Bébhinn clasped her mom's hands. "No, you shouldn't have. I shouldn't have pushed. You are doing exactly what works for you, when it works for you. I just... I wanted to get past my pain and thought if you were strong enough to try, then surely, I could."

Mom brought their hands to her mouth and kissed their entwined fingers. "The truth is, Hugh, your dad," her voice wobbled, "would kick both our asses if he saw how miserable we've been. It would hurt him to see us like this, and neither of us would want to hurt him even now."

"He would be pissed," Bébhinn agreed, a slight hiccup marring her words.

Raven and River placed hands on their sister's arm and Bébhinn's, tears in their eyes but smiles on their faces.

"Get out of here, niece," River bumped her side with an elbow. "We've got things covered here."

"Yes, baby, go," Mom urged. "Have the time of your life, pooping in dirt toilets and wiping with leaves. Text me updates when you have service."

That was hours before, and Bébhinn had used the ferry ride to give herself time to go over the trail route one more time. It was the one she and her dad had mapped out last year. There were several places where the Snowdonia Way trail's lower-level and mountain routes connected.

She subscribed to a hiking trail app to download all her trails before she hiked them. So, even without the internet, the routes were saved in her cell. This app even allowed for customization of trails, which she'd taken advantage of.

For the first time in six months, she could smile, knowing Dad was proud of her for sticking to the plan.

After talking to her mother earlier, she felt lighter and more determined to enjoy the hell out of the hike. She unpacked and packed her backpack one last time, memorizing where every item rested: insulated tarp, ponytail holders, wide-billed bucket hat and poncho for when the rain hit—and it would—thermal sheet, mini, collapsible lantern, water purifier cup, MREs and protein bars, toothbrush and paste, body wipes and deodorant, extra panties—she could only rough it so far—a compass, and a backup print-off of the route, bunkhouses and resupply stations highlighted.

Most importantly, the Benchmade Bugout knife her dad had customized especially for her. She would keep the gift zipped safe in the front of her hiking cargo pants. It would take almost two hours to drive to Machynlleth, where she would stay the night at a B&B before starting out at first light. She was so ready.

She briefly tapped the front of the envelope containing Dad's letter, praying she didn't chicken out and would finally read the damn thing.

Pushing the letter aside, not wanting to psych herself out, she pulled out the itinerary she'd be leaving at the park office, which showed her route, sleeping arrangements, and supply stops. She would be passing through several small villages where she could catch a bath, bed, and breakfast if she stayed on schedule.

Her start and finish points, and the telephone number of the transport company that would take her back to her Jeep... Everything was in order—just as it had been for weeks.

This was the biggest hike she'd attempted, which caused an extra layer of stress. The mountains would test her both physically and mentally. She and Dad had been training for this hike for months before his helicopter crash.

Her small five-foot-three stature was a benefit in some conditions and a hindrance in others. Hugh O'Faolain didn't do anything by halves, though. They'd gone to a few survival classes and even a survival boot camp in the States where they had to eat off the land or they didn't eat for a week. It had been an epic adventure all on its own.

That had been the last adventure she'd taken with her father. "Be thankful you had even that," she chided herself, shaking her head in exasperation.

When the bell chimed, announcing their arrival at the Holyhead ferry landing in Wales, she tucked the last of the gear away. Her excitement and a healthy dose of fear cramped her stomach until she stood and took several deep breaths.

Everything now would be studying her route for the one thousandth time, a high-protein dinner, and hopefully several hours of uninterrupted sleep. Once she handed over her paperwork to the park office, it would be a waiting game until sunrise.

She was about to step into the queue of bodies heading back to their vehicles when she felt her phone buzz in her front thigh zipper pocket. Mom.

"Hello, Mom, what's up? I've just landed at Holyhead."

"Oh my God, Bébhinn," Mom started breathlessly, instantly spiking Bébhinn's heart rate.

Freezing near the back of the line, she held the phone close to her ear to drown out the noises of the ferry. "What's happened?"

Her mom must have heard the beginning of panic in her voice, because she quickly added, "No, no, sorry, sweetheart, I didn't mean to scare you. I just found your sat phone on the bench by the front door. I feel terrible!"

Bébhinn's breath whooshed out in relief. "Oh shoot, I set it down when we said goodbye, and I forgot to pick it back up. Great," she chuckled, "Bran and Pat will give me a good chewing when I get home. I even went through my pack on the ferry and didn't remember that I should have had it."

"Is there any way to get it to you before you set out?"

"No. My schedule is completely planned. Waiting would require me to reschedule everything, including where I sleep, food supply, and transport. I would have to cancel. I'm sorry, Mom, but no way.

"I figured. Damn. Your ass isn't the only one your brothers will chew on." Mom was quiet for a minute as Bébhinn moved closer to her Jeep.

"I do have my small Garmin. We didn't set it up for you, but I'll send you the app as soon as I'm off the ferry. You need to remember that there is always a chance that I lose the Garmin, or drop it in a crevasse, or a fox trots off with it while I'm peeing behind a tree. Promise you won't freak out. Give me my allotted time before you call for a military rescue."

"I'm glad you at least have that. I feel relieved. I won't promise to not freak out, but I will hold off on a search and rescue unless you're five minutes past your pickup time," Mom added, amusement in her voice, which made Bébhinn smile.

"Maybe you could hide the...evidence," she suggested. "What my brothers don't know won't hurt them."

Mom snorted. "Your brother-uncles probably have my damn phone tracked and will know if I don't receive any calls. Plus, you know I can't keep anything from Raven and River, and they can't keep anything from their husbands. We'll face their wrath together. No worries."

It was nice to hear a little bit of laughter in her mom's voice. "I've got this, Mom. I'm ready. Dad made sure of it."

*six*

# BÉBHINN

*Snowdonia Way Mountain Route*
*Daily Journal*
*Day 1*
*Machynlleth to Abergynolwyn*
*Distance: 13.3 miles (21.5 km)*
*Total Ascent: 1,522 m (4,993.4 ft)*

*5 am*

*I woke up before the first streaks of light painted the sky, Dad. You once coerced me into touching my tongue to a 9-volt battery. The zap from that is nothing compared to the energy vibrating my skin.*

*This was supposed to be our day, Dad. Be prepared to hear my voice in Heaven all day for days because I plan on describing everything to you.*

*This is my first time journaling—and probably my*

last, if I'm honest. It seemed goofy to write to myself when Gray suggested it, but I agreed when she told me to think of it like I was writing a letter to you.

You wrote me a letter, so fair is fair.

You'd like my journal. It's a slim, soft brown leather number with the Three Wolves Whiskey logo stamped in gold leaf on the front cover. I picked it up the last time I visited your distillery.

Your office is still...your office. I sat in your chair for a couple of minutes. I know, I know, it sounds creepy even to me. There was a moment when I felt you standing by my side. Again, I know!

It was worth the pitying look Olive gave me when she caught me slipping out of your door.

Anyway, Dad, I'd better get going. Sunrise is at 5:39 this morning. I'll write more tonight and let you know how my day went.

Love you (even though I haven't quite forgiven you for leaving me and Mom),

Bébhinn

---

Bébhinn reclined on a giant slab of stone, taking in the gorgeous views from the side of Tarrenhendre mountain. Her thighs were granite, but thankfully, her calves were down to a lovely burn, a nice change from the fire that had licked her muscles for the hours that had come before.

Her butt, however, kept cramping. She lifted each cheek and massaged the offended glutes—moans kept slipping between her teeth. *Damn, that felt good.*

The day had been one of the best of her life. It would have been *the* best had her dad been by her side.

Still, this day had been as much for him as for her. She believed he was watching her. She had to believe that. She also had to believe he was proud as all hell.

She was actually looking forward to writing to her dad that night. Gray had been right. Bébhinn needed the closeness and the closure that writing to him brought.

It was her goodbye. One she'd been holding on to for months. Her body could gripe all it wanted as she ascended Wales's mountains because her determination would never falter. Her smile would never dim. The serenity of the terrain, trees and flowers, scurrying animals, and cawing birds wouldn't lose its beauty.

She'd lost count of the number of ravens swooping by her path, letting off their distinctive gurgling croaks. She couldn't wait for her mom to experience the wonder of nature.

She'd managed to take some great pictures for her family, but currently, she was all about appreciating the miles she'd tread with her own eyes instead of through her phone. She was four short miles to her next stop—a hot meal, a bath for her aching muscles, and most importantly, somewhere to sleep.

When Bébhinn finally peeled herself from the rock slab to begin the last leg, she felt the hairs on her neck tingle. Slowly, she turned in a circle, scanning the area around her. No movement.

The swaying branches of Welsh oak and mountain-ash held no surprises. Tall Douglas firs marched up and down the trail, silent sentinels with their tops so high and unmoving. Still, nothing caught her eye.

However, Bébhinn would swear that she was being watched. Swear it. There were no large predators in these mountains, and if it had been other hikers, they would have made themselves known. Shaking her head at her silliness, she took one more sip of water and set off for the last leg of day one.

It wasn't lost on her that had her dad been by her side, she would never have felt even the slightest unease. He'd always been her safety. She and her mom had had twenty years of handing their fears to him. It was strange not to have that, but perhaps this trip would help her break the habit and stand alone.

---

*8 pm*
*Riverside House, Abergynolwyn*

*Today was so flipping good, Dad! I have to admit, the first few miles were rough. Don't judge. The trail instantly starts ascending, like no easing into it.*

*Don't get a big head, but you were right—not about everything—but I'll give you credit for ensuring I was in the best shape. All those hours in the gym and training in the field have guaranteed success.*

*I saw no less than ten sheep—I swear they gave me the evil eye. Several raptors swooped low to capture small rodents in their claws. Remember that falconry school that Mom gifted you for Father's Day? I think it was at Ashford Castle in County Mayo. Anyway, you would have loved seeing wild birds diving for prey.*

*My supplies are good, obviously. I've only been at it one day. I'll top off my water in the morning, and then I'm off.*

*I'm sleeping in a rough, a wee cabin near the morn-*

ing's starting point. It might only boast an old wooden cot, but it has running water and a bathtub—thank you, Jesus. Tomorrow will be one mile longer and a hell of a lot steeper. The hot bath was essential for my survival.

That's it for today. I need to call Mom...and Bran and Patrick. You spawned two of the most overbearing sons known to man.

Since you ~~died~~ went away, they've become almost impossible. So have Daniel and Jonathan... Not a great time to be a female in the O'Faolain clan.

P.S. You were also right about the phones. Not having service during the hikes is lovely. I do appreciate the beauty more.

Love you (I still haven't forgiven you),
Bébhinn

# *seven*

BÉBHINN

Snowdonia Way Mountain Route
Daily Journal
Day 2
Abergynolwyn to Dolgellau
Distance: 14.2 miles (22.9 km)
Total Ascent: 1,166 m (3,825.4 ft)

4:53 am

Good morning, Dad. I feel great, so no worries. My body feels well rested and ready for today (despite the rickety cot squeaking with every movement, and the constant drip of the bathtub faucet next to my head).
Wish me luck and don't let me get lost! :)
B

It was 12° C, a perfect day for hiking unless the trail included miles of plodding straight up a narrow rocky climb to the Heavens.

"That would be a hell of a shock. Wouldn't it, Dad?" Bébhinn grinned as she swiped the persistent beads of sweat from her forehead.

Smiling, she imagined sauntering up to her dad, where she liked to visualize him leaning against a smooth, dark-wooded, heavenly bar top, handsome frown in place, and a double whiskey neat in hand, while she said, "Hey, Dad. What's up?"

Her vivid imagination made her chuckle. She could so clearly see her dad. Death wouldn't change that man. He was stronger than that. So were his sons—her brothers—and their sons—her nephews. There wasn't a man in her family who didn't carry a piece of Hugh O'Faolain.

She was proud to come from such strong Oklahoma stock, where her parents had been born and raised. Her mom and her mom's sisters were half Irish and half Oklahoma Native American and raised in both countries.

It hadn't felt like it six months ago, but Bébhinn knew she would survive the death of her father, just like she would thrive in life, and kick this mountain trail's ass.

She'd already walked through a stunning valley before reaching Tyrrau Mawr. She was three-quarters through the most challenging portion of her day—the ridge to Cadair Idris. According to several hiking blogs she'd read, it was easy to veer off path, and adhering strictly to her printed map was a must.

"They weren't kidding." She'd had to backtrack a few times, but she was close to the summit now, where she planned on taking a break to eat, use the restroom, and take some photos.

As she closed in, the view of Llyn-y-Cau lake made her gasp. It was that lovely. She had seen the painting by Richard Wilson at the Tate Britain gallery in London when she was around ten. It hadn't changed from what Wilson created in oil in 1774.

It was an otherworldly vision, but alas, she had to pee, and her bladder waited for no man or vista. The moment her feet planted on the summit, she found some scrub to squat behind, making quick work of her business. She made a face as she tucked her wet wipe in a Ziplock, tucking the clear bag in the side of her backpack.

"Disgusting," she muttered to herself. Better than chancing leaves and grass on her privates.

She walked to the edge of the summit ridge to take some photos and paused. She would have sworn she saw movement out of the corner of her eye. Just a shadow, but out of place. She swallowed down her unease and continued to take pics of the stunning lake far below, but mentally, she was going through all the scenarios in which something significant moved behind a row of trees.

"Come on, Bébhinn, quit being a weirdo," she whispered. The shadow could have been a red deer or even one of the hundreds of sheep roaming the mountains. Why was she making such a production over a shadow? But wouldn't those animals have made more noise?

"Shake it off," she berated herself. First outing without the protection of a man, and this was the front she was giving. *No thanks.* "Shake. It. Off," she said once more.

She put her phone away and stretched before finding a soft tuft of grass to rest on while she drank water and ate a pouch of trail mix and a few of the protein balls she'd made for the trip. The next leg would be as tricky and amazing as the previous one.

She'd keep following the ridge around Gau Graig and Pen Y Bwich-coch. Then it was a short descent to Dolgellau, where she had reservations at a cottage Mags had found.

"It better not be shit, Mags."

She put the weird shadow away from her thoughts, determined to enjoy the rest of the day.

———————

*7:47 pm*

*(A fancy cottage thanks to Margaret Morrow) Dolgellau*

*Another great day! I know it's only the end of the second day, but I feel like I was made for walking trails. LOL. Feet are holding up well—no blisters. I'm grateful you got me started on Salomon shoes.*

*Did I tell you that all my friends bought them too? Gray and Mags are runners, of course, and said they loved theirs. We talked them up so much that Blair bought a pair just to wear to her yoga classes (in the tiniest size they make for women—she's such a precious wee thing).*

*I miss my friends after two days apart. Seems a little clingy if you ask me. That's another great thing about spending spring break alone. I feel like since you left, I've become dependent on having them around—even Daniel and Jonathan. If that's not a 999, I don't know what is. (Mom still says an emergency at the office is a 911—you American transplants...what can be done?)*

*Mom, Raven, and River have been cleaning some of your things out of the flat. I hope that doesn't hurt your feelings.*

*It was my idea.*

*She needed to let go of a few of your things, Dad. I fear she'll never truly let you go if your place stays exactly as it was before you ~~died~~ left. She needs to make it her space. She needs to learn to be on her own.*

*We all do.*

*I just wanted to make sure you knew that even if we pack*

*away your belongings, we will never pack away our memories of you.*

*I already talked to Mom tonight. She was still with her sisters (which means I spoke to all three of them :)). You would know what a huge thing that is if you were still here. Mom has isolated herself from the family for months now. I bet Raven and River are ecstatic.*

*I know Bran and Pat are, since you know they can't function when their wives are hurting.*

*Anyway, enough of that heavy stuff. This trip is as grand as we knew it would be. I can't wait to plan my next one! For now, I'd better get to bed. No crappy cot tonight. Mags clearly loved abusing my credit card when she booked this place. I'll just say it's comfortable and leave it at that.*

*I miss you. Talking to you again is nice.*
*Bébhinn*

# *eight*

BÉBHINN

Snowdonia Way Mountain Route
Daily Journal
Day 3
Dolgellau to Trawsfynydd
Distance: 16.7 miles (27 km)
Total Ascent: 1,210 m (3,969 ft)

4:38 am

I just looked at the weather, and it's going to be a bright, clear day! You know what that means? I'll have clear views of the ocean!

I couldn't fall asleep for anything last night, so I went to Yr Unicorn pub for a double of Bushmills Black Bush. I met a few other hikers from Spain who were extremely friendly, as well as some of the locals.

*"Johnny" wasn't impressed that a little lady like me was tottering (his words) around the wilds.*

*He didn't believe me when I told him I was turning twenty-one next month. He insisted on seeing my identification. I shit you not! And then he couldn't read it, whether from poor eyesight or drunkenness, your guess is as good as mine.*

*When the bartender confirmed I was well of age, "Johnny of the Hacking Cough" wouldn't hear of it. "The wee babber cannae be long oot o' nappies." I'm small like Mom, but Christ.*

*All in all, it was lovely, and the whiskey did the trick. As soon as my head hit the feather mattress, that's right, feather mattress (thank you again, Mags), I was out.*

*I'll talk to you tonight. I've a big haul in front of me today. And yes...I already ate my hot packet of oatmeal, a protein bar, and drank lots of tea.*

*B*

---

Bébhinn crossed paths with a few other hikers, some going solo like her, and two groups doing day hikes. So far, the day had been lovely. She did get her ocean views, valleys, wooded farmland, and too many streams to count.

Summiting Y Garn was arduous as the rocky steps required a lot of scrambling, where she had to bend and use her hands for stability. Y Garn was one of the Welsh 3000s—a mountain over 3,000 feet—but worth every strenuous minute.

She was relaxing by one of the mountain streams, needing a

break after the part of the trail aptly called Devil's Kitchen. She still had many miles before checking in at Trawsfynydd, but there was no way she could pass up taking a twenty-minute break by the sparkling water.

She really wanted to cool her feet off in the stream. The water would be colder than ice, but the relief would be immense. Devil's Kitchen was a cruel bitch.

"Screw it," she announced to the trees, before standing and stripping off her shoes and socks and rolling her pant legs up. She wished she were camping out tonight because she'd wash her ripe socks in the stream and dry them by a fire. Shrugging as she laid the offensively stinky wool over a warm rock, she knew the small hotel she was staying at tonight had a launderette, which she would take advantage of.

Enjoying the rough grass and pebbles underfoot, she made her way to the edge, tentatively allowing her two big toes to touch the running water. "Jesus," she yelped. The swift current was frigid. She inched forward with clenched teeth until she was ankle deep.

"Oh, God, that feels lovely." She couldn't force herself to go further, but the icy water quickly changed from painful to blissful. "Yes," she breathed, wiggling her toes.

She arched her back, stretching her sore muscles before bending down to wash her hands. "Lovely, lovely, lovely."

Reluctantly, she waded back to dry ground and her pack to dry her feet with one of the rags she kept for that purpose. Her hand was halfway to the pack's zipper when she froze, except for every hair on her body. They were all standing at attention.

Bébhinn straightened and quickly looked around the area before returning to her bag. Where a clump of purple saxifrage sat in a neat bundle. She felt her breath whistle as she started to pant in fear.

"Calm the fuck down. It's flowers, not a bloody adder." She

forced herself to take deeper breaths, bringing her heart rate down to a comfortable level. They could have fallen from a bird flying overhead or been dropped from the mouth of a foraging sheep.

"But how would I not have heard?" she mused to herself, though she reasoned that the stream was running at a fast clip, and it became noisier the closer she'd gotten.

Carefully, she picked up the bundle, and her heart was immediately pounding out of her chest once more.

The bundle was tied with a long grass stalk... Not an animal, then. She wasn't sure how long she stood there holding the bouquet while going over any other—*any* other—possibility for its presence.

Finally, it came to her. A fellow hiker must not have wanted to interrupt her moment of relaxation in the stream and left the flowers as a "hello, I was here" kind of thing. Her shoulders relaxed. Barely.

She shook her head, not wanting fear to override her common sense. Had her dad stood beside her, she would have found the flowers and said something like, "Aren't these lovely? How sweet."

She didn't want to be dramatic. "I won't be flipping dramatic." She placed the flowers to the side and dried her feet, replacing her socks and shoes.

She had many miles left and only so many hours left before sunset. Shouldering her gear, she gritted her teeth, refusing to think negative thoughts, and set out.

---

*8:05pm*

I made it to Trawsfynydd right as the sun set, and damn, it was cold as all hell by then. I immediately took a hot shower so I wouldn't get the shakes after the grueling 27 km day. My muscles did NOT need any more tension (don't worry, Dad, I spent extra time stretching and gulped down several glasses of water with our favorite electrolyte additive).

I feel great now. I've eaten and done a small load of laundry at the hotel's complimentary launderette provided for guests. Embarrassingly enough, I must have dropped the pair of underwear I wore the first day in Wales on a trail somewhere because they are no longer in my dirty clothes baggie.

At least they were of the plain cotton variety and not some glorious silk and lace confection Aunt River likes to gift me (sorry...TMI).

Today was great except for the weird flowers I found on my bag. Today was great. I waded into a fast-running stream—ankle deep was as far as I went. Brrr! The water was so crystal clear and cold, I refilled my water filter bag. I swear it was the best water I've ever tasted.

I've gotten so used to not having phone service during the day that when I end the day, the last thing I feel like doing is answering texts and calls. I know! There's a first time for everything. But if you saw my phone log... Just wait for it, I'll give you a sample.

Bran: Call me the minute you check in at The Cross Foxes.

He had to have gotten my hotel from Mom! He's so overbearing, Dad!

Mags: How was the luxe cottage last night? Did you hump the feather mattress? 😉

I have no words for her.

Jonathan: Are you coming home yet? Daniel's been acting weird. You're better at sniffing out his secrets. Hurry up.

Ciar: Your friends are still giving me the cold shoulder from that night. I've said I was sorry like a thousand times. I'm too old for this shit. Make them stop it.

He doesn't sound too old for nappies, if I'm honest.

Patrick: River doesn't like you being gone. She misses you. Come home early.

River: I just read Pat's text over his shoulder. He's full of shit. I miss you, but you'd better not come home early. You worked too hard for this trip. Pat, on the other hand, is walking around like a lost puppy. So is Bran. Pathetic.

That was literally only a small sample of them! Mom doesn't text, but only because she knows I will be calling.

I love all of them and appreciate them thinking of me, but I know very well that if you were with me, this level of cling wouldn't be happening. I'd like to get all up into a feminist rant about not needing a man, but damnit, Dad, I know I wouldn't have a care in the world if you were at my shoulder.

So, I do worry. Sometimes. And not just about this hike.

Today tested me. I wish it could have tested you too.

Love you (you shouldn't have been in that helicopter),

Your loving daughter, Bébhinn

nine

## BÉBHINN

Snowdonia Way Mountain Route<br>
Daily Journal<br>
Day 4<br>
Trawsfynydd to Penrhyndeudraeth<br>
Distance: 11 miles (17.7 km)<br>
Total Ascent: 562 m (1,843 ft)

5:02 am

Good morning, Dad. Sorry, I got so whiny last night. It's a new day! I should never complain about how much my family loves me. I love them, too, and I know I would complain if there weren't a million messages from them.

Today is easier, though I'm slightly nervous about making my way across the marshy bog before starting another mountain climb.

*I should get in early tonight, which means time for a shot and a good meal at a local pub. I'll also have more time to talk to you tonight.*
*I think I'm close to reading your letter.*
*Until tonight, B*

---

Unfortunately, Trawsfynydd received a ton of rain overnight, making the marshy bog an even marshier bog and a bitch to trek through. Bébhinn was never more thankful that the remainder of the day was decently easy compared to what had come before and what was coming after.

Bébhinn read on several hiking websites that the fifth day, which was tomorrow, was one of the hardest sections to complete on time. She was looking forward to the challenge.

Before setting off today, she'd returned some early morning texts from her family and friends. Gray was having a semi-meltdown over a client that her mother, Josephine, had asked Gray's help to deal with. The woman was a nightmare, but Bébhinn assured her friend that the experience was well worth the pain, and that pretty soon, Gray would be choosing her own clients.

Bran and Patrick didn't need anything at all, except that texting her in the evening wasn't enough for them now, apparently.

Blair texted only to give her some exciting news, explaining that she didn't need a return text. She was just too excited to wait until Bébhinn got home. According to the botany genius, the new species of rose she'd been working on for four years showed signs of growth. Bébhinn sent a text back despite Blair saying not to, and told her how proud she was and that she couldn't wait to see her friend's newest baby.

Mags texted to complain about the "dud" date she'd endured the night before, swearing off men...for the hundredth time. The only response Bébhinn sent back was an eye-rolling emoji. Mags would rather lose a limb than not have men fawning over her.

Her usual success at dating might have made Bébhinn envious if she didn't also have her share of admirers, even though she rarely accepted dates. She'd had two semi-serious boyfriends since high school, the last, Harold, she'd broken things off with after her dad...went away.

"Christ, Bébhinn," she berated herself out loud since she hadn't seen another hiker in miles, "if you can't say the d word out loud, you can at least say it in your own damn head."

*Dad is dead.* There, she'd said it. In her mind. Good enough.

She decided to stop for a second break where she could drop her pack and stretch, pee, relax, and eat a carb and protein-dense mini meal. She snacked on the trail but kept her true refueling for when she stopped and could relax.

The view of the sea and River Dwyryd was today's high-light. She always paid attention to the beauty around her, but she found that hiking alone allowed her reflection time. Between journaling and hiking, she felt she was giving herself a day-long therapy session, which made her more determined for her mother to get out of her routine and explore too.

Sighing, Bébhinn unzipped her pack to retrieve fruit and nut mix when her fingers brushed against something soft and defi-nitely organic. Yanking her hand back, she fully unzipped the top to peer inside.

Reaching back in, she latched onto...purple saxifrage. A bunch of five tied with grass. "What the hell?" Staring in disbe-lief at the bundle in her palm, she tried and failed to make their presence make sense and figure out how the flowers had gotten on or in her pack—again— without her noticing.

There had to be a logical explanation. She hadn't gone wading like before or left her bag unattended for more than a few minutes at a time for pee breaks. And she certainly did not recall leaving her pack unzipped.

Maybe the person who'd left the last bouquet left two, and the second managed to drop in her pack with her none the wiser. It was a poor theory. She would dare anyone to come up with something better.

Clearly, an animal didn't tie grass around the stems. It had to be a person...and then it dawned on her as if a Welsh mountain sprite had thrown her a life preserver. It had to be akin to Jeep owners ducking each other. The flower bunch was some sort of a hiker duck game.

Chuckling to herself and shaking her head, she couldn't believe she'd let her mind get carried away. In her defense, her mother had endured her share of psychopath bullshit.

Before her folks married, the O'Faolain and O'Connor families had an obsessed tech-savvy, demented stalker following them. The man managed to shoot her mother as she was walking down a Dublin sidewalk, having followed the family to Ireland from the USA, where her parents had grown up. Not a year later, she'd been kidnapped because she'd gone on a few dates with the wrong man.

Talk about her mom lugging around an unlucky charm. That was before her mom and dad were totally together. Shit didn't happen with Hugh O'Faolain as a watchdog.

Her dad had forbidden anyone from telling his daughter about the incidents, but Daniel and Jonathan had eavesdropped on their parents enough to find out all the horrible drama, and of course, told Bébhinn. Her dad had been livid. She smiled, remembering how the boys had hidden from their grandfather for two weeks.

Lord, how she missed how her dad could put the fear of God in a person.

Since the beans had been spilled, her mom had explained both events, which were straight-up true crime docu material. Perhaps that's why the weird flower arrangements had sparked such a nefarious vibe. Typically, Bébhinn wasn't one to jump straight into conspiracy theories. That was more of Mags and Gray's style. Those two had never met a murder mystery they couldn't obsess over.

Stretching her shoulder blades as close as she could get them, the tension from her momentary silliness eased. Clearly, another hiker or B&B owner was trying to get one over on her, and she was nothing if not a good sport.

It would be another exciting part of her trip to tell her family and friends about. "Onward and upward, Bébhinn O'Faolain."

---

*5:12 pm*

*You know, I was thinking about dating and boyfriends today. You never liked either of my selections (consider me not shocked). You really hated Harold once Mom (the traitor) told you she'd put me on birth control because things seemed serious between us (even though I was in college at the time and could have made the doctor's appointment for myself—but oh no, I had to go to the appointment with Mom AND Raven and River).*

*I refuse to discuss that epically embarrassing day further except to add that the doctor could barely get a* word in because the Byrne Sister Trio decided it would be fun to have lunch after the appointment to celebrate the "milestone" and got distracted with choosing the "perfect" restaurant WHILE MY FEET WERE IN STIRRUPS!

Suffice it to say, I was thankful Mom had talked me into getting on the pill because a month later, I did have sex for the first time with Harold (and I'm only owning up to that because you aren't here to kill me or him).

It sucked, but hey, I was a virgin, so it might not have been all his fault. However, the eight months that came after were also a sore disappointment. And no, I don't exclusively blame Harry for those encounters either—I really wasn't that into him, which pisses me off that I was foolish enough to consider myself in love with him in the first place, and that I made him my first.

Although Mom told me about her first time, and yikes, I won that one.

I'll spare you any more details (I know you're white knuckling a whiskey glass already), but he always seemed thrilled with his performance. A total red flag. At least that's what Mags said.

I spent more time avoiding the man than enjoying his company. When I realized he would make every excuse to avoid dinners with you, I made sure to invite him constantly.

Anyway, breaking up with him was not a hardship, and this is the first time I've even thought of him since your funeral. I'm only thinking of him now because I realized that even though I would get furious at your background checks and the death glares you would send my dates' way. I hate that I'll never get to be sideways for your behavior again.

My phone won't be tracked, my car won't be tracked, you don't get to threaten anyone about my curfew (even though I had started third year at uni and I HAD MY OWN HOUSE). Yeah, I wish you were here for me to yell at and get mad at...and get hugs from and be told how proud you are of me.

You will miss me falling in love. For real, falling in love.

Who will walk me down the aisle?

Who will be the best grandpa ever to my children?

It's hard to even consider falling for a guy when I know how different it will be. I'll never hear you say, "He's the one for you, sweet girl."

And I know what you're thinking right now, with your lip curled in smug satisfaction. You're thinking Bran, Patrick, Daniel, and Jonathan will pick up your baton of overbearing ass—it won't be the same.

They aren't you.

Glad I got that off my chest. I feel better. I hope you don't feel worse for my honesty. You know, it turns out this letter-writing my thoughts to you is kind of turning into my thing. I don't think I'll leave off after the hike. Maybe I should get extra journals and write to you again. Not every day and not about everything, but I think I would like to make sure you're never left out.

In other news, today was a great hike. It was easy and beautiful. Because the trail I was on today connected with the Cambrian Way trail, I saw more people I enjoyed speaking to.

I even exchanged numbers with a couple with a hiking blog page. They said they would love it if I could send them some of my pictures and insights about Snowdonia. I was hoping they'd be staying at Penrhyndeudraeth (Jesus, do the Welsh ever get exhausted writing out their long-ass words—their love of consonants is impressive), but they were taking a different trail than me.

Speaking of where I ended up tonight, I'm staying at Taldraeth. It was an old vicarage once upon a time that the owners remodeled into a B&B. Gray found this place for me—I think her grandma, Mary O'Connor, knows the owners. It has several rooms and a small dining parlor. Really pretty. You and Mom would love it.

You would have loved it...if...

Love you. Goodnight. B

# *ten*

## THE WATCHER

IT PISSED him off to no end that the love of his life wasn't keeping the bouquets that he'd taken great pains to collect for her. He took solace in knowing that she would have kept them if she'd known they were from him.

He was dying to approach her, but trailing her from a distance was a thrill he wasn't ready to relinquish. He wasn't ashamed to admit that after months and months of watching her movements at home, being this close to her was intoxicating—one-on-one time was just what they'd needed to grow closer.

He would surprise her on the final night. From her itinerary, he knew that she planned on splitting the last section into two days—he knew because he'd been the one to help fine-tune the excursion. It would be the night she would be able to admit her feelings for him.

His body tightened with expectation. No other man could anticipate her needs like he could. Patience. It was all about patience. He settled in for another few miles of shadowing his soul mate until she was safely settled for the night.

He hated that he'd caved to his jealousy the night before and sneaked into her room to borrow her journal. He'd watched her on the few occasions she'd sat near a window writing in it, and he had to make sure she wasn't writing to a boyfriend. That wouldn't have ended well for the boy.

It was a letter to her dead dad, which meant he would have to return it. She'd loved her father, and he wouldn't cause her more heartache than necessary. He would slip back into her room by tomorrow or the next day and replace the journal.

He hoped to see his own name on those pages someday.

Watching her sleep had become an obsession soon after he'd met her. It had been so easy to plant a camera in her bedroom once she'd moved into her own place. She'd rarely brought her boyfriend, Harry, over, which was a blessing. His rage had almost escaped his tight control when he'd had to endure seeing another man put his hands on what was his.

The only reason that pansy-ass boy was still breathing was because his girl hadn't returned any of the boy's feelings.

She was saving her heart for him. It had been obvious. Continually, and in every way, she let him know that she was keeping her authentic self for the time they could be together.

It had taken over a year, but he'd put together a life plan to suit them both.

A home. He'd found the perfect flat and decorated it with her tastes in mind.

Children. One.

Work. She would work with him. Once they were a couple, they wouldn't want to be separated all day. She hadn't graduated yet. She could always change her major to suit him. It would keep her in school longer, but she wouldn't mind if he asked her to.

Eventually, she would understand that cutting ties with her family and friends was for the best. She would want to spend all her time with him, and other people would get in the way.

Over two years of careful planning were about to reap the biggest reward of his life. From the moment he'd seen her in the science of nutrition class, her first year at university, their future was as good as written.

Her father's death had been one of the best days of his life. He would never tell her that, of course, but her father had been the biggest obstacle to their relationship. With him removed, all the pieces had begun to fall into place.

He watched her sure strides eat up the rest of Day 5's miles, his binoculars making him feel as though he was striding by her side.

# eleven

DAGR

THERE WASN'T A TRAIL, mountain, or cave that Dagr hadn't run, climbed, or explored across Wales—not only Wales, of course, but as he was raised in Cymru, there wasn't a country more special to his heart.

Going through his pre-hike stretches, he looked toward the trailhead he'd take in a few minutes. The Glyderau mountain range was a beauty of a site from his vantage point in the town of Machynlleth, where he'd spent the night.

As a pastime, he'd become an assistant ranger for Wales's National Trust. He had a lot of friends in the Trust, and they called him periodically to run through the longer trail routes. He'd done alternate routes of the Snowdonia Mountain route several times over the years. He was more than happy to check the route's safety.

It was a simple matter of doing what he loved—anything outdoors and adventurous—and filling out minimal paper-work, marking areas that could be improved or revamped. A perfect mini vacation from work.

Growing up, he'd spent more time outdoors with his father than in. He'd advanced to trail running years ago. His body was never more in tune with nature than when he was silently gliding up the side of a mountain.

He was a big man like his father. Both men should have been runner-lean with as much time as they spent in the wild, but Dagr's main moneymaking gig landed him more often than not in a high-rise office building where the only form of physical exertion was in the gym. Consequently, he carried a lot bulkier muscle than the typical outdoorsman. He relished the challenge of pushing said bulk up mountains, doing it every chance he could.

The mountain route he was about to begin took even seasoned hikers nine to ten days. He planned on knocking it out in five by moving fast and sleeping rough. He tracked the weather when he woke up that morning, and a late spring snowstorm might hit the tail end of the last leg. He should be able to just skate by.

He grinned at the challenge. What adventure wasn't made better by a bit of danger? He was about to swing his heavy pack from the ground when his phone started buzzing in his jacket pocket. Pulling it free, he looked at the screen. "Dad," he sighed before answering, not surprised his father was calling.

"Hey, Dad. You're up early."

"Surely not much of a shock for you, son, since I've gotten up early every day of your life."

His dad was in a mood, but Dagr knew his old man would eventually tell him what was troubling him. "It's a beaut of a morning. I'm about to take off, so if you need something from me, now's the time. I plan on hitting some unmarked trails this time and not staying in any towns."

His dad sighed heavily, and Dagr could picture him pinching the bridge of his nose. He and his father were extremely close. They spoke every day, and never more than a week went by that they didn't see one another, so his dad knew his son's schedule this morning.

Finally admitting to the reason for the call, his dad said, "I pissed off Gerry Langdon last night, but only because the bastard pissed me off first. I would've called you then, but it's taken the night to see my blood pressure down."

"Christ, Dad, Gerry is one of INCC's biggest donors." INCC, or Initiative for Nature Conservation, was a charitable organization without government funding. Pissing off a man like Gerry...

"I warned my boss that making me speak to donors was a bad idea. I belong in the field. I *only* belong in the field."

Stubborn. "Dad, for fuck's sake, man, you're usually the last man in the room to allow a blowhard to rile you up. You're more educated, wealthier, and as for your "my boss" comment. You don't have a bloody boss. You only pretend to follow protocol when it suits you.

"You're still pissed that INCC wouldn't let you fund and run the new nature preserve. Let me guess, Gerry wanted a special favor for his donation."

"The twpsyn asshole wanted one of the trails named after his granddaughter. Seriously, Dag, the man is too old for that level of nonsense."

Dagr coughed to cover his amusement. "I understand what you're saying, Dad, but in the man's defense, I've seen several of my friends with little children do the damnedest shit when teary eyes and quivering lips come out."

Changing the subject, his dad added, "My boss," emphasis on the word boss, "needs you to look over a contract to do with the new park information station. INCC is purchasing a fair bit of land outside Carmarthenshire—close enough to the reserve and the already popular tourist attraction, Carreg Cennen Castle."

"Fine. Fine. Email me the particulars, and I'll run through it when I get home." Dagr was a solicitor with offices in London and Wales. His specialty was transactional law, focusing on contract drafting and negotiation, mergers and acquisitions, and ensuring compliance.

Dad's boss—the pretend one—occasionally used Dagr's services. Dad always tried to pay him, but that would never happen. He might not have the consuming passion for wildlife and land conservation that his dad toted around, but he'd been raised to respect the planet.

"Before I let you go, you know what you have to do to smooth things over with Gerry. Take him to lunch, buy him cigars and whiskey. He'll forget all about the custom trail name."

"Christ. Fine," his dad spat out. "Weather coming your way, son. Best cut your run short this time."

"I'll make it," Dagr blew the weather worry off. "Plus, I have a sat phone. If I get into trouble, I'll be able to call my daddy," he teased.

"Aren't I lucky?"

# twelve

## BÉBHINN

Snowdonia Way Mountain Route
Daily Journal
Day 7 (Journal went missing on the fourth night and turned up this morning)
Pen-y-Pass to Capel Curig
Distance: 9.8 miles (15.9 km)
Total Ascent: 966 m (3,169 ft)

7:44 pm

Dad! You can't even believe what's happened! I would swear you're haunting me, but you would never do anything that would put me through hell, so... I don't know. The weirdest things have been happening on this hike.

I haven't wanted to bring it up, just in case you

can talk to Mom in her dreams and rat me out, but when I say weird, I mean weird.

Here is some of the crap I haven't told you about. Flower bouquets on or in my pack—tied with grass. Definitely not an animal thing to do. Sometimes, I swear I see large shadows in the trees with my peripheral vision following me. (Okay, that could be my imagination. Still, it feels eerie, especially when we both know Wales doesn't have big predators like you grew up with in Oklahoma.)

Missing panties. Dirty Panties!!! Now that I would put down to small animals, but I don't leave my pack lying open. Never (or at least I think it's never).

You may have noticed that this journal entry is for Day 7, and the last entry I wrote to you was at the end of Day 4. Yeah...my journal was missing from my room when I woke up the next morning. Like gone. Gone, gone.

I left a message for the B&B owners about the missing journal, begging them to please mail it to me if it turns up. I cried most of Day 5. I know you weren't going to really read my letters, but... No but. In my mind, or my dreams, or whatever, you would read them. You would live this adventure through my words and read some of my feelings that I was too chicken to tell you...before.

So, how am I writing in the lost journal now? I found it in my pack this morning when I was checking supplies. That's right. It was in my pack.

I get goosebumps just thinking about finding the damn thing snuggled up all perfect, untarnished brown leather and gold embossing in my pack's pocket.

I mean, I'm not crazy, right? No seeing person could possibly miss a damn book in a backpack, no matter how thin. So what do you think? I mean, I'm half Irish and have lived in Ireland my whole life.

I know all about Irish folklore. Nan told Daniel, Jonathan, and me all about the "lore." I'm going to come out with my theory. Don't laugh. I think I could be plagued with a mischievous púca.

I said not to laugh, Dad! I know it's ridiculous, but they love creating mischief. They're shapeshifters, and when they change into animals, their fur is black—hello, shifting dark shadows on the trail.

Okay, here's a less make-believe theory. I've got some local kids screwing with me. Today had only a few ascents, just an easy hike full of gorgeous views that allowed me to hit the village of Capel Curig early enough to enjoy a lovely dinner with the owners and three other hikers at the B&B I booked.

I was able to ask the local family if they'd ever heard of hikers getting pranked, and guess what, the answer was yes. The owners grimaced before chuckling and said they had heard a few stories over the years.

Mostly, ornery teens who take turns slipping stones into unaware travelers' packs. There were a few other "amusing" stories. I have to tell you, Dad, the relief I felt at finding out my woes were probably caused by a group of bored Welsh teens on break had my body shaking in relief.

Teens, I could handle. Púcai not so much. A creeper (which I've hated to even think about), not at all.

They probably realized the importance of the journal they poached and drove to another village to find me. I haven't worked out how they knew where I would be, but I suppose living here, most hikers follow the same trail, and last night I did eat dinner at a local restaurant. My pack was at my feet, but I suppose someone could have sneaked it back in.

Whatever, I'm tired of thinking about it. I only have two and a half to three days left, and I want them to be epic where my only worries are not peeing on my feet.

Oh, I almost forgot. I took a selfie yesterday on top of Mount Snowdon—the tallest mountain in Wales! I would have framed it for my room if you had been in it with me. I think instead, I'll tuck some of the pictures in the pages of this journal.

I really need to go to bed sooner rather than later. Do you remember what Day 8 will be throwing at me? What am I asking? Of course, you remember. According to blogs and your research, the day will see me through several scrambles and over several summits.

I'll be just one more mountain goat. My stomach is cramping in excitement.

I feel better for the writing tonight. I was letting myself get weirded out over silly crap, but picturing you rolling your eyes over my dramatics straightened me out.

*I love you.*
*Always. You are still taking care of me.*
*I'm less upset with you than I was yesterday.*
*Love, Bébhinn*

*I love you.*
*Always. You are still taking care of me.*
*I'm less upset with you than I was yesterday.*
*Love, Bébhinn*

# *thirteen*

## THE WATCHER

THE JOURNAL WASN'T what was really bothering him, though. She would begin the eighth stage of the hike the following morning, and even though they were both members of the same hiking club in Dublin, her endurance and experience with scrambling outstripped his own. He didn't have a death wish. It would wreck all his work to get injured at this late date, which was why he finally made the difficult decision to leave her to Stage 8 while he drove to the next destination on her route.

He might not be able to follow her today, but tonight would be fun. He'd helped her pick Stage eight's accommodation himself. Smiling at the access he would have to her, he stooped to squeeze into the back of a compact taxi. The driver was a young twenty-something boy and a cousin of the person who ran the taxi service. Many of the car services were family-owned in these parts.

After the short drive to Bethesda, he was handing over the fee when the boy dropped some disappointing intel.

"Not sure how long you plan on staying, but I see you're a hiker," he said, nodding to the backpack in his fist, "and my grandad told me this morning to expect some nasty weather tomorrow or the next. Snow and wind. It should only be a problem higher in the mountains, though."

Hiding dismay, he quickly thanked the boy and headed to the public bunkhouse where she would sleep tonight. He needed to get the layout of the place before he found somewhere to hang for the day.

Tonight, he would see if she changed her plans because of the weather and then change his if need be.

He was so close to the one thing he'd dreamed of having.

Bébhinn Clarissa O'Faolain.

# *fourteen*

## BÉBHINN

*Snowdonia Way Mountain Route*
*Daily Journal*
*Day 8*
*Capel Curig to Bethesda*
*Distance: 13.3 miles (21.5 km)*
*Total Ascent: 1,522 m (4,993.4 ft)*

*5:12 am*

*Before you start, I'm monitoring the weather. Today is holding clear, thank God, because I'm about to scramble my way over 21km! I admit the weather might be a concern for the final stage.*

*Remember, we decided to break Day 9 into two days, and I still will unless weather moves in. If that happens, I'll just have to push through. I really hope that doesn't happen. My body might not be 100%, but it's pretty damn close.*

*Talk to you tonight, B*

"Damnit!" Bébhinn cursed. She'd slipped for the third time in an hour on one of the toughest scrambles of the day and had the bruises and abrasions to prove it.

Three more miles, if her map-reading skills were on point—and they were, considering she'd been doing a killer job of following the miles of unmarked trails for days—but damn if her legs and arms didn't have a slight tremor of fatigue.

The second slip was the one that caused her first real injury of the trip. She could feel the bruising across her ribs and down to her hip with every breath.

No matter. Today had been epic. Bébhinn fist-pumped the air as she stood atop the last summit of the day, thoroughly enjoying the vista and standing straight versus bent over climbing with her feet and hands up the rocky side.

"I came, I saw, I conquered." She couldn't help the chuckle of relief that escaped as she turned in a complete circle, taking a 360° video to show her family and maybe even to send to the blogger couple she'd met.

For eight days, she'd pushed her body, and for eight days, she'd succeeded in completing the stages. Better yet, today she'd not seen any odd shadows or had anything taken or put into her pack. The kids, if it had been kids, must have grown tired of inflicting their shenanigans on her.

She'd thought more about the journal's disappearance. It could have been lifted by some little shit on the fourth night because Bébhinn had decided to restock her pack at a small grocery near the B&B before going to bed to save time the next morning. Most likely, another hiker found it where the thief had dropped it. Probably someone she'd met at dinner, and once their path crossed hers again, they returned it.

Everyone discussed their routes and destinations, so it was

only a matter of time before they saw her name registered as a guest. The finder could even have been one of the B&B owners. They heard her discussing her route and might have sent it to her. Whatever way it happened, she was thankful to have it back.

Admittedly, the flowers had taken her aback the most. Thankfully, her pragmatic father taught her not to jump to conclusions. It had to be a sweet passerby on the trail.

As she made the day's final descent that led to the village of Bethesda, she thought over all the messages she'd need to return before she went to bed. Her phone had been flooded with texts from her family and friends as she'd finished breakfast that morning, but since she didn't have a moment to spare before setting out, she didn't answer them.

Thankfully, the bunkhouse was right where she'd marked it on her map. After a day like she'd had, it was unfortunate that there wasn't a 5-star luxury hotel awaiting her pleasure... Massages, whiskey, and a down-filled bed topper held considerable appeal.

The bunkhouse she'd booked had Wi-Fi, hot showers, and a small communal kitchen. It was better than sleeping rough. She'd gotten extra supplies for the last stage the evening before, knowing there was nowhere near Bethesda to buy supplies.

She stomped her boots on the concrete pad in front of the bunkhouse to dislodge any debris from the tread of her boots, noticing that the owners had graciously provided a grill, firepit, and chairs for guests.

Ignoring the outdoor amenities for now, she trudged up the three steps—moaning only once—and went in search of a hot shower and her bunk for the evening.

Bébhinn had showered, heated up a soup packet, washed it down with tea, and had a protein bar for dessert in less than thirty minutes, even managing to call her mom between bites. She was clean and her tummy was satisfied. She was ready to answer her texts and write to her dad. Then she would crash because tomorrow, the last two days of her journey began.

Taking her phone out, she dug into her messages.

Mags: Call me.

Mags: Why are you ignoring me?

Mags: Are you almost home? I've been back in school for days and days without you. ☹ The least you can do is return my damn texts.

Bébhinn: I'll be home in 2.5 days. Stop being dramatic.

Mags: So, my friend does remember how phone etiquette works. I text. You reply. So simple and yet, you struggle.

Bébhinn: You should take your comedy to the stage. Mind telling me what the 999 is? I've got a bunch of texts to return before I get to meet my pillow, and if this isn't an emergency, I'm moving on.

Mags: Yours truly is currently working on a piece for the president's wife!

Bébhinn: What?! Was it commissioned? That's huge.

Mags: Of course not. No one knows me or my talent. Yet. This will be a birthday gift for her. I imagine she'll love it so much that it will eventually hang on a wall at Phoenix Park.
THEN I'll get plenty of commissions.

Bébhinn: I love your ambition and positivity, Mags. See you in two days. X

Mags was an incredible artist. Her medium was as unique as she was—hand embroidery. Mags was mad for stranded cotton. Round 2.

Bran: Raven would like you to come home early. We can go out to your favorite pub and celebrate. Early.

Seeing through her brother's nonsense, she sent off a reply.

Bébhinn: See you in two days. Love you.

Round 3.

Gray: Tell Ciar, Daniel, and Jonathan to stop texting me, Mags, and Blair. Please. I beg you.

Bébhinn: Since when am I the chat president?

Gray: Since Blair is keeping her phone off more often than not, and Mags is still only speaking to the boys with middle finger emojis and knives. They are YOUR family.

Bébhinn: Two. Only two of them.

Gray: I win. Zero are mine. Plus, they're only still being annoying because everyone hates

hurting Blair (and you if we're being honest).

Bébhinn still winced when she thought of that moment at the party where she'd threatened to tell her dad on them. *Damn. Damn. Damn.*

Bébhinn: Fine, you whiner. I'll try to straighten it out when I get home (even though I thought this shit was quashed days ago), but only when I get home.

Gray: I'm sighing and rolling my eyes, but fine. See you soon. x

Round 4.

Daniel: Jon is keeping shit from me. Jesus, Bébhinn, would you come home already? I need you to find out what's going on with him.

She could only roll her eyes. Jonathan had said the same thing about his cousin not five days ago. "Needy bastards."

Bébhinn: I'll be home in two days! Have you and Jonathan considered that it's healthy to keep a few things from one another?

Daniel: No.

Daniel: Fine. Call me from the ferry on the way home.

Bébhinn: Fine. I won't have service after tonight until I come out of the last stage. I'll call you then.

Round 5.

> Raven: Your mom isn't back to being the sister I remember…but she's getting closer. Packing a few of your dad's things up has done wonders. I hope your adventure is having a similar effect on you. See you soon, sweetheart. Bran wanted me to remind you about the weather coming your way.

> River: Do you have a rash on your butt yet?

*Jesus, River.* One last text blinked into existence before she could set her phone aside.

> Mom: I forgot to tell you to sleep well.
> Love you.

She had the best mom. Smiling to herself, she took out her journal. It was time to write the one who couldn't call or text her anymore. Dad.


*8:52 pm*

*I'll start by saying that I should have been asleep an hour ago. I blame your family, Dad. Needy, messy, messy people.*

*I don't mind too much.* 😊

*Today was another epic one. God, Dad, 80% of my day was scrambling up one mountain after another. My hands might be permanently flexed into claws. I'm thankful the bunkhouse is empty right now, because when the hot water hit my lower back, I know I must have sounded like a bawling calf.*

I can't believe I'll be heading home in two days. Can you believe it? There were a few tough days where I wondered what in the hell I was doing, but all in all, this time by myself allowed me to truly reflect on my new life. A life where you aren't there...one where I know I'll be okay.

My brothers will be relieved.

Tomorrow isn't going to be easy. Hell, this whole damn trail hasn't been easy, which is probably why I feel so smugly satisfied that I've done it. Almost done it, anyway, and by myself.

My body feels good. Great actually. I think it's adapted to the all-day grind. I thought of the different hikes Mom and I can start taking together. I can't wait.

I know you'll enjoy it if I write to you about those adventures. Especially if Mom talks her sisters into joining us. Can you imagine???

You O'Faolain men spoiled your ladies. Hey, you spoiled me, too, so no complaints. It's only that you taught me how to enjoy all the luxurious things while also teaching me how to rough it. I'm a fire-building machine thanks to you.

Mom and her sisters have forgotten what it was like growing up in Oklahoma and running wild at Nan's. I'm determined to get them in tents. Hell, maybe I can persuade the whole family to an annual camping trip. I bet if they did something that you loved, it would make them feel closer to you, like it makes me feel closer.

Oh, I almost forgot. The weather is iffy, but I've

been watching it. I won't have service once I leave. I promise to study the weather before heading out in the morning, but it looks like the cold front is holding south of the range.

I've got to go. A few backpackers just walked in, and I'd like to say hello before I sleep and ask them what they're thinking about the weather.

The bunks have drapes that I can pull as soon as I shut my bunk light off. Not 5-star but not too bad either.

I'm reading your letter tomorrow night. It's time, and I promised myself I would.

I ~~think believe~~ know I've forgiven you for leaving us. Leaving me.

Love your daughter,
Bébhinn

# *fifteen*

## THE WATCHER

HE HAD A DECISION TO MAKE. Stay and follow, or leave and meet her at the end. He'd listened to her speaking to her mother earlier, the windows in the bunkhouse weren't double-paned, thank the Lord, and she confirmed what he already assumed—the final stage was a go despite the weather.

That's why he loved her so damn much. She was fearless. He wanted to be fearless for her.

He didn't want to chance getting stuck in a snowstorm, but there was no way he wanted her to be stuck in it by herself.

Follow it was, then.

He'd been dreaming of surprising her on her last night, and God willing, the weather would hold, and he would get his wish.

He knew from her journal that she planned on reading a letter her father had left her on her last night on the Snowdonia range. He wanted to be there for her when she did. It would be an incredible bonding moment.

Christ, but her father had been scary. He'd only met him

once, but Hugh O'Faolain could scare the piss out of any man. When she'd first moved into her house, Bébhinn had held a get-together for their Dublin hiking club, The Ramblers, and O'Faolain had shown up unexpectedly. The rest of the group had been thrilled, but he'd almost been caught coming out of O'Faolain's daughter's room, where he'd been setting up a camera.

He disliked invading Bébhinn's privacy, but it was the best way to observe her habits and tastes when she was at her most vulnerable. He hated the few nights her then-boyfriend had stayed over, but he would be lying if he denied how aroused he'd become watching their intimate moments.

Soon, she would only ever do those acts with him. He doubted she'd like the consequences otherwise.

The bunkhouse was silent, as it should be for the tired hikers inside at a quarter after midnight. Since he would follow her in the morning, he decided to cancel his alternate lodging in favor of staying close.

He let himself in as silently as he could and showered, finding an empty bunk. He pulled the curtain closed, cocooning himself in darkness. He loved being so close to her—he loved even more that tomorrow night would see them much closer than that.

Propping his hands behind his head, he stared at the bottom of the bunk above him and daydreamed about how his life was about to change.

He was the type of man who had always been overlooked. He was neither intelligent nor foolish, witty nor dull. His life was all about being in the middle, but all that would change with someone as magnetic as her at his side.

He wasn't traditionally handsome, but he wasn't ugly either. He'd spliced enough pictures of him and Bébhinn to know that he was a perfect complement to the petite, dark-haired beauty. Her hair was long and thick and hung to her tiny waist. He'd seen pictures of Bébhinn with her mother and two aunts in her living room and bedroom. The four women were freakishly similar, though Bébhinn was the most beautiful.

Bébhinn was at least five inches shorter than he was, and he knew from previous group hikes that she was lean and muscular while still maintaining a round ass and mouthwatering tits. He should know. He'd seen her naked in her bedroom many times. He couldn't wait to replace the camera lens with his own eyes.

Tomorrow would be the first day of the rest of their lives, he thought as he quietly parted his bunk curtain to peek at where his future was sleeping peacefully.

## sixteen

## DAGR

DAGR WAS EXHAUSTED and aching to high Heaven. In the trail running world, those symptoms equaled euphoria.

He was hunkered down on the side of a mountain under a thick rock ledge. If he kept pushing hard, he should be able to avoid the worst of the coming storm. He'd spoken to his father that morning. He'd cautioned Dagr again and asked him to call it quits. That wasn't how Dagr rolled, though. Pushing the limits was his specialty, in and out of the courtroom.

So far, he'd only logged two areas on the main trail that needed tending, where rockslides had created a dangerous crossing between two of the summits and several large, downed trees were partially blocking a river. The mountain creatures and plants wouldn't like their water source at such claggy strength.

Otherwise, the past few days had been precisely the mind numbing and body workout he'd needed. Not to say that the dissatisfaction he'd been feeling for months hadn't managed to creep in during the dark of night.

"And what in the bloody hell do you have to be dissatisfied about, boy?" he asked himself as he tied off the ends of his tarp between the two stout oaks bracing each side of the rocky overhang. His makeshift bed was nestled in a dense thicket of trees and would create a snug sleeping nook to pass the night.

He couldn't pinpoint what had triggered the months of unease and restlessness plaguing him. Nothing unusual, and certainly nothing catastrophic, had triggered his disquiet. In fact, it had been years since anything tragic occurred. His mother passed from cancer when he was twelve. He and his dad had managed.

His dad's folks, Dagr's grandparents, passed away ten and sixteen years ago. They'd adopted dad late in life...very late. It was grand to have had the years they'd had with them.

Dagr had turned thirty-nine a few months past, and since then, he could feel that his typically sunny nature had begun to compete with bad moods and sullenness. The busier he stayed, though, the better he felt, which meant he was always working or hiking. His body tended to function well with minimal sleep.

Dad had called him out more than once for his shitty attitude. Dagr definitely needed to get a handle on himself.

He'd considered getting serious about finding a woman with whom he could have a serious relationship. He'd had numerous brief flirtations, where witty banter and great sex were his only criteria. Perhaps he needed to dig deeper.

The problem with going deeper was that it was almost impossible to find a partner uninterested in his bank account, and even harder to find a woman who held even a few of his wish list traits.

They weren't even that difficult, but one would think he was asking for perfection.

Educated—He wasn't talking about a uni degree, just well-read and an intelligent conversationalist was plenty.

Independent—Happy with her own company. No pouting if her boyfriend goes out with his friends occasionally and never complains about him spending time with his father.

Funny—Not like a comedian or anything, just that she could find humor in small things, especially that she could laugh at herself.

Love her family and friends—A person could tell a lot about a partner by how they interact with the people closest to them.

Adventurous, e.g., hiking—A must.

The list was far from out of line. As he made a small fire to give him warmth and light for the evening, he nodded to himself, secure in the belief that his expectations were average. It's not like he was asking for a runway model. In fact, appearance wasn't on the list because he'd been taken in too many times by a pretty face in the past.

His resume was filled with past stunners—unfortunately, he'd even dated a woman from his office. As it turned out, her beauty and brains couldn't erase her complete lack of personality. He'd sworn off women, at least casual women, months ago, which meant the closest interaction he'd had with the opposite sex was boardroom meetings and standing in line at the dry cleaner's.

Lying down on his pallet, he sighed as he covered up with an ultra-thin, insulated blanket as he watched the fire. Mesmerized by the growing flames flickering in the moonlight, and with no one near to pass judgment, he admitted, "You're lonely, Dag."

*Damnit.* He was lonely, and nights were, of course, the worst. One thing that the past few days had made him face was that he wanted a partner. A forever partner. That one person besides his dad that he could count on, rely on, tell his secrets to, and obsess over.

He knew how a man, a real man, treated a partner. His

father had loved his mother with devotion. He'd trusted her absolutely, and she'd trusted him the same. His father never faltered when his mother went through chemotherapy, when she vomited, when she lost too much weight, when she slept for hours a day, or when she lost her hair. His father's love never wavered. Not for one minute.

Dagr wanted that. Desperately wanted that.

He should try a dating app.

Or maybe he should just get a dog.

# seventeen

BÉBHINN

Snowdonia Way Mountain Route
Daily Journal
Day 9
Bethesda To Conwy
Distance: 17.9 miles (28.9 km)
Total Ascent: 1,134 m (3,720.4 ft)

4:47 am

Since I decided to fully forgive you, I feel lighter this morning—and nostalgic. Remember when you, me, and Mom would binge The Hobbit and The Lord of the Rings movies when I was little?

It's one of my favorite memories.

So, how's this for you? "Not all those who wander are lost." Bilbo Baggins got me thinking. I realized that you aren't lost, only wandering. I will see you again.

*I can live with that.*

*My stomach hasn't stopped fluttering. More so than on any other day. There are days it feels like you've been gone for years, and others that feel like it's only been hours. I think the fluttering is because I woke up thinking about what you meant to me, what you'll always mean to me, and I felt..happy.*

*I need to call Nan. No need to scold me. I know I need to visit my grandma. I miss her, and with the exception of Mom, she'll be the happiest to know I'm doing better. Since Pa Dunn passed, I haven't made nearly enough time for my namesake. I swear that woman has the second sight.*

*I've avoided thinking about where you are, but now that I'm coming to terms with our new relationship, I wondered if you get to see Grandma and Grandpa O. I bet your folks were so mad at you for being there too early.*

*Today is going to be a great day. Watch out for me, Dad.*

*Seriously, though, I feel like something important is coming my way.*

*Wish me luck! I love you.*

*B*

---

Bébhinn felt her stiff shoulders tense further as the same feeling of being watched swept her back. Why today of all days? She'd even bragged in her journal about the epic last stage.

She'd started early. It had been dark except for the clear moonlight when she'd left the bunkhouse. The weather was enough of a concern to make her push hard.

Alternating between a jog and a swift walk, she managed to cover eight miles before lunch. Her pace wasn't the problem. The darkening sky and the ever-present creeping sensation of being watched were bringing down the day. However, she hadn't felt like eyes were on her for over two hours.

The creeper vibes could have been her nerves talking. The weather was not holding like the weather reports had predicted early this morning. An hour ago, she'd ensured her emergency Garmin locator was active just in case.

She was pushing her body hard because she wanted to reach the rough bunkhouse before dark, and she should, easily. The question was whether to blow by the night's shelter in the hopes of beating the storm, or at least get closer to Conwy and her ride back to her Jeep.

The bunkhouse had no water or electricity, but it did have a roof and a door, and a cot. If she didn't beat the weather, the alternative was sleeping rough. She had a tarp, but the black and gray clouds gathering above didn't bode well for a dry night's sleep if she didn't make Conwy.

She stopped by a fast-running stream to wash her hands and face and to refill her water skin. She wouldn't admit it to her brothers, but damn did she regret not remembering to bring the sat phone they'd bought her. She could at least call for accurate weather reports instead of trusting her eyes alone.

There was nothing for it but to press on. She was making excellent time. According to her map, she should hit the bunkhouse in another five hours if she kept at a slow jog. She would assess then.

Without a doubt, Bébhinn's panting breaths could be heard for miles. She bypassed the bunkhouse two hours ago and had regretted the decision for approximately an hour and thirty-five minutes.

Visibility was down to twenty percent; heavy snow, wind, and fog were a treacherous combination. Hoping for the best was over. She needed to make a decision and fast, or she would be putting her life in jeopardy.

Cursing her foolish decision yet again, she slowed to a walk and looked for a reasonable spot to hunker down until the weather let up, which probably wouldn't be until morning.

She attempted not to be spooked about the abrupt darkness and lack of visibility, taking several deep, calming breaths.

"Think. Think, think, think. There are rock outcroppings everywhere," she reassured herself out loud. There were hundreds upon hundreds of small caves throughout the Snowdonia range. Surely, she could find one.

Turning on her phone, she went to the downloaded maps and found the one with the most detailed topography of her current location. It was dangerous to go off-trail when visibility was limited—she didn't have a choice.

She'd studied that particular map last night and again this morning to prepare for the type of situation she was unfortunately in. The map showed a promising ridge not more than three hundred feet north of her position. Making up her mind, she struck off the path. Her body was shivering from the quick drop in temperature. Finding shelter and starting a fire was fast becoming critical.

Twenty minutes of slow, careful steps later, the long branch she'd been using as a measuring stick hit rock—falling into a crevasse wasn't on today's agenda. Straining her eyes to see through the blizzard-like conditions, she could just make out several ridges of rock under the snow, leading to what had to be the line of boulders and outcroppings from her map.

"Thank God." She wanted to run to the possible promise of shelter, but forced her feet to move at a steady pace and kept poking her stick left, right, and center as she went.

Thankfully, another line of trees began several feet ahead, running parallel to the rock face, creating a wind and snow break and allowing her to see more clearly.

When she spotted a dark break in the gray rock, she knew she'd found a cave and prayed it was deep enough for her needs. She wanted to rush to the opening but forced her trembling legs to keep steady.

Finally reaching her goal, she could bend and shine her pen light inside the cave. She was relieved to see the narrow opening widen enough to make a pallet and build a fire. She could almost stand to her full height as she moved inside.

Her body shuddered in relief as the biting wind ceased buffeting her body. She took a deep breath as she pulled her face guard down and assessed the cramped but completely acceptable space.

There wasn't any sign of animal occupation. "Thank you again, Lord, for that." She had no desire to share her bed with critters or creepy crawlies. Mostly leaves and twigs littered the floor, which she could use to build a fire.

Before settling in for the night, she needed to brave the outside once more to relieve her bladder—a miserable process in this weather—and gather twigs and anything else that would burn.

Her chest felt considerably less tight having found shelter. The storm had descended sooner than predicted, but she prayed that the prediction of the storm being short-lived was still accurate.

Pulling her face mask up, she told her dad, "It could be worse, Dad. My phone could work, and I'd have to listen to your sons chew my butt for an hour." She hated that her mom would worry, but the moment she was close to the pick-up location, she would have service again and call her mom immediately.

With renewed determination, she left the cave for supplies.

# *eighteen*

## THE WATCHER

"FUCK THIS WEATHER!" he bellowed while kicking one of the rough wooden cots in the bunkhouse that he was forced to take shelter in. The same bunkhouse that the love of his life clearly chose to bypass, putting her life in danger.

He balled his fists, angry enough to burn the bunkhouse to the ground. There was no other option but to find Bébhinn as soon as the weather allowed.

He had to remind himself that she was highly trained in survival. She was one of the strongest long-distance hikers in their Dublin club.

She wouldn't panic. She was smart and strong. Fierce and beautiful.

There was not a savvier outdoorsman than his love. She was so worthy of his worship that he was embarrassed for doubting her decision to press on even though he couldn't follow.

The weather might have crushed his plan of surprising her in her bunk. He would have parted her tarp curtain, offering her a purple saxifrage bouquet...and his heart.

She would be lying on her back, with her piercing amber eyes staring up at him. She would open her arms for an embrace, realizing it was him she'd loved all along, begging his forgiveness for not seeing him sooner.

Sighing, he shook off his disappointment and lay down on a cot so he could envision a new surprise.

A better surprise.

As the snow continued to fall outside and the wind continued to howl, he could only smile in anticipation.

His forever...Bébhinn.

# nineteen

## DAGR

"DAMNIT!" Dagr cursed, frustrated that he'd miscalculated the weather front's speed. He'd slowed to a walk an hour ago and had only gotten as far as he had because he knew the trail well.

He could keep going, but the snow was accumulating fast, and the fog could quickly become disorienting with or without his compass.

He needed to pack it in. He might know the trail, but the deepening snow would hide rocks and branches that could easily trip him, causing anything from a twisted ankle to a fall and possible head injury.

"Damn," he cursed again. Shaking his head in disgust that he hadn't made it to Conwy in time, he sighed and turned off what little of the trail was still visible and started toward a line of rock outcroppings that had a few caves big enough to settle in until the storm passed.

He hadn't gone a hundred feet before he saw an orange glow through the thinning trees. If another hiker had gotten stranded, perhaps they wouldn't mind sharing their fire. That would save him from starting one himself.

As he approached a second row of trees, he scouted for bits of wood beneath the trees yet to be buried by snow. The least he could do was not show up empty-handed when he was hoping to mooch a spot.

Cradling what wood he'd managed to scavenge, he brought his fingers to his lips and blew, whistling loudly to make whoever was in the cave aware that they had company.

He was close enough to see a shadow flicker behind the flames at the mouth of the cave. "Hello, in the cave! Mind some company?"

Silence for a beat greeted his salute and then, "Of course. Come in," a woman's voice called.

The mouth of the cave was surprisingly wide but low enough that he had to practically crawl until the space opened up enough to shuffle on his knees. He dropped the wood behind him before scooting further toward the fire. *Christ, but the heat felt amazing.*

"Hell of a storm," he said while pulling off his balaclava. "It came up fas—" He was interrupted when the woman launched herself at him.

"Bran, you bastard!" she laughed and wrapped her arms around his back where he kneeled, half turned her way.

Her smiling face landed on his surprised one, and she froze, going stiffer than one of the frozen puddles outside.

She quickly scrambled back so fast she fell on her bottom before rapidly rolling up to her knees, mirroring his position. Her mouth was opening and closing, hands raised in a helpless "what the hell" gesture.

She was young, in her early twenties maybe, and...stunning. She was a tiny thing with a long, thick black braid draped over one shoulder. It was her eyes, though, that drew his attention.

Even widened in surprise, they were slightly slanted, almond-shaped, and a stunning golden amber. Striking didn't come close to describing them.

"I'm not sure who Bran is, but I guess you've figured out that I'm not him," he chuckled, trying to lighten the mood.

She finally shifted, easing back to sit on her feet. She grinned, making her dimples deepen. "Good grief," she started, shaking her head. "You must think I'm a lunatic," she laughed.

"Were you expecting Bran?" He glanced out of the cave and noted the snow was heavier now. "Should we search for him? I've a sat phone if you think he got turned around."

Her hands flew up in a stop gesture. "Oh no! I just mistook you for one of my brothers. He's just that level of overprotective that I instantly thought he'd tracked me down because of the weather and was here to 'save me,'" she said using air quotes.

"You thought I was your...brother?" he asked, not understanding how she'd come to such a conclusion when she hadn't even seen his face until he'd turned.

Seeing his skepticism, she grinned and pointed toward his head. "The hair."

He touched his hair automatically. Not a week past, he'd had the sides shaved and the top trimmed. It hung in a waterfall of loose waves that reached mid-ear. He kept it shaggy and falling across his eyes when he wasn't working and slicked back and out of the way for work.

"It's white," she continued. "My brothers and nephews have white hair. It's unusual enough, and if you knew my family and their overprotective tendencies, you probably would have jumped to the same conclusion. Anyway, I'm Bébhinn O'Faolain. Dublin."

At her outstretched hand, he automatically took her hand in a respectful shake. "Dagr Griffiths. Carmarthenshire and

London." He felt ridiculously off kilter. Her self-assured, no-nonsense demeanor was refreshing but also...something else.

She made him feel like a young, brash teenager facing a beautiful woman for the first time. He wanted to appear like the confident man he was, but was surely coming across as a back-wards simpleton.

"Here," she began, rustling around in her pack and pulling a packet of field rations free. "I was just making some soup. I'll add another to my pot for you."

Not waiting for an answer, she got to work making him dinner.

twenty

## BÉBHINN

BÉBHINN TRIED to hide the slight shake of her hands, hoping to appear nonchalant as she dumped another chicken noodle soup packet into the boiling water.

Dagr. Dagr Griffiths. *Jesus.* How had she ever thought the man at her side was remotely related to her *brother*, for the love of God? He was tall, maybe as tall as her dad, but it was hard to tell since she hadn't seen him fully upright.

It was the hair that had caught her off guard. That plus his height had thrown her for a moment. But besides that, they were nothing alike, and thank goodness for that, because no one wanted to look at a sexy stranger and think, "Hey, he looks just like my brother."

Besides his mannerisms and Welsh accent, another thing that was completely different about him were his eyes. Her brothers' eyes ranged from honey amber to dark brown—variations of their father's.

Dagr's eyes were... They were impossible to describe. She needed Mags' flair for description to come close, but if forced, she would call them clear. *You're an idiot, Bébhinn.* Clear? She could do better than that.

They were so light blue, they appeared colorless.

Mesmerizing.

Attempting to drum up a coherent bit of conversation, she blurted, "The weather hit fast." That was all she had?

She watched as he maneuvered his big frame into a more comfortable position. He fed the fire a few pieces of kindling before turning his unnervingly gorgeous eyes back to her.

"It caught me off guard, and that rarely happens."

She believed that the man watching her wasn't caught off guard often. Every movement he made seemed capable. She really needed to stop staring. The man would think he was holed up with a nutter.

Glancing to her left, she noticed that her father's letter was lying on a rock shelf next to her pack, and she discreetly pushed the envelope under her discarded face mask.

Tonight was supposed to be the night she read her dad's final words. *Damn. Damn. Damn.*

"I can't believe we found the same cave."

"Oh, I knew the cave was here. I hike all over the world, but Wales is my home. Dad and I have explored every mile. I am surprised that you found it, though. Unless this isn't your first time exploring these peaks."

"It's my first, but I did study the topography maps of each stage, and thank God I did or else I'd have had to push through." She shivered thinking about it. "I was getting pretty cold before I decided to find shelter."

She stirred the soup, which was ready. It only took a minute to hydrate the noodles and chicken. Dagr rummaged through his pack until he pulled out a small metal pan similar to hers. She held her hand out and he handed it to her so she could split the soup.

As she divvied dinner, he tugged off his shoes, placed them near the fire by hers, and shed his jacket.

"Hopefully, this thing will dry fast. I've been using it for my pillow at night." He explained while he laid the jacket between himself and the fire.

"In the meantime, I've been staying at lovely B&Bs with feather mattresses and hot showers." She smirked before adding, "I like my travel agent better than yours."

He laughed before picking up his pot to sip the hot soup. "Ahh, so you're a princess hiker. I must have missed seeing your matching luggage because it was covered in snow."

"Hey! I travel light, Mr. Judgy. And to think, I was about to offer to share my pillow."

"Oh Christ, I knew it! The princess needs a pillow."

"No, the princess was smart enough to pack a blow-up pillow that takes up no room in her pack but provides much more comfort than a zipper jacket."

"Fine, fine. I concede. I'm sure as hell not going to argue with the woman who built this fire and made me dinner."

"Ha ha. Mom and my aunts have always said that the way to a man's heart is through his stomach. Well," she smirked, enjoying their banter, "Aunt River says a lot more than that, but I won't repeat her words of wisdom in polite company."

The shocked look on Dagr's face before he burst out laughing was priceless. Her immediate thought was that she wished her dad could have met him. Dad rarely liked anyone, but something told her he would like Dagr Griffiths.

"It sounds like you have a close family. Do you all live in Dublin?"

"We are. Very much so, and yes, most of us. My mom and dad grew up in Oklahoma, in the States, though my mom and sisters split their time between Ireland and Oklahoma. Only in recent years, once Dad's mom passed, did he sell most of his properties there.

"Dad was already retired when he married my mother, and she and her sisters had already started their interior decorating business in Dublin. So, smart man that he was, he moved to Ireland. Do you have a big family here in Wales, then?"

"It's just me and Dad." He shrugged like it wasn't a big deal, but she got the feeling he might have loved having a big family. "Dad's folks passed a few years back, and I'm an only child. My mother died when I was a kid. She was a competitive eater and choked during a hot dog challenge."

Bébhinn felt her eyes widen and her mouth drop. Surely, she'd heard him wrong. A...hotdog? "Umm, gosh...wow, Dagr. That's terrible. I'm s—" She was cut off by his laughter.

"God, Bébhinn, you should have seen your face. Never play poker, lass." His shoulders were still shaking in amusement when he divulged, "Mom died from a severe stroke. It was sudden. A complication from her cancer. She died within hours."

She let out a huge breath, torn between laughing and crying in commiseration of losing a parent suddenly. "I'm sorry. I bet she wanted to kick cancer's ass for you and your dad's sake." Then, to lighten the mood, she added, "You can't have many friends with that type of humor, you asshole. Hot dogs..." Her pfft of exasperation made him smile.

He only grinned and shrugged. "I don't. Not really. Dad is my best friend, and he's all I've ever needed."

She tried to hide her wince, but his admission landed close.

"So," he changed the subject, glancing toward her pack, "what's with the letter?"

He must have noticed her tucking the letter away earlier. "Family business," she replied, with a touch more irritation than she liked.

Dagr held his hands up in a sign of peace. "Apologies. I'm an attorney. I recognized the legal embossing on the envelope." He must have noticed her discomfort, because he immediately said, "I spoke out of turn. I'm sorry."

Her face flamed with embarrassment. "No. I'm sorry. I overreacted. It's...it is... I meant to read my father's letter to me. He passed just over six months ago." She felt her face tighten with the need to cry and quickly turned, busying herself with fiddling with the fire and taking a sip of her soup.

He was silent for so long, she thought the awkward moment would never pass, and then he said, "I understand the pain of losing a loved one. You meant to read that letter tonight. Let me find another shelter so that you can have the privacy you obviously planned for the evening." He was already rolling to his knees and reaching for his pack.

Bébhinn whipped her gaze to the man. "Oh, Lord, no. I'm sorry if it came across that way. You aren't going anywhere in this weather. Don't even think it. Dad and I were supposed to go on this hike together. I'm hyper," she stuttered, "hypersensitive. I miss him, but I've had a great hike. He'd be very happy.

"My family, on the other hand, will be foaming at the mouth with worry when I don't check in," she chuckled, still blinking rapidly to dam the tears wanting to sneak out. "Even though I warned them that the weather might delay me."

"No shame. My father still blows up my phone with dire warnings and demands. In fact, I can't believe he hasn't already called me."

When he grinned at her, Bébhinn felt her stomach flip. The man was...all man. If her friends were here, Gray would raise one patrician brow in caution. Blair would give her a cautious look that meant "He's hot, proceed, but use caution." Mags would be giving her two extremely obvious thumbs up and elbowing her forward.

"I've got at least twenty years on you, young lady, and I'm still about to use my sat phone to let my dad know I'm safe. You can use it to contact your family, too, if you want."

Twenty years? Surely not. "I'll take you up on that. My brothers bought me a sat phone, and in my hurry to leave, I forgot it." He began to rummage through his pack, eventually pulling his sat out. "I would rather call one of my brothers, but I should probably call my mom. Since dad, she's...she struggles."

"Of course she would be—"

He was cut off when the sat phone started to ring. "Jesus," she heard him mumble.

"Hello," he answered.

She was fascinated when she saw the seemingly unrufflable attorney's cheeks turn red. He glanced her way once and winced, turning his body just enough to avoid eye contact.

From the one-sided conversation, she ascertained that his father was as protective as hers had been.

"Aye, Fa. I'm fine. I said I'm fine. Christ, Dad! I'm warm enough. We're snug in a cave with a fire." His muttered "idiot" was meant for himself. He hadn't meant to mention her, she assumed, smiling at his expense. "Another hiker got stuck like me. Yes, it's safe. Jesus! Dad! Enough. I'll call you when I get to Conwy. Fine. Fine. Yes." And then the best part. "I love you, too."

He looked at her with a sheepish expression after he hung up. "Pretend you didn't just witness a thirty-nine-year-old man being raked over the coals by his father."

She covered her grin with her hands until she could suppress her laughter. "Hey, listen, I'm only thrilled that it isn't just my family that's so extra."

"Oh no. It might only be the two of us, but my father is mighty in his extra-ness." He wiggled the phone at her. "Give me your mom's number."

With a nod, she took the phone from him once it started to ring. Her mother answered before the first ring finished.

"Hello."

Her mother sounded like she'd been crying. *Damn.* "Hey, Mom, it's me. Sorry, it's so late."

There was a squeal, then arguing voices, and finally, her mother cleared her throat. "Bébhinn, sweetheart. No worries, I'm just so happy to hear your voice."

She made a vow when she heard the quiver in her mother's voice that she would never forget the sat phone again.

"No fucking worries. No worries, Row? For fuck's sake, sister! You made your mother and aunts worry," Bran's growly voice shouted over the line, loud enough for Dagr to hear if his raised brows were any indication.

Bran must have taken the phone from her mom, or Bébhinn was on speaker. "I'm literally only three hours later than I normally call, Bran. I hardly think your tone is necessary," she warned.

"Are you safe? I don't like this." Speaker then. That was Patrick.

Before she could answer, Raven said, "I'm glad you called. My husband has been impossible."

"Ignore your brother, babe. He's grumpy because I had a treatment on my vagina and he's been cut off for two days."

"Jesus, River, stop! Now I'm snowed in and gagging." She glanced at Dagr, who had his hands covering his face to stifle his laughter.

Another thirty seconds went by when all she could hear were people saying "Stop," "Christ, Riv," "I'm officially sick," and the go-to, "Dad, make her stop."

Jonathan piped up next. "Where are you staying tonight?"

"There are several caves just off the main trail. I found one and started a fire. I just finished eating dinner. I'm cozy. Hopefully, the snow breaks by morning, and I can start early."

Her mother gasped, "Oh, Bébhinn. A cave? That doesn't sound safe."

"Never mind that, Auntie Row," Daniel cut in. "Where'd you get the sat, Bébé?"

*Nosy bastard.* As casually as she could, she said, "Oh crap, I forgot to tell you that another hiker got stranded too, and we're sharing the shelter for the night."

Cue...silence. Dagr's hands dropped, and he shook his head, grimacing. He could see where this line of questioning was headed.

"Name?" Bran demanded.

Before she could reply, Dagr answered for himself. "Dagr Griffiths." His deep voice held a hint of warning.

Not good. Not good. Not good *at all*. Now it was her turn to cover her face with her hands, but not because she was laughing. No. It was pure mortification.

Without hesitation, he said, "Solicitor with a practice in London. Pro bono work for wildlife protection, predominantly in Wales. Avid trail runner. Assistant Ranger for Wales National Trust. I inspect trails and assess maintenance needs.

"I'm thirty-nine. Single. My mother's passed, but my father loves me. I'm not liking your tone with Bébhinn, but I understand your worry, so I'll let it go. I have no intention of making a pass toward your sister...niece, as she's far too young."

River's snort of amusement only made her face burn hotter. *Lord, take me to my father. I'm ready.*

"Fine." Bran.

"Take care of her." Patrick.

"She snores." Jonathan.

"I love you. Call me from Conwy." Mom.

"Keep your hands to yourself." Daniel.

When the call ended, I could only shrug and say, "Welcome to the O'Faolain family."

# twenty-one

## THE WATCHER

IT WAS three in the morning, and he'd woken up after only two hours.

He wouldn't sleep again until she was in his sight. He knew that. The fear that she was unprotected in the blizzard-like conditions was debilitating.

He'd spent a few hours dreaming about all the things he had planned to do to her the moment she agreed to be his.

What bit of skin would his fingers or lips touch first? He'd pictured tracing his fingertips across her full lips and down her neck to follow the line of her collarbone.

Whispering all the dirty things he wanted to do to her. What he wanted her to do to him.

He would tell her that he lived for her pleasure.

Through a camera, he'd seen her face in the throes of passion. He knew exactly what she'd look like when he played with her body. Picturing her bright, whiskey eyes wide, looking up at him, her body quivering as he laved and then sucked a nipple into his mouth had him grinding his hips into the rough canvas of his cot.

She had the best nipples. Her areolas were a stunning deep brown and the size of a fifty-euro cent.

In his dream, her nipples would make a decadent popping noise as he lifted his head and allowed them to pull free of his mouth.

He was sweaty and panting as he woke from the erotic dream. Groaning into his blanket, he realized he wasn't too old to make a mess in his boxers.

He cleaned himself up and now stood at the lone window watching swirls of snow batter the landscape.

She was out there. Alone.

"You'll never be alone again, baby."

# twenty-two

## DAGR

DAGR COULDN'T REMEMBER when he'd enjoyed a dinner more. Instead of a perfectly cooked steak or fish filet with veg and potato sides, he slurped down a scorching portion of some bland, protein-packed watery soup and savored it.

Dessert had been his treat, having shared half of a blueberry protein bar with the woman sitting across the fire from him.

His dinner date was currently grinning around her puffed cheeks as she blew up her "princess" pillow. Done with the resuscitation, she pressed the rubber plunger back in its cradle and triumphantly held a standard-sized pillow up for his inspection.

"See? It even has a soft outside for ultimate comfort," she said while running her fingers over the pillow's textured material.

Bébhinn O'Faolain intrigued him. She was the whole package—intelligent, funny, adventurous, and though he would prefer not to admit the last, he would. She was stunning.

Not in the way some women were beautiful with perfectly-applied makeup, salon hairstyles, and tailored clothes. Bébhinn was an all-natural beauty. She radiated health and passion. The absolute best thing was that they were complete strangers, and he felt more comfortable around her than anyone except for his father.

"I appreciate the earlier offer of sharing that blowup toy, but I've done the calculations, and they show that even with your small head, once you add my big head, we definitely won't fit."

"We'll fit," she assured. "With my body wrapped around this side of the fire, and your body wrapped around the other, I'll put the pillow lengthwise between our heads. We each get an end."

He paused for a moment, realizing he hadn't considered that layout. "Perhaps. To be decided."

Her eyes lit with amusement, and she gave him a considering look. "You didn't think I meant to sleep next to you, did you? Surely, Mr. Griffiths, we haven't known each other long enough for the big spoon/little spoon step in our relationship."

He felt the pale skin across his cheeks and ears heat even knowing she was only teasing him. Clearing his throat, he busied himself with putting enough wood on the fire to last a few hours before answering. "Very funny. Although this," he waved a hand between them, "could go down as one of my longest relationships. Sooo," he grinned, "you know." He shrugged, taking great pleasure when he saw her cheeks pinken this time.

"You must be a great attorney. You're brilliant at turning conversations around to suit you." She lifted her eyebrows in mock censure.

"Speaking of, thanks to your brother's interrogation, you know something about my life, but I don't know anything about you. What do you do in Dublin?" *Please say you're a very young-looking divorcée.*

"I'm a student at Trinity."

*Fuck my life.*

"I've one year left for my History of Arts & Architecture degree. I already work part-time at my mother's and aunts' interior design studio. When I graduate, they plan on making me a partner.

"One of my best friends, Gray MacGregor, works for her mother's company, O'Connor Hospitality. Gray and I plan on working many of the jobs together in the future since I'm more passionate about decorating commercial spaces over residential, and she's brilliant at opening businesses."

He was impressed with her passion as she spoke about her work. He knew the feeling of satisfaction that came with understanding your path in life. He had a lot of friends who went to university and fell into whatever job was eventually offered. They never appeared fulfilled.

"Sounds like you have it all figured out. You should be proud to be so young and driven. Now," he started, removing most of his outer clothes since the cave was warm and he could use his layers as a pallet, "do you mind explaining your family...tree?"

She snorted in amusement while she mimicked his actions of getting ready to bed down for the night. "Ahh, you caught that, did you?"

She looked at him and rolled her eyes heavenward, blowing out a regretful breath, which only intrigued him more.

"Had I had a legal notepad and pen, I might have been able to keep track of the names and familiarities, but alas, I'm only a man, stuck in a cave with no paper or laptop in sight."

"Fine, but you asked for it. Try not to interrupt," she warned. At his nod, she continued. "Mom has two sisters. My mom's name is Rowan, and her two older sisters are Raven and

River. Older is quite a stretch as they are no more than nine to ten months apart.

"I won't get into their parents' lineage tonight except to say that my grandfather was a Byrne and Irish, and my grandmother was a Bond, Creek Native American from Oklahoma. They were both college professors in Oklahoma and died in a tornado years before I was born.

"Fast forward. My mom and aunts started an interior design business while still in college. They first had a brick-and-mortar shop in Oklahoma before moving permanently to Dublin and opening the shop they still have now. Triskelion Territory Designs. The reason for their move is an even longer and convoluted one, entailing my aunt Raven and her then-boyfriend breaking up. With me so far?"

"Yes, but damn if I'm not missing a computer right now."

"Wait. It gets better," she promised. "Enter the O'Faolains. Wealthy Oklahoma oil tycoons who decided to open an Irish pub in Tulsa, Oklahoma, in memory of the family's patriarch, who'd passed years before, Jonathan O'Faolain.

"Hugh was the head of the family and had two grown sons, Bran and Patrick. God, in His infinite wisdom or more likely His sense of humor, led the men to hire the sisters.

"Long story shortish, Bran fell in love with Raven. Patrick fell in love with River, and Hugh fell in love with my mom, Rowan. Bran and River had a son, Daniel. Patrick and River had a son a few months later, Jonathan, and Hugh, my father, and my mother, had me a few months after that, making me Bran and Patrick's sister and niece, and them my brothers and uncles. Daniel and Jonathan are my nephews and my first cousins. Oh, and Mom is Bran and Patrick's sister-in-law, and their stepmother.

"Dad bought a four-story stone relic next to Triskelion and had the whole thing remodeled. The bottom floor is a realistic pub and great room for hanging out and entertaining, with guest rooms in the back. The remaining floors are for the three couples, so they were never far from each other.

"Would you like even more convoluted information to blow your mind?"

"Christ, why not?"

"Okay. So, Dad bought the townhouse I live in with my three best friends. He also bought the historic brick townhouse attached to mine. Can you guess who lives there?"

"My guess is your cousins...or nephews rather."

"Correct. Plus, Ciar Murphy. He is a few years older and the son of Ciaran Murphy. Ciaran and his brother Cormac own a successful pub in Dublin. Murphys. Ciaran, by the way, used to have a thing for Mom. Dad never stopped hating him," she laughed.

"Your dad sounds like he was very protective of his family."

"You have no idea. Anyway, my mom and aunts' best friend is Josephine O'Connor MacGregor. She grew up in Oklahoma but has since permanently moved to Scotland with her husband, Thomas MacGregor. You'll recall me mentioning my friend Gray earlier. Jo is her mom.

"Thomas has another daughter—whom he raised but isn't the biological dad of—with his ex-wife, whom he was married to in name only because she fell pregnant in college and her folks are dickheads. His ex-wife, Aileen, is now married to their daughter's bio dad. Margaret, or Mags, is that daughter and another one of my best friends and roommates.

"Aileen's older brother, Coll, is also Thomas' best friend. The three of them grew up together. Coll married Thomas' little sister, Catriona. They have a daughter, Blair. She is also one of my closest friends and lives with me too.

"There you have it. The inner workings of my inner circle."

He was a very successful attorney. Pouring over dusty tombs

of complex law was light reading for him, but Bébhinn's regurgitation of her family and friends' connections had his head spinning.

"Wow. Seriously. Wow."

"I did warn you. You've only yourself to blame." She placed the pillow between them and was about to lie down. "I'll call you next week and give you an oral exam. Good luck."

"Your smug tone suggests you don't think I'll pass."

"Mmm," was her reply.

"I never put failure on the table as an option. Hand me your phone." She unlocked it with a curious but amused look and handed it over. He unlocked his phone and handed it to her.

He went to her contacts and added his name and number, and because he was thorough, he added his email and birthday. He was pleased she was entering her information too.

"I'll take one hour tonight before I go to sleep to recite everything you told me. It's all I'll need."

"You think I won't call?"

She had already lain on her side facing the fire, taking up an extra small portion of pillow. He lay down too, taking up more than half the space.

"If you're even half so diligent as your late father and brothers, I would bet that you already know the day and time you'll be placing the call." He grinned when he heard her snort of amusement.

"We'll see," was all she gave.

"The snow has almost stopped. We can make an early start of it. I know the trails well. With the snowfall, it should take between eight and ten hours to reach Conwy. I had a service take my car to Conwy. I've been summoned to Carmarthenshire. My father has managed to piss off one of the new park's biggest donors, and he needs me to smooth things over."

She sighed deeply before answering. "Dads can be the worst," she said wistfully.

"And the best."

"That too."

"You mentioned you have a lift from Conwy to transport you to your jeep, but you still must drive to the ferry. Let me radio my friend's son and have them take your jeep to Conwy. It's less than an hour to Holyhead ferry from there. Did you leave your keys at the ranger office?"

"I did, but for crying out loud, you don't need to go to the trouble," she insisted.

He picked up his sat phone, dialed Joey, and set it up before Bébhinn could protest further. "Done."

"You're bossy."

"Something tells me you like bossy." Her silence was answer enough, so he pushed his luck further. "Read the letter. Tonight was the night, and you aren't a coward. Read it."

# twenty-three

## BÉBHINN

READ IT. Read it. Read it.

Perhaps it would be easier to have Dagr to take some of the loneliness from her while she read whatever her dad chose to write down for her.

Bébhinn wasn't afraid, not really. More reluctant than anything. Once she read it, she couldn't look forward to receiving more.

It would be over. Really over. Dad would be gone.

She didn't speak, letting the crackle of the fire and the whistling wind outside settle her reticence. Ten minutes passed before she slowly slid the letter out from the bag at her back, tracing her name scrawled in her dad's bold, slanting strokes.

*Bébhinn Clarissa O'Faolain*

**Hugh Darcy O'Faolain**
posthumous letter

*My dearest Bébhinn,*

I must have died, my sweet B. I hope it happened later than sooner, but that's the thing about death, the one doing the dying hasn't a clue.

I have decided to write you, your brothers, and your mother a letter once a year. I hope Lee, our family attorney, dumps at least twenty letters in everyone's lap when I finally peace out, even though that puts me in my nineties.

For reference, I wrote this letter to you on your twentieth birthday. I can't explain why I decided that it was the perfect time to be morbid, and this will sound as though I was losing my mental faculties, but I assure you, I have not. I had a dream.

Mom and Dad spoke to me (and for the last time, I am of sound mind). They told me they loved me and that they would be seeing me soon and not to be scared.

They must still be working out the afterlife kinks because it scared the fuck out of me.

I double checked my will, making sure your mom and my children are well taken care of—not that your mom isn't the best interior designer in the world, or you and your brothers aren't successful in your own rights.

You're young, sweet girl, but you carry the best of the Byrnes and O'Faolains in your DNA.

I'm proud of you, Bébhinn. There isn't a father prouder of his daughter.

I hope this isn't the last letter, but just in case, I'll try to fit in most of what's in my heart.

You will become a partner in Triskelion with your mom, but I also want you to take a seat on the O'Faolain board of trustees. Your brothers will always take care of you, but you need to have a voice in the family businesses.

All of them.

Especially Three Wolves Whiskey. I don't know why that particular venture is my favorite. I do know my father would have loved it, and maybe deep down, I'm still trying to make him proud of me.

I don't like your boyfriend. Get rid of him, or I will. If he were worth your time, I wouldn't be able to get rid of him so easily—and it would be easy.

You need a man who isn't easily scared. The boys and I can be intimidating, so don't date anyone easily intimidated.

I hope there are many letters to follow this one. I hope I'm there to see you successful in business and love. I hope I'm still here to walk you down the aisle someday. I hope I'm here to break up the fights between your brothers and cousins—and there will be many.

I want to see you smile at me from across the room. I want to raise a glass of Three Wolves to toast your many successes.

I want desperately to be here to slay every one of your dragons, but we both know, as does your mother, though she refuses to discuss it, that I'm an old man now and only getting older.

I chose to marry your mother because she was and still is the absolute love of my life. I did fight her on it, but you know your mother. You get your stubbornness from her.

Your mother.

Christ and all his angels as my witness, I have never loved another person more. She made me a better man, son, father, and friend.

When I tell you that your mother's strength, generosity, and love shine in you stronger than any other, there is no greater compliment.

I will be writing Row her own letter(s). I think I know her better than anyone else, including her sisters. When I do die, she will move on from her grief at her own pace, and nothing will change her itinerary.

She will let me go.

Eventually.

My letter will leave her no choice. I can assure you. She won't read it for a goodly while. Don't force it. And don't worry about grief carrying either one of you away. That would be selfish to everyone else who is still living and loves you. Neither of my girls is selfish.

Heaven is real. My folks taught me that. I hope I don't see you guys for a very long time, but I believe with everything in me that we will meet again. There is comfort in that.

As for you, I'll make it simple. I'm dead, but you will never not have me. I am a part of you as you have been a part of me—from the moment your eyes looked at me from your sweet face...my eyes.

You may be the image of your mom, you may have her artistic flair, but you are MY daughter. My advice, hopes, and dreams for you are simple.

Never limit yourself.

You are capable of anything.

No dream is too big.

I love you. Now and forever.

Dad

~Warning — I've made sure in my other letters to make sure the boys don't let their baby sister get serious with anyone they don't approve of. Don't roll your eyes at me, Bébhinn. Like I wrote earlier, if he's worth you, your brothers and nephews won't be able to run him off.

~~I've been thinking about a few big hikes we could do together. One is in Wales. What do you think of getting your mom to play in the mud with us?

~~~Call Lee after you read this. His firm has a gift for you from me.

~~~~I'm going to let you go now. No more post-scripts. Live your life knowing I will always watch over you.

Bébhinn carefully folded the letter back into its neat trifold with one hand. She was surprised to feel her other hand in the firm grip of Dagr Griffiths. She breathed a shaky breath out, silent tears tracking her cheeks, finding herself so very thankful for the gift of her father's words.

His words weren't just about his love for her. They were also permission, or a demand in his case, to go on living life.

To live and love and laugh.

She would always carry her father's memory, and it *would* be enough.

Bébhinn gave Dagr's hand a tight squeeze of acknowledgment, and he tightened his grip in response.

He didn't let go, and neither did she.

# twenty-four

## DAGR

LUCKILY, the wind during the storm last night kept the snow from packing the trails too heavily. There were still spots that might have been treacherous if Dagr hadn't been familiar with the terrain. The two and three-foot drifts easily changed the landscape and could give less experienced map readers trouble.

Undoubtedly, the petite woman walking behind him would have had no problems. Her father had made sure she was a highly competent outdoorsman.

Bébhinn had doused the rest of the fire's coals with snow while he stacked the remaining firewood against the cave wall that morning. They'd already eaten a breakfast of protein bars and water and dressed.

Before he crouched to lead the way out of the cave, he'd given her a stern look. "Do you want to talk about anything? About the letter?" he added unnecessarily. She hadn't pulled her face mask up yet, so he saw her cheeks pinken. He hoped she wasn't embarrassed about sharing such an important moment with him.

She smiled softly and shrugged. "The letter is … it so encompassed Dad. Wonderful and sweet and exasperating. I'm glad I waited to read it. I wasn't ready six months ago."

Bent at an uncomfortable angle, he took an awkward shuffle step back to where she stood upright and took her gloved hand in his. "I'm glad to hear it."

"Thank you for being there. I'm not sure I could have done it without you beside me."

"You could have. You would have."

She used her free hand to lightly touch his cheek before saying, "I think we were meant to meet."

He felt his body shudder and heat. "I agree." Before he could do or say anything inappropriate, he dropped her hand and backed out of the low opening. "Best get on with the last section."

They trucked along for almost eight hours at a steady pace, but far from his normal trail running speed. He was no longer in a hurry and had no plan to risk an injury on the covered trail. He was also in no hurry to part with the present company.

He heard a gasp behind him and turned in time to catch Bébhinn's arms as she stumbled forward.

"Good grief," she grimaced. "Sorry about that. I didn't place my foot in your footstep and stepped on a branch or something that shifted. If I don't pull it together, you'll think I'm a green hiker."

Her laughter proved that she wasn't concerned about his reaction. Even with the shit weather, she was excellent at summiting. Her ability to pinpoint their location and read terrain changes was impressive.

"Yeah, you are so clumsy." He forced himself to let her shoulders go and step back. *Remember, dumbass, you're entering middle age, and she's still at uni.* "Another hour and we'll find Conwy. I'm sure my buddy's son parked your Jeep beside mine."

"And thankful I am that you did that for me. I wasn't looking forward to driving a couple of hours to grab my Jeep before driving on to the ferry."

They began their final descent, enjoying the warm sun on their faces, chatting like old friends. He told her about some of his more extraordinary cases in London, his work for INCC, and his father's nature reserve passion project.

"My friend Blair is a botany genius. I'll have to tell her about the reserve's internship."

"It's an unpaid internship," he warned.

"Besides the fact that it would look crazy good on a CV, Blair would pay your dad to work with wild plants. When I say she is a genius, I'm not exaggerating. Her mother has a successful nursery in Scotland. Catriona and Blair can spend days wrist deep in potting soil without coming up for air."

"I'll have Dad send me the information. I'll forward it to you. In the past, the positions were highly sought and tough to get."

He smiled when he looked over his shoulder and saw her wave her hand in front of her like she wasn't concerned.

"Pfft. She'll get it."

"What are your plans when you get home?"

"I would like to tell my family that I'm spending one more night in Wales and give myself a few hours to go home, shower, and snuggle in bed with no familial interrogations until tomorrow, but alas, Blair and Gray's dads own a security firm, and they'll know the minute I step foot on my block and alert my brothers."

When he started to chuckle, she groaned, saying, "I'm not joking."

"Wow. Your family is..."

"Yeah."

As the sun melted more snow from the trail, they could pick up the pace until they stood side by side at Conwy Mountain's summit overlooking the town's castle and quay.

"How does it feel to complete Wales's most grueling hike, Miss O'Faolain?"

"Pretty damn good, Mr. Griffiths."

"I'm glad we met," he dared to profess.

She remained silent, staring over the picturesque landscape surrounding them. Finally, she said, "That sounded like a goodbye."

He didn't dare look at her, keeping his eyes forward. "It wasn't."

She made a humming sort of growl in her throat. Acceptance? Agreement?

"Race you to the bottom, old man!"

She squealed and took off before he could trounce her for the "old man" comment. He barked out a laugh before following.

As he raced after the woman throwing smack talk over her shoulder, her long braid beating against her pack as she pelted down the rocky slope, he realized something important. Since he'd ducked into the cave the night before, he hadn't felt a moment's discontent.

Somehow, Bébhinn O'Faolain had snatched him out of whatever monotonous trajectory he'd been living.

Dagr upped his pace, easily overtaking her. "Sucks to be short and slow," he said as he easily maneuvered around her to lead them the rest of the way.

"Hey," she shouted as he pulled ahead, "a gentleman would have let me win."

"I'm a man, but I never claimed to be gentle," he shouted

over his shoulder. He was still chuckling as he slid on the rocks leading up to the lot where their Jeeps were parked.

Bending at the waist, he grasped his knees as sweat dripped from his forehead despite the chill in the air. Bébhinn skidded to a halt next to him, her good-natured personality intact but equally out of breath and sweaty.

He couldn't help it. He tapped the end of her nose before announcing, "I won."

"Shithead. I'm a hiker. Not a trail runner," she sniffed, pretending offense.

They stored their gear, and then it was time for goodbyes. Reluctant goodbyes, at least on his part.

When he could no longer comfortably stare at her, he stuck his hand out. "It was a true pleasure to make a new friend, Bébhinn O'Faolain." He inwardly winced at the word friend, but that was what they had become. He only winced because it sounded like he was drawing a line in their relationship—a line he should have drawn but didn't want.

She didn't take his proffered hand.

# twenty-five

## THE WATCHER

HE WAS REELING FROM SHOCK. His body was shaking from exertion, having left the bunkhouse soon after the snow had stopped. He couldn't stay there, knowing Bébhinn was alone and with him wondering if she'd found shelter to wait out the storm.

It had been dangerous and foolish to leave while it was dark, but the headlamp had provided enough light, even though he'd gotten turned around three times and had to backtrack.

He'd been cursing himself for hours. He was tired, thirsty, and sore from where he'd fallen over hidden debris.

Hours ago, he'd found tracks leading off the path and followed them to ensure she hadn't gotten turned around in the storm.

They led to a cave. He sighed in relief. She must have stayed there. When he turned to backtrack, he noticed something he hadn't registered in his hurry to follow the tracks. His booted tread was clear to see heading toward the cave but when he studied the tracks leaving the cave, there were two sets.

One large, one small.

Fear like he'd never felt filled him. Were the small tracks Bébhinn's? The larger ones had to have been made by a man. They were huge compared to the smaller ones.

He blew a breath out, shaking the negative thoughts away. She probably hadn't even stayed in the cave. Knowing her perseverance, she pushed on through the weather and slept snug in Conwy. The tracks could belong to anyone. Lucky for him, once he got back on the main trail, he was able to follow their trail.

Whoever they were, they were headed in the direction he needed to go. Knowing where to step, he'd been able to pick up his pace to a jog, even though his heart had felt like it could explode hours ago.

He stopped briefly four times, costing him time, but it couldn't be helped. He'd almost cried in relief when Conwy came into view.

His plans could still pan out. Her transport time with the car service wasn't for another two hours. He would find her yet and hopefully surprise her. He would admit to his feelings, and she would admit hers.

They would laugh about how scared he'd been for her safety before sharing her ride back to their vehicles in Machynlleth. They would spend the ferry ride to Dublin holding hands and talking about the future.

There was still enough snow on the ground, even at this elevation, so he kept following the tracks, noticing they were heading to a public parking area next to the town's community information center, where most hikers parked or waited for transportation. With luck, she would be there.

He had convinced himself that the tracks he'd been

following weren't hers. She had been solo hiking for days, and as far as he knew, Bébhinn hadn't changed her mind, but the scene in front of him told a different story.

There she was, standing way too close to a man he'd never seen before, who was looking at his girlfriend with way too much possession.

He stilled on the small path leading to the lot and watched in horror as Bébhinn smiled and laughed. Her level of comfort around the man didn't scream friends.

Worse, her Jeep was parked and running next to the pair. She'd changed her plans and had it transported to Conwy.

No admittance of feelings.

No shared ride.

No ferry ride holding hands.

All his months of planning were ruined.

Who was the white-haired man? Not family. Not with how she was looking at him.

He spun around and ducked behind a line of trees before she noticed him. He lashed out in rage, punching the bark of the tree repeatedly until the pain in his knuckles brought tears to his eyes.

He slid down the trunk until he could spy the pair between a break in the trees.

He watched them embrace.

The man cradled the woman he loved to his chest as if she were *his* most precious treasure.

He felt his heart breaking. Beyond his pain, he only knew confusion. This was not a man she'd ever been around. Her family had that hair, but the intruder was not one of them.

Her body was plastered to the man's. He watched as the man cupped the back of Bébhinn's head lovingly to his chest.

The scene was nauseating. Maddening.

Nothing about this scene was right. In fact, the wrongness of it had bile building in his throat.

How had his plans gone so awry?

Clenching his jaw, he admitted defeat. In this moment. Only this moment. There would be another chance for them to connect. He would make sure of it.

# twenty-six

BÉBHINN

"COME ON, man. A handshake. Really? You helped me through the scariest night of my life, and I don't mean the snowstorm. Give me a hug, you big brute, and mean it."

Air whooshed out of her lungs when he did as she commanded, lifting her until her toes barely touched the pavement and crushing her to his chest.

The thump of his heart against her ear was Heaven and over all too soon. Once her heels touched the ground, she forced herself to take a step back.

Looking up into Dagr's serious, intense expression had her stomach flexing. "Come on, Dagr. A hug shouldn't put that look on your face," she teased, when in reality, she was shriveling from embarrassment.

He made it clear that he considered her a friend, not girlfriend potential. She went and made it awkward. *Damnit!* Though he was the one who took the hug from casual to "I don't want you to leave." Confusing, after the friend comment.

He didn't comment on the hug, moving past it with, "If you leave now, you'll easily catch the four o'clock ferry."

*Ouch.* She was pretty sure she'd just been dismissed. "Oh, right. Sure. I'll get out of your hair, then." She opened her Jeep door and slightly hopped to reach the seat before shutting herself in. Flicking the window button down, she waved as she backed out of her parking spot. "Safe travels, Dagr."

She took several deep breaths as she left the park station, refusing to look in her rearview mirror to see if he was watching her drive away.

---

An hour later, Bébhinn was walking across the ferry's deck to make her way inside and hopefully grab a drink and a calorie-laden cheeseburger before starting the arduous task of returning the innumerable texts from her friends.

She kept trying to get her elation back to what it had felt like to complete her first crazy solo hike, but her brain was stubbornly stuck on Dagr Griffiths.

She sat at the same table she'd occupied the first time and dug into her burger while she opened her texts. She'd called her mom on the drive to Holyhead. She would let her sisters, Bran, and Patrick know that Bébhinn was on her way home and would see everyone tomorrow for a mandatory family lunch.

She pulled up her friends' group chat, Devils & Angels.

Daniel: I hope that prick with the sat phone kept his hands to himself, B.

Jonathan: Dad said he looked him up, and he is who he said. Still, when he saw that it was only Bébhinn in that cave, he should have bailed.

Mags: Love that you two think Bébhinn needs or wants your opinions.

Bébhinn grinned at the support.

Gray: I have a hot date tonight. Tall, dark, and Nigerian. I might be in love. Wish me luck.

Daniel: Has your dad vetted him yet?

Gray: Jesus, Daniel, you're annoying. Blair— you never told me if you want to go on a double with us.

Mags: If I weren't visiting my parents, I'd go. Your guy's friend is a smoke show. I just found out the guy I'm seeing doesn't read, AND he called my embroidery cute. Idiot. You should go, Blair, and stop fiddling with those Bell things.

Blair: Nettle-leaved Bellflower. Campanula trachelium, to be exact, and it will be part of my thesis. They'll go extinct without help.

Mags: Which isn't happening until next year!

Blair: Exactly! I don't have time to waste on going out with someone I'll never see again.

Gray: When I get home, I'll help you babysit your green babies. Dad said he didn't want you sleeping in the back garden anymore.

She laughed, knowing the rant that was sure to follow that comment.

Mags: I swear to God, between Uncle Colly and your dad, Gray, I'm going to lose my shit. I'm going to invite our sister to visit. Mirren is excellent at finding their hidden cameras. I'm tired of those two overprotective wingnuts spying on us.

Ciar: You girls need spying on.

Mags: And with that, I'm out.

Gray: Off to work.

Blair: See you soon, Bébhinn.

That conversation had taken place the night before. Her friends wouldn't have been worried because her mom would have let them know she was safe. She was about to text the group when her phone dinged.

Ciar: Hey, Bébhinn. Figured you're on the ferry. I forgot to tell you that Uncle Cormac and I are throwing my old man a birthday party tomorrow night at the pub. Hope you can make it.

She sighed. She would prefer not to go out, but she would never miss something to do with Ciar's family.

Bébhinn: Sounds like fun. Maybe the girls and I can make his favorite soda bread biscuits with extra currants.

Blair: We knew you'd say that and made up a big batch today.

Gray: We knew you had a family lunch and would be tired. We put your name on it.

Mags: We even made a small tin for Ciar since they're his favorite too.

Ciar: Damn. Score! I'm not sharing with my roommates.

Daniel: Dick.

Jonathan: I'll ask Auntie Raven to make me some. Mom should never attempt baking.

Daniel: I want some, too, since it's MY mom making them.

Bébhinn: Thanks, guys. I am worn out. BUT I DID IT! See you all soon.

Before she could add anything else, her phone pinged again but not from the group chat. "No way," she said, sipping her iced tea and staring at the name on her screen. She almost didn't want to open it in case it was bad news like, "Hey, glad we shared a cave, but lose my number," or something equally as bad.

Dagr: Did you make it to the ferry on time? I just got to my flat in Carmarthenshire. I'm meeting Dad for dinner and then heading to London tomorrow.

Devastation avoided. He wasn't friendship breaking up with her. She couldn't explain it, but meeting Dagr Griffiths felt destined, and even if he wasn't interested in her the way she wished, friendship was enough. It would be nice to have a friend that no one else knew.

Who knew she'd be so drawn to an older man. Maybe she was more like her mother than she thought. She needed to play this cool. She didn't believe he was interested in her the same way— though she hoped she might grow on him—so she couldn't scare him off with being too exuberant at hearing from him.

Bébhinn: I made it.

# twenty-seven

DAGR

I MADE IT. What did that mean? Had he irritated her by texting so soon? *Damn. Damn. Damn.* Dagr knew he should have waited a few days, but he couldn't help the impulse to see what she was doing.

> Dagr: Oh, good.

*Please, Samsung gods, set my phone on fire.* What was he, twelve? A charging American grizzly bear couldn't have taken his eyes from the screen when he saw dots appear, letting him know she was responding.

> Bébhinn: Don't forget to get the internship info from your dad for my friend, Blair. When I tell you that she would be doing INCC a favor and not the other way around, I mean it. 😊 You can email me the info. I put my email in my contact. And in case you've forgotten, there's a family tree pop quiz in your future.

He chuckled as he read her message, relieved that she seemed at ease enough to tease.

Dagr: I won't forget. IF she is as great as you say and does get the position, it would be a miracle if she tolerates Dad outside of a week.

Bébhinn: Your dad is the one who will learn not to fuck around with Blair. She is quiet, but that doesn't mean she isn't plotting your downfall. LOL. Do you leave your Jeep in Wales and fly to London?

Dagr: You have interesting friends. I charter a jet from Flywales. It's the only way to get a straight flight to London.

Bébhinn: My, my, my. Private, Mr. Griffiths. Sooo fancy.

Dagr: Your family isn't the only ones who like to background check new people. I think you probably travel fancy yourself, Miss O'Faolain.

Bébhinn: I'm rolling my eyes. What will you do when you get back to London tomorrow? My Sunday is having lunch with my family and going to a birthday party for my friend Ciar Murphy's dad, I think I mentioned him to you. He lives with my cousins next door.

Ciar Murphy. Yes, she had mentioned him. He sounded like an annoying little prick, though he had to admit that Bébhinn didn't seem like the type of person to suffer fools.

> Dagr: You have a full day, then. I'll spend a couple of hours going over the cases I'm currently working before having dinner with the man who is the wildlife preserve's biggest donor. The one Dad pissed off, and that I hope to smooth things over with in case he didn't manage to on his own. Your plans sound better.

> Bébhinn: I hope I get to meet your dad one day. He sounds interesting.

> Dagr: He is equally the best and the worst. LOL. Like most family. Have you written in your journal yet?

She had told him about writing letters to her father in a journal and how it was helping her feel closer to him and yet also giving her closure. He saw waving dots appear and disappear several times, and he winced, hoping he didn't make her sad by bringing it up.

> Bébhinn: I have another hour and a half left on the ferry and plan on doing it in a few minutes. I'd really like to sip on a whiskey and relax. There's so much I have to tell him about the trip. And you. But alas, drinking and driving…

*And you.* He was excruciatingly curious to see what she would tell her father.

> Dagr: Don't forget to tell him you forgot your sat phone AND brought a pillow to a cave party.

> Bébhinn: Shithead. I'd better go and commit all my sins to paper. Tell your father I said hello. I'll talk to you soon.

> Dagr: Take care.

He felt good about their chat and, quite honestly, couldn't wait to chat again. It was nice to have someone outside his father, friends, and work to talk to.

# twenty-eight

BÉBHINN



Dad,

I'm on my way home, Dad! I did it! I completed the mountain route, and God, I wish you could have been by my side when I stood above Conwy Castle. I know exactly what you would have said in that moment. "We're not in Oklahoma, sweet girl, that's for sure."

You'd be right. No red dirt here, but surely Wales and Oklahoma have the same stunning blue skies.

I just finished a greasy ferry meal and returned messages to my friends—I already called Mom, of course.

I couldn't wait to tell you how the last few days of the hike went until I got home, so here we are.

For starters, I got stuck in a snowstorm (yeah, I know, my sidekick, Hubris, thought we could beat the weather) and slept in a cave. Good news, your teachings and that badass survival course you made me take made navigation and building a fire a breeze.

Side note: I had a guest. His name is Dagr Griffiths, and he also got caught in the storm. See! I wasn't the only one who thought they could make it out in time.

When I first saw Dagr from behind, I thought it was Bran or Pat. I know. Crazy. In my defense, how many people do you know with white, WHITE hair besides your sons and grandsons?

Well, it's that white and his frame is similar to my brothers'. What was I to think? Anyway, he is great. He's a solicitor in London. He grew up in Wales, though. I'll tell you more about his job when I get to know him better.

I should have mentioned that we've decided to stay friends. I admit that I think he's handsome, but I think he is only interested in friendship. Since I've gotten on the ferry, I've decided that it's probably for the best.

He came along when I needed someone who was just mine. I know you know what I'm saying. You loved your whole family, but you had Mom. She was your person. I think Dagr could be mine.

You would like him. Of that, I am sure. Who knows,

someday he might become friends with the rest of the family. For now, though, I'd like to keep him to myself.

I do promise never to forget the sat phone on any big hikes. #Regrets.

Mom sounded good on the phone. I know you probably always worry. I do too.

Back to the hike, I took a ton of pictures and plan on developing some of them to stick in this journal. Wales doesn't have big predators like the States, so the pics are mostly of small, scurrying animals, sheep, goats, and wild horses. No big predators around these parts, thank Christ. Your home country can keep them.

So, I intended to write daily on this hike. There were a few impediments to putting pen to paper every day. I will still write to you, but not every day.

I want to give you my thoughts and feelings, and when they're important enough, I will. I want to mark important events by talking to you this way. It helps me, and I'd like to believe that you know I'm doing it.

You will always be my dad.

You'll always be my best friend.

You'll always be my hero.

Until I pick up a pen again, you have my love, Dad.

Your daughter,

Bébhinn

# twenty-nine

## THE WATCHER

HE HAD BEEN STEAMING with frustration, wishing that his was a personality that lent itself to violence so that he could vent some of the aggression thrumming in the pit of his stomach onto someone else.

Regrettably, he was a pacifist who enjoyed a low-key lifestyle. He'd joined the hiking club in Dublin because Bébhinn was a member, and then studied night and day about the outdoor activity.

Truly, it was a miracle that he'd been able to find his way to Conwy after the storm, and he probably wouldn't have if he hadn't had tracks to follow.

He'd never been the best student in class or entrepreneurial. He wasn't boring, but he was far from charismatic. His only tech skills included linking a Ring camera to his phone, which was how he was currently inside her bedroom.

By the time he'd gotten a ride to his vehicle and driven to Holyhead, he'd barely made the last ferry. He was finally home, in their new apartment, sipping on wine and watching Bébhinn sleep.

She was in her favored position. Her legs and head were slightly twisted to the left while her back remained flat on the mattress.

He was disappointed she chose to wear such a large shirt and shorts to bed. He loved to prop his phone on his nightstand and watch the tiny tank tops she preferred to sleep in shift while she moved, where he could catch glimpses of her smooth, creamy skin and the top swells of her firm breasts.

He couldn't imagine going to sleep without her soft breaths and sighs next to him. The Wales hike hadn't ended as he'd hoped, but she was still his. There had been no romantic gestures between Bébhinn and that man who must have sheltered through the storm with her.

She hadn't strayed. She was still his.

There would be another opportunity for grand gestures.

He would make sure of it.

# *thirty*

## BÉBHINN

"I'M SO glad you're home and that you had so much fun, sweetheart." Bébhinn's mom hugged her tightly before they sat down at Aunt Raven's dining room table in her third-floor flat.

Family get-togethers always switched among the sisters' flats, or for larger groups, they would meet on the first floor of the O'Faolain building.

Raven and Bran made one of their all-time favorite Oklahoma dishes for lunch today. "God, I love chicken and dumplings," Bébhinn said as she inhaled deeply over the big pot set in the middle of the table.

"Raven makes it the best of the three of us," River admitted.

"That's because I still order Bisquick to make the dumplings," Raven laughed. "Nothing beats it. Everything turns out fluffier."

"It's true," Rowan agreed. "There was nothing Mom couldn't whip up with the stuff.

"I don't care what it's made from. I'm starved," Jonathan whined.

Before Bébhinn could retort about Jonathan's impressive skill at inhaling anything, no matter the taste, her phone vibrated in her lap. She expected to see a text from Gray, who'd been bemoaning earlier about not having anything "good" to wear to Murphy's tonight, but when she glanced at the screen, her stomach curled tightly.

> Dagr: Are you at family lunch?

> Bébhinn: Just sat down. Chicken and dumplings at Aunt Raven's. Yummmmm.

> Dagr: Sounds…good?

She was grinning as her fingers flew over the keys.

> Bébhinn: You don't know what you're missing. I'll have to make it for you sometime. It's an American dish and a family favorite.

> Dagr: You do that. My grandmum taught me to make a mean shortbread. It became our thing as she got older. I would bake her a tin every time I visited. I'll be responsible for biscuits and whiskey for dessert.

"Who are you texting with such a huge grin on your face, Bébhinn?" River asked. "It must be Mags."

Caught off guard, Bébhinn felt her face flush and her eyes widen. Dead giveaways to the family now staring at her. "Oh, yeah. Mags." She prayed it sounded more convincing to their ears.

Her mom and aunts gave her a sharp look, but true to their loyal hearts, they began dishing food onto everyone's plates, diverting the men's attention.

As casually as she could, she replied to Dagr. Already

knowing what she would type and mortified at how forward she might come off.

> Bébhinn: Deal. A few more weeks and classes will be over. I've been wanting an excuse to shop in London. I could meet you and create my culinary masterpiece.

> Dagr: Damn. Client calling. Text later?

She sent a thumbs up, disappointed that the conversation was over but exhilarated that he'd initiated one in the first place.

Turning back to her plate, she scooped pillow-soft dumplings into her mouth, humming in pleasure at the gravy-covered carb ball. *Thank you, Oklahoma.* Her pleasure evaporated when she caught Bran's eye. Her brother was staring intently, raising an eyebrow in query.

Apparently, food hadn't been the diversion she'd hoped.

---

Ciar and his uncle cordoned off part of Murphy's Pub for Ciaran's party. No decorations, of course, but the food and drink were plentiful. She'd tried to convince her mother to come, but she'd declined, and because of her dad's letter, Bébhinn accepted the decision and didn't push.

Her dad had been right. He did know his wife better than anyone. His words freed Bébhinn from the constant worry for her mom.

She looked at Mags, Blair, and Gray lining the bar and laughed. Mags must have goaded Blair into taking a tequila shot, if the look of horror on Blair's face was any indication, which was the exact moment Mags snapped a selfie. Blair would kill her.

Bébhinn joined her friends and all of them took turns taking goofy pictures, talking over each other, and singing Ciaran happy birthday, to which he shouted, "Feck off!" to the lot of them.

She was leaning back against the bar an hour later, flipping through some of the pics while laughing at the sight of Gray and Daniel performing some ridiculous dance moves to an old Irish tune.

She'd noticed a few of her friends from her hiking club, The Ramblers, had taken a table in the main room. Before she went to say hello, she chose a photo of her, Blair, Mags, and Gray and sent it to Dagr before she could talk herself out of it.

They'd all been laughing at Ciar, who was gyrating like a stripper behind Jonathan's unknowing back, while her cousin tried to take the girls' picture.

She and her friends were all wearing party dresses. Bébhinn wore a simple mahogany colored slip dress paired with a delicate three-quarter-length sleeve sweater in a lighter shade to dress the look down for a Sunday out.

If the picture she chose to send Dagr happened to be one where her sweater opened just wide enough to showcase her breasts in the best light...well, she wouldn't apologize.

When her phone vibrated, she barely contained a grin.

Dagr: You had an American feast for lunch, and now you're looking lovely and partying it up in an Irish pub. I'm not usually a jealous man.

She couldn't stop the smile that bloomed. She would have preferred he had professed her gorgeous or stunning, but lovely would certainly work. He didn't have to comment on her appearance, after all.

Bébhinn: Poor you. You must try harder to have more fun. Thank you, by the way, for the internship info. I forwarded it to Blair. I swear, she almost fainted. I won't keep you. I only wanted to say a quick hello.

Dagr: Call me when you get home. I'm ready for the O'Faolain family tree pop quiz. I realize you want to make me wait in the hopes that I'll forget, given enough time. It won't happen.

She saw a shadow loom at her shoulder and barely dodged Daniel, pulling her phone from her hand.

"What the hell, Daniel. Are you five years old again?" While her cousin ordered a drink from the bartender behind them, she used the moment to text Dagr back.

Bébhinn: Be ready.

Before she could escape to go say hello to her hiking buddies, Daniel's attention was back on her again.

"Tell me who you've been texting, Bébé."

The use of her childhood nickname grated. As he knew it would. "Are you under the impression that I answer to you, Danny?" His jaw flexed at hearing *his* old nickname.

"You weren't texting Mags during lunch, and you aren't texting her now, so don't bother lying." They both looked at her friend, who was trying to teach Blair the Texas two-step. Bébhinn's mom and sisters had taught the girls when they were younger, but Blair hadn't picked it up. Her deafness made dancing trickier but never impossible.

Blair could feel the beat of the music, and because Murphy's system was currently beating out an old American country song, Mags probably thought it was a perfect time for Blair to practice. Unfortunately, since Mags was currently acting as a dance instructor, Bébhinn couldn't use her as an excuse.

"I didn't say I was texting Mags," she sniffed in feigned offense. "You are only two years older than me, Daniel. Stay in your lane. I'll put up with some overstepping from my brothers but not from you or Jonathan."

At least Daniel had the good grace to wince. Holding his palms up in peace, he said, "You know how Dad is. How Uncle Pat is. Everyone is trying to find a new normal without Grand-dad...your dad," he added softly, nodding in her direction.

"You've got to cut us some slack, Auntie. Granddad would have our balls in a basket if we didn't look after you. You know that."

Bébhinn felt guilty for her sharp attitude. He was right. Her dad had been way more overbearing, and he would expect his children and grandchildren to take over the hovering.

"Fine. I promise to tell you if there is something to know. Right now, though, I swear I'm only texting a friend."

Daniel looked at her for a solid minute, possibly waiting for more, but finally accepting that she wouldn't tell him more.

"Promise you'll tell one of us if something...someone new comes into your life."

"I promise. I'm going to say hello to some of my hiking club friends. Do you want to meet them?" she offered.

Gray joined her and Daniel as they made their way across the bar. Gray knew most of her hiking buddies, and of course, they all loved Gray. Daniel's silent, looming presence would probably make the group uncomfortable, but it was a price she was willing to pay to end his curiosity about who she was texting.

When she got to The Ramblers' table, she smiled and said hello to Sarah Dillon, an emergency room nurse, Billy Nance, a local Dublin mechanic, Mr. Todd, a teacher at TU Dublin, Tina

Fields, an owner of a nail salon, and Justin Turner, a student at Trinity that Gray and she both knew. Justin used to be Jina two years ago before she changed her look and name.

Bébhinn didn't care about what Justin identified as now. He'd always been quietly kind and a great partner on hikes. They'd had a few classes together over the years.

Unfortunately, it had been clear for months that Justin had a thing for Bébhinn, and their interactions had become increasingly uncomfortable with each interaction. All she could do was treat him as a friend and hope that she wouldn't have to actually speak the words that she wasn't interested.

Justin had tried three times to get her to go on a solo hike with him, but Bébhinn had always kindly declined, claiming that it was more fun to go with the other club members.

He'd always taken it well, and recently it seemed Justin had recognized she wasn't interested in anything but friendship, so it was less uncomfortable now than previous interactions.

Daniel, for all his earlier prickish ways, bought everyone a round. It was a great evening, mainly because Justin never tried to flirt with her.

However, Bébhinn's mind barely managed to stay at Murphy's, already imagining calling Dagr. She laughed at something Mr. Todd said, but her smile was all for the evening to come.

# thirty-one

## THE WATCHER

IT HAD BEEN a pleasure and absolute torture to see Bébhinn at the pub. She was so beautiful it'd taken his breath away. Their time in Wales had brought them closer. He knew she had to feel that new closeness. Her bright eyes and big smile said it all.

She laughed when he'd told her a funny story, and her eyes sparkled. It had all been for him. He'd felt like a giddy teenager.

She joked with him and their fellow Ramblers members. She spoke to everyone and listened to their stories. She gave them the highlights of her Snowdonia hike, which he already knew most of, having walked the trail with her.

Even after they'd shared a few moments that evening, he could feel her pulling away from their table, wishing to leave. He tried not to take it personally. He was still tired from the trip as well.

He was soothed, however, when he'd asked her if she'd seen any lovely animals or plants and flowers. She admitted that there was a lot of purple saxifrage and that it was beautiful.

*Bingo.* She had secretly loved his bouquets. He'd known it.

Three hours had passed. It was now eleven o'clock in the evening, and he was resting against the headboard—the one he bought because of its similarity to hers—observing Bébhinn as she lay across her bed.

It was a relief to know she was alone. He hadn't seen that prick she'd spent the night with in the cave again. She'd shown up at Murphy's with her friends and family—no date in sight.

"My God, you're beautiful."

Her covers were thrown aside when she rolled to her stomach, her perfect ass framed by green lace with a matching pine green tank hugging her fit back and waist.

She had a notepad propped on her pillow and appeared to be making a list. He tried zooming the camera in, but the quality wasn't the best and became too grainy to make out any words.

If they didn't come together soon, he'd have to find a way to upgrade the camera in her room. He desperately wanted sound so that he could not only see her when she slept beside him but hear her soft breaths.

His breath caught when she rolled to her back again and propped herself against the cream cushion of her headboard. Her hair spilled over her shoulders and chest, so lovely that he didn't mind that it covered her perfect tits.

He was planning to suggest an overnight hike to the club as soon as uni classes ended. Picturing him and Bébhinn sharing a tent sent an ache of longing between his legs.

He was surprised when she palmed her phone. She rarely made calls or texted this late. She lived with her best friends, and they'd already been in and out of her room that evening.

He cursed again over the lack of sound when she began talking animatedly to whomever she'd called.

"Damnit!" he yelled. He could feel his control slipping. He

hadn't needed medication for months, not since he'd been so close to achieving everything he'd ever wanted. Now... Now, he could feel himself slipping.

"No. No, no, no!" he screamed. He would not go back. Only forward, and forward was planning an overnight hike to get Bébhinn alone.

Just the thought soothed him. He was smart. He would find an opportunity to bring them together organically. Screw the meds. He was slipping because of stress, stress he wouldn't have the moment she became his.

He watched her speak to whomever was on the phone with sick fascination. She was an animated woman. The person on the other end of the line couldn't see her, but that didn't stop the grins and wild hand gesturing. Once they were a couple, he would know everyone she spoke to.

Who *was* on the other end?

# *thirty-two*

## DAGR

DAGR LEANED back against his office chair's soft, black leather, taking in the London skyline. He had finally finished a deal for one of his largest conglomerate clients, who had recently acquired property near a natural water source.

His focus was on ensuring that the clients understood the many conservation regulations and restrictions that owning the land entailed.

He enjoyed the hours of research, especially when he knew his efforts helped conserve the land. He enjoyed his efforts, but he was wiped out. The only reason his ass was still seated behind his desk was because he was too tired to take the lift to his flat.

He tapped a finger on his phone screen, pretending he wasn't waiting for a message from Bébhinn. They had been communicating daily for two months. He readily admitted that he looked forward to those moments more than anything else.

Theirs was a platonic friendship, yet he knew her better than any woman he'd ever dated. Gone was the melancholy that had plagued him for months before meeting her. He felt satisfied and rejuvenated in his personal and professional life.

His personal life consisted solely of staying in touch with his friends, with the occasional drinks out. He hadn't asked a woman out on a date since he'd met Bébhinn. His jaw flexed in frustration at himself.

Mentally, he was back to being at the top of his game. Why wasn't he dating? Why did the idea seem like a waste of time?

He'd made up his mind before that hike to stop dating casually and look for a real-life partner. That couldn't happen if he never looked.

Knowing what he should be doing, but what he was contemplating doing—what he was going to do, rather—was driving him crazy.

"Fuck it." He picked up his phone and texted.

> Dagr: Want to grab a drink tonight?

Nervous sweat prickled his neck even as wavy dots appeared on his screen.

> Bébhinn: Of course, but you never mentioned you were coming to Dublin. Business?

*Shit. Shit. Shit.* Should he lie?

> Dagr: No business. I planned to fly to Wales and thought I'd detour to see one of my favorite people.

*Christ, you idiot. What are you, a seventy-year-old doting granddad?*

Bébhinn: I'll even let you buy me an appetizer. Let me know when your flight arrives, and I'll pick you up.

Dagr: Not necessary. I'll rent a car. I'm taking the ferry after we meet anyway.

Bébhinn: I'll pick you up. You can rent a car at one of the places near the ferry when you buy your ticket.

Dagr: Stubborn. Fine. I'll text you the info soon.

She hearted his last text. He realized he was still sitting in his office grinning five minutes later.

"Shit!" He cursed as he jumped up. His earlier exhaustion evaporated. He had to get home, pack, and make flight arrangements.

He'd barely made it to Heathrow before his flight left, running through the terminal like a madman. Grabbing a commercial flight took less time to book than hiring a private one, so he booked the first available.

He emerged from the stifling, over-peopled maze of the airport onto the equally crowded outdoor ride pickup zone. He'd texted Bébhinn ten minutes ago and knew she had immediately gotten in the car queue.

And sure enough, he saw her Jeep six cars back and immediately hustled toward her. The minute their eyes met, they both grinned and waved. He didn't even have to wonder about his reaction. He'd missed her. They'd met briefly by chance and had become close friends by an even greater chance.

He tossed his duffel and briefcase in the backseat and shut

himself inside the lavender-infused Jeep cab. He knew from their many conversations that she loved lavender.

She pulled out into the passing lane, maneuvering competently between the lanes of traffic, leaving the airport before they spoke.

"So where are you taking me, Miss O'Faolain?"

She grinned at him briefly before returning her eyes to the road. "A quiet pub near my place that has the best loaded fries."

"Fries? How very American of you," he teased.

"Hey, both my parents might have Irish surnames, but I am half American for all that. You don't even want to know what an Oklahoma calf fry is."

Dagr instantly googled it and regretted it immediately. "Christ. No, thank you." Bull testicles. He felt bile rise in his throat.

"Tell me you've not, Bébhinn."

Her only answer was a toothy smile.

They chatted easily until she parked her Jeep outside the pub she took him to. No, that wasn't right. It was easy until they were walking in, and he placed his hand at the base of her back as they walked through the heavy old oak door.

It was a possessive move. A gesture to warn other men she was taken. If he could have kicked his own ass, he would have. She hadn't pulled away from him, but as soon as he realized that he'd crossed a boundary, he'd let his hand drop. She glanced up and made eye contact but said nothing.

They ordered their drinks and "loaded fries" as conversation returned to normal. If their legs happened to touch on the swiveling barstools, it was not by design.

She was in the middle of telling him an outrageous family story about a stalker that followed her family across the globe when a heavily tattooed man suddenly swooped between them and kissed Bébhinn's cheek.

"How's my favorite Bébé?"

He saw her eyes widen in surprise, but no more than the young man's when he faced Dagr.

"Ciar! What are you doing here?" she gasped. "Let me introduce you to my good friend." She looked between the two, clearly taken aback.

"Ciar Murphy, this is Dagr Griffiths, a good friend of mine. I've told you, Dagr, that Ciar lives with my cousins next door to me."

Dagr held out his hand to shake. "Or nephews, as the case may be," he chuckled, trying to put the man at ease.

Ciar shook his hand, a bewildered look on his face. "Fuck me, if I didn't come over here thinking you were out with one of your brothers, Bé," he shook Dagr's hand firmly. "Sorry mate, if I came across as shady, but it was a shock to see you weren't Bran or Patrick."

He didn't want to like the younger man, but it was clear immediately that he was genuine. Chuckling, he replied, "No worries. Bébhinn mistook me for her brother when I ducked into her cave that night. The hair, I guess." He patted his head and smiled.

"Ahh, so you're the man the family is talking about." Ciar clapped Dagr's back good-naturedly.

Dagr'd wanted to dislike the man who had such easy access to his...friend, but he seemed like the kind of intellectually direct man that he tended to favor. In the meantime, Bébhinn was turning a remarkable shade of red.

"What do you mean by that?" she asked, her voice a higher pitch than usual.

"Come on, Bébhinn. You had to know the family would notice you trying to hide dating someone." He chuckled and elbowed her side.

Her red cheeks went to the deepest crimson he'd only ever

witnessed in nature. Giving mercy, Dagr attempted a casualness he wasn't feeling. "No secret. We're friends. Hiking buddies," he tacked on. He looked at Bébhinn, and she looked at him.

They didn't feel like *just* hiking buddies.

He would never claim more, and he sure as hell wouldn't embarrass her by admitting that he considered her...more.

Ciar was sharp if the look he was currently giving them was any indication. Clearly, Ciar was trying to force a truth on them that neither he nor Bébhinn was willing or ready to admit to. Dagr looked back steadily, showing the younger man that he had no power over him. Dagr would not be tricked into admitting anything. He was way too good a solicitor for that shit. The young buck holding his gaze would find him harder to push over than the average Joe.

Ciar flicked his gaze to Bébhinn. "I won't mention seeing you out tonight, Bébhinn, but I suggest you introduce your *friend* to the family sooner than later."

# thirty-three

## THE WATCHER

HE WAS THANKFUL THAT THE RAMBLERS' monthly meeting had been at Bébhinn's. He'd been able to change out his camera with a new model that had color and sound. Sometimes he would go weeks without video when the battery died before a meeting.

The new camera would notify the app on his phone when there was movement. He could also pull the camera up even when there was no movement, like when she was sleeping or went to the bathroom. He loved listening to the shower start and picturing her clothes coming off.

He'd gotten off to that a lot.

He would have put a second camera in the bathroom, but there was no hiding place. He shrugged. It gave him something to look forward to. Another bonus was that he could print off stills from the video. He was acquiring quite a collection already.

The best part about the last club meeting was that everyone loved his suggestion of an overnight hike. He looked at the kitchen table and grinned. His new two-person tent sat in all its new, packaged glory.

His first plans were derailed by weather, but he was confident that this time would work. Plus, they would be with a few of their hiking friends to witness him and Bébhinn committing to one another.

He got a notification on his phone, and his stomach tightened in anticipation. His back fell back on the couch in horror as he watched that white-haired man from Conwy walking around her bedroom.

She was there picking things up to show the man, who was smiling and chatting. He turned up the volume, dread singeing his insides.

"I'm so glad you came to town," she said, while leaning against a heavily framed floor-standing mirror.

The man's back was to the camera, but he could see his face in the mirror. He was older than he'd thought when he'd seen him in the parking lot, but handsome. He clenched his jaw in irritation.

Very handsome. "Damn."

"One of my better decisions," the man replied. "I would have come sooner, but I know how hard the last few weeks of the semester can be."

"One more year before I get to work full-time for Triskelion. I can't wait."

Triskelion was her family's interior design shop. He'd found that out after they'd first met. He wasn't above a little social media snooping.

"I hate this evening to end, but since you insist on taking me to the ferry, we'd better go. I don't want you driving home too late."

He watched as the man stepped close, and drawn like a

damn magnet, she stepped toward him. He watched as their hands twitched, clearly aching to reach out to the other.

The man cleared his throat and spun on his heel to leave her bedroom. His camera was able to catch the misery on the man's face. He hoped the man, whoever he was, choked on his feelings.

Bébhinn looked sad as she followed the stranger out of her room. The man was leaving on the ferry, and hopefully that was that.

He knew Bébhinn wasn't serious about this white-haired man. She might try to hide her feelings, but after so many months, he knew her better than she knew herself. A woman as gorgeous as her would naturally attract and be attracted to extremely handsome people.

He wasn't near her standard type, but their compatibility would more than make up for his lack of...certain attributes.

Only a few more weeks, he thought, glancing once more at his new tent.

# thirty-four

BÉBHINN

BACK IN HER ROOM, she would have sworn Dagr had been about to do...something, anything besides turning tail and practically sprinting from her bedroom.

He was inside the car rental place now. Bébhinn was twisting her fingers together, sick with worry that she had read him all wrong when she'd taken that step to close the distance between them.

"What a mess," she sighed, thumping her head against the seat's headrest.

She'd done well to keep up a steady stream of conversation like they always did over the phone. She enjoyed hearing about Dagr's cases and encouraged him to speak of his latest one as they drove.

He was responsive and funny like normal, but there was a forced element to their discourse that hadn't been there before that moment in her bedroom. It could be something as simple as work stress that he didn't wish to discuss, and she was blowing it way out of proportion.

She knew she hadn't imagined his leg or hand touching her tonight at the pub. His fingers had rested on her lower back more than once. It was familiar and hot as hell all in one go.

When he'd asked her to go out for a drink, and not only that, but flew to Dublin instead of Wales to do it, she couldn't help but feel like they were moving toward something.

Now...she wasn't as sure.

She had turned down a few dates the past few months, and not solely because of Dagr—mostly but not wholly. She was happy and busy and still recovering from losing her father. She had her mother and her family to think about, plus school, and her "internship" at Triskelion.

Her best friends took up time with their own daily dramas, as did her damn brothers and nephews, who loved nothing more than to poke their noses into her business.

She was satisfied. "I am satisfied just as things are." She was thankful no one was around to hear that pathetic vision board quote.

He had just shoved open the rental place's glass door and was going to her Jeep. "Don't make this weird," she whispered to herself before he opened the passenger door.

"I'm all settled. I can't thank you enough for the ride," Dagr said as he leaned into the cab.

"No problem. Your bags are in the back seat." As if he didn't know that! "Have a great weekend with your dad. Let me know if you go on any cool adventures without me," she pretended to pout.

He hesitated like he was about to say something, but changed his mind and said, "Nothing planned."

He dragged his bags from the back and set them on the passenger seat, still staring at her with an intensity that made her skin prickle. *Stay cool, damnit.*

"Thanks again for visiting." *Stop talking, you immature child.*

"I've a fundraising charity thing in a few weeks in London. It's for several nature reserves, including the one my father runs. Go with me."

Her throat was suddenly as dry as the Atacama Desert. "Formal?"

"Black tie," he confirmed.

"Shopping for a new ball gown…" she pretended to think, tapping her chin. "I'll be there."

Dagr's frame seemed to lose some of its tenseness at her agreement. "I'll send you all the information and arrange a private jet to bring you to London."

"That's not—" she started to protest.

"It is," he said in such a serious tone that she felt her cheeks flush.

He took his bags without another word and shut the door, leaving her blinking in bewilderment until her driver's door opened. He dropped his bags on the pavement and reached in for a chaste embrace.

"Text me the moment you're home."

"I will." What else was there to say?

***

"Here, try this on," Gray said, handing her a dress, "while you explain lying to your best friends for months."

Bébhinn glanced around Gray's shoulder, where she stood blocking her exit from the changing room that she was currently standing naked in, with the exception of a simple pair of navy cotton briefs.

Her eyes found Blair, who was leaning against the opposite wall, but as soon as she saw Bébhinn looking lifted her hands and signed, "I would not have told anyone."

Her frown was slight, but Bébhinn felt like shit that she'd not told them about talking to Dagr. How was she supposed to explain that he was only a friend with platonic texts and calls, not benefits? The night they'd met for drinks was the first inkling she'd had that he felt anything other than friendship for her.

Mags shoved her arm past Gray, handing her another dress. "Yeah, spill already."

Bébhinn pushed the two girls back from the door. "Move back so Blair can follow." Blair just smiled and rolled her eyes. She was pretty used to what it was like when the four of them were together, and excitement was high. Blair was excellent at reading lips, but she did have to see them.

"How's this? I find a dress, then we find a pub, then I tell you guys everything, and then you tell me how I'm going to tell Mom that I'm going to London next weekend to see a man she's never met."

Once they agreed, they got down to business, and she found a dress quickly. She felt beautiful and couldn't wait for Dagr to see her in it. Blair found the winning design. The color was a rich champagne with a floor-length maxi hem. The boat neckline rested against her collarbones, with a darted bodice and flowing cap sleeves.

The silk fitted at her waist before skimming her figure until barely draping her strappy-heeled toes. It was elegant and sophisticated in its simple lines. The back was her favorite part. A soft cowl revealed her bare back to her natural waist.

No bra, but thankfully, she wasn't as busty as her mom and aunts. Her breasts were a perfectly rounded, firm C cup. Her friends assured her the dress was perfect from all angles. She was relieved to have that part of the day dusted.

Bébhinn wasn't hugely interested in shopping for clothes. Now antiques and homemade household goods, that she could spend hours at. In fact, she'd asked Dagr to make her flight earlier so she could visit a shop that supposedly carried a stunning array of hand-painted wallpaper.

She wanted to surprise her mother with a roll since she was slowly redecorating her flat, and if it wasn't to her taste, her mom would have many clients who would want it. Either way, she would be happy to give her a gift for no other reason than that she loved her.

Shopping bags hanging from the back of her high barstool chair and drinks ordered, there was nothing left to do except explain Dagr to her friends.

Once she started, the telling became easier. From their first meeting in the cave and how she thought it was her brother, to three weeks ago when she felt like he might want more than friendship.

She took a sip of Three Wolves, which the pub carried, much to her delight, and sat back, satisfied that her friends would be as pleased about Dagr as she was.

"Wait," Gray started, sounding confused, "you've never even kissed the man?"

"Forget kissing. No sex. Seriously." Mags looked between their friends, incredulous.

Blair signed, "Phone sex?"

Bébhinn tried to tame her blush, but it was no use. "No, you assholes. I've told you for the past hour that we're only friends. Jesus!"

"But you want more?" Gray asked.

"He wants more?" Mags asked.

"I hope it works out. I'll be a shoo-in for his dad's internship."

Bébhinn rolled her eyes. "You're already overqualified, Blair. As for the other, I've wanted more from that first night, but I haven't a clue about his feelings. Only hope."

"Your family is going to shit about the age difference," Mags pointed out.

"Your brothers and the boys will put up a fight," Gray agreed.

Blair asked, "You only said he was quite a bit older. How much?"

*Here we go.* "He's just turned thirty-nine. Eighteen years older."

"Like mother, like daughter." Mags winked over her glass.

"Hey! Mom and Dad were way more years apart than that, and the family didn't bat a lash."

Blair touched her hand. She was wearing a look on her face that said, "You poor delusional girl."

"Rowan didn't have parents. Rowan and her sisters were already under the O'Faolain influence," Gray started.

Mags interjected. "By 'influence,' Gray means under the influence of their dicks."

"Never speak of private parts and my brothers again. Gross."

"Anyway," Gray elbowed Mags to shut up, "your mom didn't have parents to protest the age difference. You've lost your father, though I think even you can admit that Hugh would have handled the news poorly, regardless of him and your mom. Despite that, your brothers—"

"Will lose their shit," Mags finished.

"And Daniel and Patrick won't be much better," Blair finished.

Bébhinn felt her shoulders slump. She couldn't deny any of their points. They were all true.

"We've got your back, however, and can help out as we may," Gray said and smiled. "If something more than friendship does begin with you and Dagr, it will be an uphill battle with your family, but never impossible."

"I've never known an O'Faolain to take no for an answer," Blair quickly signed.

"Okay. Thanks, you guys."

"I know our families," Mags nodded toward Gray and Blair, "would murder me for saying this, but I think you should lie until after London. Find out after you stay with him and see if it's going to progress. Then you can have a family meeting, and they can like it or love it. Either way, it'll be too late." Mags shrugged like her idea was faultless.

"And my mother? My excuse for going to London?" Bébhinn couldn't believe she was considering a plan Mags had devised.

"Your mom, Raven, and River share a hive mind. If you tell your mom, she wouldn't be able to keep it from them, and in turn, they would tell their husbands, who would then tell their sons. Your London charity gala would have some gate crashers, guaranteed." Blair wasn't wrong.

"Tell her that you're visiting Liv and then make sure you do so it isn't a lie. You aren't outright lying that way," Gray suggested.

"Only omitting," Blair signed while nodding in agreement.

# thirty-five

## BÉBHINN

Dad,

Catch up news first. I finished another year at uni. Only one more left. Grades are excellent, btw. I've gotten a few small interior jobs that Mom and the aunts have thrown me. They approved of my work.

Bran and Patrick put on a brave face, but I wonder if they will ever stop missing you. If Mom and I are anything to compare to, they won't.

I imagine it's a matter of endurance. Learning to live with part of yourself missing. I'm glad they have Raven and River and the boys.

Proper warning. I'm giving Mom a year, maybe two, to begin to consider dating. I know you probably just cracked the glass of whiskey you're holding at the thought, but she has so much love to give.

You know she is a woman who loves someone with everything she is. There is someone out there who deserves to have that love directed their way—even if it is only half as much as she gave you.

Daniel and Jonathan are shitheads. Okay, not always, and I love them. Daniel is following in your entrepreneurial footsteps, and Jonathan is close behind as he graduated this year. I'm sure you don't need me to tell you everything, you are surely watching your grandchildren. Their taste in women is still questionable.

Mags is still diligently working on her embroidery masterpiece, which she believes the Queen will "swoon over." For all her mouthy ways, she is an exceptional talent. Her sister, Mirren, is visiting soon and has promised to root out the security cameras that Gray and Blair's dads have hidden around our house.

I know you know where they are. Send me a dream or something. There is no line those Scottish bastards won't cross to keep an eye out on us. What am I saying? I'm sure you approve of their methods. Don't deny it. (I'm rolling my eyes.)

Let me see. What else is happening around here? Blair has an incredible opportunity for an internship in Wales, which you know she'll get. She is that smart and doubly passionate about botany. The nature conservation would be lucky to get her. Oh, and she went out on a date last weekend—like the first one EVER and didn't give me or the girls an ounce of detail!

Gray and I will graduate next year. We still plan on working closely together (and I'm sure any businesses she opens and I decorate will have Blair's plants and Mags' embroidery tucked in some odd corner of them all).

Gray works more for O'Connor Hospitality than I do for Triskelion. My hobby is hiking. Her hobby is checking real estate adverts. She's obsessed.

Speaking of passions, I'm hoping to get Mom some gorgeous hand-painted wallpaper for one of the rooms in your flat. She's already redecorated a couple of rooms. I'm so proud of her.

If I were being strictly honest, I think the changes help her, but I also believe that nothing will make that flat any less "Hugh and Rowan's."

Okay. You're caught up on family and friends. Now it's my turn.

I'm in need of advice and...forgiveness...maybe?

So, listen—Dagr Griffiths—you'll remember him. Hike. Cave. White hair. Remember? The hiker who didn't forget his sat phone.

Well, we've become friends. Good friends, actually.

He came to Dublin a few weeks ago to have a drink. With me (in case you missed the obvious).

I'm afraid I have a bit of a crush on him that I'm not sure he reciprocates, but I hope he does.

He's older than me, and before you jump on your high horse, nothing like you and Mom. I'm afraid of how the boys will react. I wish you were here to talk them down, but if you were here, you'd probably be leading the charge, soooo.

I know all his bests and worsts. Favorites and

hates. Foods, movies, and books. His favorite color is white. I said, "How boring," he said, "A wash with bleach makes it good as new."

See??? Funny and practical.

Anyway. Oh Lord, why is this so hard to write? Damnit! Anyway, Dagr invited me to a charity gala. It's in London. I don't know if it's as friends or an actual date.

I want it to be a date.

I haven't told the family that he and I are still talking. We talk every day.

Mags, Gray, and Blair think I should lie about why I'm going to London, but you know I don't like to lie.

I'm not sleeping, I'm so conflicted. I toss and turn and stare at the ceiling. Don't mistake my guilty conscience for a change of heart. I am going.

It's just... God, Dad, I want your approval so bad my stomach aches with it. It isn't fair that I met a man that I see a future with.

And. You. Aren't. Fucking. Here.

I have the perfect dress, and I think he might kiss me, and all I can think of is that you'll never know Dagr. You'll never grill him over drinks or threaten to ruin his career, or...or tell him he better not hurt me. That he better love me above all others, and I know that's ludicrous when we are ONLY friends.

But I think it. I want it.

I want you to still be here.

B

*O'Faolain Building*
*4<sup>th</sup> Floor*
*Dublin Departure for London Day*

Bébhinn was SWEATING. Buckets. She needed to grab a taxi in the next hour to make it to the private airport if she didn't want to be late for the flight Dagr had set up. She'd just finished sending a message to The Ramblers, only remembering minutes ago that she'd never sent one to let them know she wouldn't be going on the hiking trip that weekend.

She cringed at the bad manners. In her defense, the London trip had taken over most of her thinking power.

She wasn't worried about canceling, even late, because the group had decided to make it into a family affair. Those who had spouses or children could bring them along. The hiking spot was only a three-hour drive from Dublin.

She'd been looking forward to cooking hot dogs and marshmallows over a fire with the kids, but not enough to say no to London.

Now here she was, reading messages from the group as they came through in one hand and struggling with her luggage in the other. She *should* have been feeling exhilaration at embarking on what might be the start of...something as she was walking through the door of her mother's flat, and yet...

Lying, it turned out, was for the birds. She could misdirect her brothers, but her mother? No.

Her mom was in the kitchen feeding her sourdough starter. She and her sisters all kept the starter in their refrigerators. Her dad and brothers loved it. Her mom rarely ate the stuff, but Bébhinn guessed old habits died hard—like spouses.

"Hey, Mom," she called out as she let herself in.

"Sweetheart! I didn't know you were coming by. I was just thinking about you. I have a new client I'd like to bring you in on as a full partner. Mrs. Dennys wants a complete upper story redesign, and it includes a child's playroom, which I know you love to design."

Bébhinn couldn't help but clap her hands in glee. "I can't wait! The colors, the story, the books, toys, and board games—consider me hired."

Her mom grinned at her enthusiasm before saying, "I have lunch plans with Saoirse Kennedy, but I would gladly cancel if you wanted to grab a bite together. River's favorite potter has a new toad and frog design that I've been dying to see."

"I can't actually, but please don't go without me. That design sounds perfect for your new clients." Bébhinn winced when she saw her mother's smile fall.

"I came here to talk to you about something. Important," she added. Her mom's attention was immediately focused.

"I'll wait for you for the potters. What is it? I've felt like you've been distant lately. I'm embarrassed to admit that I worried you were outgrowing your old mother."

Her mom tried to use a teasing tone, but there weren't enough months since her father's passing for too much levity.

"I'll never outgrow needing my mom. Don't even speak it."

She smiled at the reassurance, wiping her floury hands on a kitchen towel and walking around the counter to join Bébhinn at the bar. "What is it?"

"I'm going to ask you for something I've never asked for before."

With only a slight flair of her eyes, Rowan O'Faolain said, "Ask. Anything."

"I need you not to tell anyone what I'm about to tell you. Even your sisters."

Her mom's eyes widened further at that, but she nodded affirmation. "Unless it's to do with your safety, I promise to keep this conversation to myself."

No going back now. "I'm flying to London in an hour to meet Dagr Griffiths. He's taking me to a charity gala to raise money for nature reserves across Europe. I'm staying with him tonight and coming home tomorrow." Her mom resembled a deer in headlights, so she quickly added, "We are only friends."

Two long, long minutes later. "Friends?"

"Definitely."

"Definitely?" Her mom sounded suspicious. With reason.

"Fine," she sighed, knowing she wasn't walking away without giving her mom more. "We are just friends. Good friends, actually. We've talked every day since Wales.

"I swear, there isn't a whole lot we don't know about each other. We encourage each other every morning and discuss how our days have gone each night. He's become the best part of my day."

"I remember what that is like. It makes you feel invincible." Her mom smiled softly, surely thinking about her husband.

"Gray, Mags, and Blair are my best friends, but I swear, he's become one too. The whole truth is that I want more, but I don't know if he does," she rushed the last, relieved to tell her mom about Dagr.

"He's never...umm, given you a reason to believe he might want more?"

Bébhinn felt her cheeks warm before admitting, "He flew to Dublin a few weeks ago just to take me out for a drink before going on to Wales."

"That seems like a pretty big gesture for casual friends. Nothing was said or...done to make you think he might think of you as more than a buddy?"

Bébhinn had thought a lot about that evening. Every touch

or brush of his fingers. At the pub, his hand had touched her back and his leg had casually touched the side of hers. "A few very minor things. Nothing extraordinary but not nothing."

"I appreciate his caution. Patrick mentioned that he is older than you. Bran looked up some of his background when you guys were hiking."

"He is. Older, that is." *Don't start stuttering around the facts now, Bébhinn, she chided herself.*

"Yes, we've just confirmed as much," her mom chuckled. "By how much?"

"Eighteen years." Bébhinn closed her eyes and swallowed hard. She trusted her mother, but she was laying a lot on her.

When she remained silent, Bébhinn added, "Less than you and Dad." Her mom blinked several times, but thankfully didn't tear up over the mention of her husband. And because she was feeling extreme stress at the moment, Bébhinn included, "I wrote to Dad about Dagr in my journal."

"Oh. Oh, well. Oh." It took a moment, but a grin broke across her mother's face. "I bet Hugh had a few thoughts."

They both hugged and laughed, each hearing his voice in their heads. He was saying different things to each of them, of course, but every comment would have been opinionated as hell.

They dried their eyes and stood together for a while, thinking about what they'd lost but what they still had to live.

"I'll keep your news, Bébhinn, if only because I know your father would bellow the house down, and it amuses me to remember some of our bigger rows. I won't tell my sisters, though I'll probably almost break at the seams from the secret.

"I'll keep your heart to myself but only if you promise to tell me when there is new news."

"I promise. I've wanted to tell you for weeks, if only to get your advice." They embraced and sniffled tears during which she promised to call her mother upon landing, in the evening, in the morning, and before takeoff the following day.

"I love you, Mom."

"You're my heart, Bébhinn."

# *thirty-six*

## THE WATCHER

HE SAW there was a message from The Ramblers' Facebook group. Nothing new there. Everyone was excited for the trip. He had his bags packed a week ago. The anticipation was nearly strangling him. He'd barely slept more than four or five hours a night once the club gave the trip a green light.

He would need to be on the road within the hour if he was going to make it on time. Everyone was driving separately or carpooling. He wished he and Bébhinn could have made the trip together, but it was for the best.

He wouldn't have had enough room in his tiny Nissan Micra to fit the huge suitcase she'd been packing yesterday. She must plan on leaving the suitcase in her Jeep, because it would never fit into the two-person tent he'd gotten them. It was probably spare clothes and supplies in case someone forgot something. She was always the most thoughtful in the group.

In only a few short hours, they would see each other at the designated hiking spot, where they would pitch tents before heading out on a day hike.

Since the trip was family-oriented, the hikes today and tomorrow morning were shorter with little to no difficulty. The location was chosen for the picturesque trails and lakes for the kids to play in and explore.

The leisurely pace was exactly what he needed. He and Bébhinn could sit by the lake and talk, smiling and laughing at the kids having fun. She would touch her fingers to his as if by accident, like she'd done during a hike last year.

He watched her at night and imagined kissing and touching her body—like her ex-boyfriend used to do to her. Except he would be better at it. She would praise him for how good he made her feel.

He finished mixing the batter for the sweet biscuits he made for the trip and placed dollops of dough on the waiting baking sheets before putting them in the oven. While they baked, he would load his gear and then check the group messages. He'd heard it ding several more times.

He let himself into the apartment just as the buzzer went off. He set the sheets on the counter for the biscuits to cool, grabbing one as he sat at the table and opened Facebook.

"No. No!" His mangled cry was one of disbelief and anger as he read the messages.

**The Ramblers Hiking Club Community**
**Bébhinn**
**Hey everyone! Sorry to be posting last minute, but I won't be able to make it today. I hope everyone has so much fun. Post plenty of pictures here so I can see them! Happy hiking!**

He stood so fast his chair tipped over and slammed against the tile. He fisted the half-eaten biscuit in his hand and, in a fit of rage, swiped the two baking sheets from the counter.

He read the message again. And again.

That suitcase had never been for the hiking trip. She was going somewhere, and it wasn't with him.

He didn't want to believe that she was intentionally ruining his plans, but he was having trouble seeing an alternate motive.

And where was she traveling? Who was she traveling to see?

He had to stop attempting grand gestures. In trying to create a special, perfect moment, he was taking the chance of losing her.

He couldn't lose her. He wouldn't.

# thirty-seven

## DAGR

DAGR WAS ALREADY at the airport, pacing nervously in the lounge provided for private jet customers. Bébhinn should be landing in four minutes.

He couldn't believe he'd asked her to come. Even though it was a charity event, it felt very much like a date.

"Because it is a date, you pillock," he chided himself.

Had he given himself thirty extra seconds from the time he climbed out of her Jeep that night to when he opened her driver's door, he might have kept his mouth closed.

All he could remember was that he didn't want the night to end. He didn't want months to pass before he could see her again. He wanted to walk by her side and feel her warmth on his arm.

So, he'd asked her out and not to a simple dinner. A black-tie affair that would have many people wondering about who she was and what she was to him.

He'd looked up the O'Faolain family, and though they were more well-known in the States, their business dealings in

Ireland were impressive enough that once Bébhinn's name was discovered, there were many people who would recognize who she was.

A good friend of his, Lee Whiten, a London-based solicitor with a second office in Dublin, mentioned to Dagr a few weeks back when they'd met for drinks that his biggest clients in Ireland were looking to buy a considerable tract of land. He would like to hire Dagr's firm to oversee that the wildlife preservation compliance laws were followed.

When he found out the clients were Bran and Patrick O'Faolain, he'd about shit himself. The thought of entangling himself further in Bébhinn's family had him breaking out in a cold sweat.

He knew from the hundreds of conversations he and Bébhinn had shared that her family was close and clearly loved one another, but if he were to help Lee on the case, he feared that they might think he was attempting to ingratiate himself into the family once they found out that he and Bébhinn were good friends.

And they would find out. He hadn't told Bébhinn about the offer to work with Lee because he knew what she'd say. She would ask him to do it because her family deserved a solicitor who cared about the land.

Consequences—he was currently reaping them with his spontaneity.

The good news was that Bébhinn hadn't been acting differently since she'd said yes. Texts and calls remained as light-hearted as ever. They always discussed their days and work.

She was on summer break, which meant taking on more responsibility with the family's businesses, including board meetings. He loved hearing about her design ideas, and he could listen to the stories about her mom and aunts' antics for hours.

He'd almost convinced himself that he was making too much of the so-called date when he saw Bébhinn through the terminal's windows disembark from the plane, and sweat immediately beaded his brow, and his heart tried to beat out of his chest.

She was wearing loose-fitting blue jeans and a navy t-shirt with white sneakers. Her stunning dark hair was swirling around her shoulders and down her back. She smiled at the attendant as she passed, looking fresh and lovely. And young.

Swallowing his nerves, he shoved out the heavy glass door and started in her direction.

She yelled, "Dagr!" and waved, picking up her pace even though she was dragging a huge suitcase behind her.

When they were close, there was an awkward moment where they both had their hands stretched toward one another, each going in for a hug and then thinking better of it.

He settled for placing one hand on her hip and leaning in to kiss her cheek. A hug would have been less intimate. She looked bemused and patted his arm like she was placating his odd behavior.

He pulled away and pointed to the cream-colored monstrosity at her side. "That suitcase is bigger than you are. I promise, my guest room has perfectly good pillows. You needn't have packed bedding," he teased.

"Shithead," was her immediate response. "You clearly don't know how much space is required to pack for a fancy dress event. Gray said I was being foolish for not shipping it straight to your place."

She rolled her eyes at the thought, but as he took over pulling a suitcase that had to weigh eighty pounds, he couldn't say Gray's idea didn't have merit.

"I told you that you didn't have to meet me, Dagr," she complained as they made their way to his black and white

Range Rover parked in the small lot next to the lounge. "Though I can't say I'm sorry to see your handsome face."

He felt his face flush at the compliment even though she was clearly teasing him. He really needed to pull his head out of his ass and stop overanalyzing...her...their relationship... everything.

"I'm happy to see you." At his serious tone, she looked across her shoulder where he walked next to her, surprise widening her eyes.

"I'm happy to see you too," she admitted before asking, "is it me? Or are we less awkward over the phone?"

He coughed out an unexpected laugh at her honesty. "You aren't wrong," he answered as he placed her suitcase in the rear and opened the passenger door to let her in.

Before he could shut her door, she touched his hand to get his attention. "How about we agree to have the same relationship in person as we have online. I'm not an indecisive person, and you sure as hell aren't. From now on, we say what we want, when we want. Deal?"

"Has anyone ever told you that you're brilliant?"

"Often," she grinned.

After that, the drive held no side glances or silences. They were back to their comfortable selves. They spoke of the evening ahead and how long she would need to "beautify" herself. He couldn't imagine a woman as stunning as Bébhinn needing two hours to accomplish what was already done, but what did he know?

They headed straight to the antique wallpaper place to pick up some paper for her mother before going to lunch and then his flat. When she was silent for more than a few minutes, he glanced over, not wanting to take his eyes off traffic for longer than that.

She was typing on her phone with a strained look.

"Everything okay?"

She sighed heavily before answering, glancing at him with a sheepish expression. "There's a member of my Dublin hiking club that's got a thing for me. I've known her—him—I should say for quite a while now. Justin, who used to be called Jina, has made his interest known for over a year.

"My friends think Jina became Justin when I made it clear I wasn't into girls, but I would certainly hope someone wouldn't change their whole identity just to date a person. Justin is a great person to hike with, and I've always enjoyed his company, even when he was still Jina.

"I'm trying my hardest not to hurt his feelings, but our group communicates through our group Facebook chat, and Justin keeps private messaging me."

"It's never a comfortable place to not reciprocate a person's feelings. I've had that happen in the workplace before. Not a good time," he admitted.

"Oh, really? I'll want those stories and their names in case I need to fend off women tonight. That way at least I'll be prepared," she joked.

Bébhinn sounded like she might not be joking, and he couldn't help but feel the satisfaction that came with knowing she might be the tiniest bit jealous.

"Tell me what Justin messaged."

After explaining that she'd forgotten to message the group until that morning, that she wouldn't be able to make it, she said that Justin had messaged, "I hope everything is okay. I'm so disappointed you won't be able to come. I was hoping that this was a trip we could get to know each other better."

"He isn't subtle, I'll give him that."

"Not at all," she said glumly, still staring at the message. "What would you reply?"

He thought about it for a minute as he maneuvered into a

parking spot a few blocks from the antique store. "If it were me, I would want absolute honesty. Make sure there is no room for misunderstanding or hope. How about, 'Everything is fine, I just completely forgot to message everyone.'"

"Speak slow," she interrupted, "I'm typing."

"Okay," he chuckled, "then write, 'I'm spending the weekend with my...'" He hesitated. "'With my boyfriend.'" *FML.*

He saw her fingers falter. "I only thought if you wrote boyfriend, it would soften the blow. A 'It's not you, it's just that I'm already taken' kind of a thing," he quickly added.

"You're a genius." She looked up from her phone and grinned. Pressing send on her phone, she said, "Done and done. Whew! That's a relief. Let's go look at wallpaper."

# thirty-eight

## BÉBHINN

I'M SPENDING *the weekend with my boyfriend.* Bébhinn was still feeling tingles in her belly over Dagr's words. Obviously, her brain knew he hadn't meant it, but her poor, hopeful heart enjoyed hearing those words come out of his mouth.

Thankfully, she had been able to concentrate at the wallpaper store and found stunning early 19th-century floral paper mounted on two Masonite panels that her mom would die over.

The profusion of flowers and deep colors reminded Bébhinn of her great-gran's garden.

She'd grown up listening to her mom talk about how she and her sisters used to run wild through Nan's gardens. She couldn't wait to see her face when she opened them.

They'd left the store with the owner's promise of packaging the panels. The shop would make sure they shipped to Bébhinn's home.

After a long, relaxing lunch at a pretty bistro, Dagr took her to his flat, which happened to be above his fancy London firm. The black and glass building was impressive. His firm owned five floors and shared the penthouse with the other building's owners, which had a gym, spa, and pool.

She spun around, taking in his personal space. She assumed his décor would be all blacks and grays and was surprised by the warm palette—creams, golds, browns, greens, and blues.

"What do you think, Miss Interior Designer?"

"Both surprised and impressed," she answered honestly. "I expected a much darker color story. This," she spun around once more, "is perfect. It couldn't be more lovely if you'd hired Triskelion."

She could tell her opinion pleased him. "You'd better show me to my room so I can get ready. What time is the car picking us up?" She already knew they would be having dinner during the auction with dancing to follow.

"Six," he said over his shoulder as he led her to a stunning guest room that was all done in shades of cream.

"Oh, Dagr, it's like the room was made for me. If you weren't a successful attorney, I would beg you to work for my mom." She laughed when he shook his head and held up his hands in a stop gesture.

"The only thing I did was tell the decorator that I prefer natural colors and comfortable furniture. No matter how grand a house my grandparents lived in, it always felt like a home. Their style influenced Dad and me a lot. Neither one of us cares for cold and austere."

"Super sleek and modern has its place, but my preferences run very close to yours. I hope someday you get to visit my family's place. It's got a similar feel to this."

"I'd like that. Well, I'd better leave you to it. From past experience, I know women can take an extraordinary amount of time to prepare for these things," he chuckled.

She smiled as he left her room, shutting the door behind him. Her smile faltered once she was alone, wondering over his comment. How many women had he had "past experience" with?

"Stop being a jealous weirdo," she berated herself. He was older and would have had many relationships.

"He's not in a relationship with you anyway, numpty. Friends only," she growled under her breath.

Putting Dagr's past to the back of her mind, she slipped into the luxurious en-suite bathroom and turned on the steam shower. It was time to see if she could loosen up Mr. Griffiths' strict code of conduct, she thought, smiling at herself in the mirror.

# *thirty-nine*

DAGR

IT HAD TAKEN thirty minutes to get from his flat to the event. Thirty minutes in which Dagr tried his best not to stare at the woman sitting opposite him in the backseat.

When Bébhinn emerged from her room, his tumbler of Glenfiddich 21 came close to slipping from his grasp. Her dress flowed over her stunning body like silky ripples of water. He realized she must be wearing high heels once she was close enough. He was still much taller, but no longer loomed over her like a giant.

It made her mouth that much closer to his.

Her hair was in a smooth bun at the nape of her neck. It was a simple style that perfectly showed off the dress and the diamonds in her ears and at her neck. Her makeup, he noted, was also simply done. She was the first woman he'd taken to something like the charity event where they didn't wear gobs of the shit and eyelash extensions.

He definitely preferred her natural beauty over the artificial kind. It was impossible to tear his eyes from her silk-covered breasts, his mouth watering to suck the slight outline of her nipples through the thin barrier of material.

Impossible—that is, until she turned around and he caught his first glance of Bébhinn's bare back where the material was draped low enough to see the dimples on her strong, lower back.

When he'd told her he'd never seen anyone so lovely, he'd meant it. She blushed at the compliment and told him he looked elegant in his Armani tux. He blushed, too, unfortunately.

The driver was opening their door, and he was about to slip out when Bébhinn clasped his hand.

"There won't be a more handsome man here tonight, Dagr."

The look on her face made him want to climb back in and forget the charity. Instead, he said, "I doubt that very much, but I wouldn't mind you thinking so."

He drew her out of the car behind him, ensuring her matching silk cape was set correctly around her shoulders before offering his arm. Names were given, and pictures were taken before they were allowed through the open front doors of the opulent home of tonight's host.

A smartly-dressed hostess led them to the ballroom, offering glasses of champagne and a brief property history. He listened to none of it, too focused on the woman at his side.

He was fighting to remove her hand from his arm and pull her close. He was fighting with himself over every desire he'd had for months. He didn't want to take advantage of their friendship and, most importantly, her age by trying for more.

She made keeping things platonic difficult with her subtle touches and stolen glances. He'd caught her watching him with interest more than once. He'd only caught her because he was watching her as well.

Before he could ponder their relationship further, they were led into the great dining room where guests were already mingling and sipping cocktails.

He was stopped repeatedly by acquaintances, his and his father's. Land preservation was definitely not the only thing being discussed that evening. Events like this charity were the perfect place to mix high-powered businessmen, politicians, and men like him, who closed whatever deals were made.

Bébhinn leaned into his side and whispered an hour later during dinner, "I wonder if this feels more like work than your normal work week."

Without thinking, he squeezed her thigh with the hand that had been resting on his lap and raised his eyebrows, smiling. "You are very observant." And because he was a masochist, he leaned over to whisper, "You're the most beautiful woman here tonight."

She laid her hand lightly over his, where it was still warming the top of her thigh. They looked at one another, both trying to read each other.

Bébhinn broke the silence. "Do you want to see what others see when we stand together?"

Dagr felt his brows raise in confusion. Was she referencing their age difference? His chest tightened with the beginnings of embarrassment. She picked her phone up with the hand that wasn't still covering his and began to flick through apps. He felt his body grow more tense.

"Did you research my family much?" she asked without looking up from her phone.

"Only a brief history—businesses, holdings, that type of thing," he answered, wondering again where this was going. And then she held up a picture that blew his mind.

"No wonder you thought I was your brother," he laughed. He was looking at a tall, white-haired man with a woman so similar to Bébhinn, that he found himself taking her phone to get a closer look.

She chuckled. Pointing at the picture, she said, "That's my oldest brother, Bran, and my Aunt Raven." She swiped to the next photo. "And that is my brother Patrick and my Aunt River." She swiped again. "My nephews, Daniel and Jonathan." And the last swipe. "Mom and Dad."

Hugh O'Faolain was younger than when he'd passed, with dark hair silvering at the edges. Dagr stared for several beats at Bébhinn's mother.

Though Bébhinn looked extraordinarily similar to her aunts, she was the mirror of her mother. Looking at the photos, he realized her comment had nothing to do with their age and everything to do with their similarity to her family.

She with her mom and aunts, and him with her white-haired, identical brothers. They were also all tall like him, but where the brothers had high-cut cheekbones and a slightly golden tint to their skin, his jaw was squarer, and his skin was as pale as his father's.

He blew the pictures up and saw that their eye colors ranged from dark brown to amber—a honey amber like Bébhinn's and her father's. He and his father were so pale blue that they tended to be sensitive to bright lights. The differences were many, but if you didn't look too closely, their hair and height would throw any stranger into thinking they were related.

"Wow." That was all he managed to say as he handed her phone back.

"I know." She grinned before tucking her phone back into her clutch while still maintaining contact between their hands.

"I can assure you, despite our first meeting, I've never looked at you again and thought of one of my brothers," she laughed softly, mindful of the long dining tables full of important guests bidding on various pieces of art, spectacular trips abroad, and jewelry. There was also the recognition of several guests who gave religiously every year.

"I should hope not." He squeezed her thigh once more as the dinner, auction, and speeches ended. The guests were then herded toward the ballroom, where more drinks and mingling awaited.

They entered the ballroom, and he heard his name being called within seconds. The minute he turned and saw who was hailing him, he sighed in frustration. Lauren James was a researcher for his firm, and a woman he dated briefly last year —and by dated, he meant they slept together a whopping three times.

He realized after the second encounter that she was the type of woman who said she understood that sex for him was nothing more than that—companionship at its most basic. He was upfront and clear.

She was thirty-five, a divorcée, and a mother. When he told her he wasn't interested in anything serious, she said it was the same for her, and then the homemade treats started showing up in his office, and her clothes went from business attire appropriate to strip club.

The third time was a colossal mistake. He'd conveniently avoided her for weeks, but she'd come to his office late, he'd had a bitch of a day in court, and she came bearing his favorite whiskey.

He bluntly told her he was no longer interested in anything other than friendship, but when she'd dropped to her knees and took things in hand, literally, the third and last bad decision where she was concerned commenced.

He'd managed to avoid her for months.

Lauren must have wrangled a date from some unsuspecting

man who didn't realize she would become their next stalker. He really despised clingers.

He lightly wrapped his hand around Bébhinn's waist and placed a casual hand at her hip. She glanced at him but didn't move from his side as Lauren landed.

"Dagr, love, I didn't know you'd be here tonight," Lauren crooned, completely ignoring Bébhinn. There was zero chance of her not knowing his schedule. The woman stalked his secretary and spoke to her more than he did.

"Lauren." He prayed that for once she would hear the fuck off tone of his voice. Clearly not, with the inappropriate hug that resembled a human boil, where Lauren tried to elbow Bébhinn to the side, and her cheek kisses were akin to a pestilence.

Bébhinn's kindly smile faltered, but her elbow was now pressed firmly on top of his hand, making it clear that she didn't wish him to remove it.

"I've missed you, babe," she flipped her bleached blonde hair behind her shoulder, presumably to show off her gigantic breasts erupting out of the top of an inappropriate gown. How in the absolute hell had he ever found that woman attractive? Her personality alone should have been a three-kilometer red flag.

"I'm going to make this short. I am not your love or your babe. We are not friends or even friendly. You will cease making a spectacle at this charity event, which happens to be extremely important to me. I am here with my—"

"Girlfriend," Bébhinn interrupted. "Enjoy the rest of your evening, ma'am. Take me to the bar, my love. I'm dying for a Jameson."

Lauren's face flushed with anger, and when it looked like she was about to cause an even bigger scene, he pivoted on his heel and led Bébhinn away.

The second they were out of Lauren's hearing, Bébhinn said, "Sorry about the 'my love' thing, but yikes. That woman is desperate."

His past screw ups weren't something he wished to discuss, but he owed Bébhinn an explanation. "Obsessed might be a better designation. Unfortunately, I got the warning from a buddy of mine too late."

There were three separate areas where drinks were served. Dagr led her to the one furthest away from where they'd left a sputtering Lauren.

Drinks in hand, he finally looked at Bébhinn and grimaced at her questioning gaze. "Right. So, I fooled around with Lauren a few times. Three exactly. The last time, I knew I was being foolish since her personality had begun to show itself." He shrugged in a juvenile manner, as if he had no control.

She surprised him by covering her giggle behind her hand. "My, my, my, Dagr. You must be quite something in bed," she teased.

"Christ, don't you dare try to embarrass me more than I already am." They laughed at that point, the encounter absurd enough to tickle their funny bones. "But I am."

"Am what?"

"Quite something." He winked and nudged her side, causing another round of snickers.

Despite the Lauren encounter, the evening turned out to be one of the best evenings he'd enjoyed. Bébhinn was sharp, witty, and an excellent conversationalist. She'd spoken to his clients and friends alike—all unabashedly curious about his relationship with the young O'Faolain.

It hadn't taken long for the presence of an Oklahoma oil billionaire's only daughter to get around. She fielded questions and curiosity about her family with calm grace.

He should have expected his presence, but when Lee

Whiten joined him and Bébhinn, he felt tension creep into his shoulders. He should have realized his friend would be at the charity. Both he and Lee had several land preservationists as clients.

Bébhinn, of course, knew Lee. Lee didn't let on that he was shocked at who Dagr's date was. He spoke to her like the caring granddad that he was. He did give Dagr a brief look, which was meant to convey that he expected an explanation.

Dagr was under no illusion that Lee would insist on the details of their relationship. He only wished he knew what those details were.

"I know I've told you this, but your father is a man that I will remember the rest of my days. He is very missed by me and my staff."

Cheeks flushed with emotion, she gave a small, circumspect hug to his friend. "I appreciate that, Lee."

"You haven't contacted me yet, like I thought you would." Lee raised his bushy brows in question.

"I will. Soon. I promise. Dad said he left me a package, but I just wasn't ready to have it all over with yet."

"In your time, Miss O'Faolain," he said, patting her hand. "Though I admit, my curiosity might be greater than yours."

"I'm sure Dad left me something special, which I will appreciate, but I know it will make me cry. I've just...put it on a back burner. If you would bring it to the next board meeting, I'd appreciate it, Lee."

"I'll make sure of it," the older man assured.

"I'm so glad I got to see you while I was in town. You and Dagr must know each other?"

"Oh yes," Lee nodded. "Your man, here, is one of the best solicitors I know."

Dagr cut in. "At least the one you know that you can still beat at poker," he teased.

"There is that," he chuckled. "Your father couldn't make it, Dagr?"

Rolling his eyes, he admitted, "You know, Dad. He'd rather chew on nettles than attend such a 'ridiculous waste of time.'" He air-quoted the last.

"Your father has never fallen in line a day in his life. Good to know that Ulf is still very much, Ulf. Did he—"

A young man breezed up, interrupting Lee. He was a twenty-something adonis straight off a Paris runway, his presence instantly irritating Dagr. "Bébhinn. My God, I can't believe you're here. I wish I had known. We could have come together."

"Harry," Bébhinn whispered back.

# *forty*

## THE WATCHER

HE HAD LOST all interest in going on the weekend excursion with the club, but he knew if he stayed home, he would only stew on what she was doing and who she was doing it with.

He pitched in where he could, threw rocks in the ponds with the kids, and helped with the meals. It was torture to be doing all those things without Bébhinn.

He did them anyway, because he planned for them both to stay club members. It was their thing, after all, a beloved hobby that was all theirs.

She was with her boyfriend…that had to be a lie. It had to. He would have seen evidence of a relationship with the bedroom camera if that were the case.

No. She made up the story because she forgot about the trip, and spending the weekend with a "boyfriend" was an easy story for the other members to believe.

But what if she did have one? She had clearly packed a large suitcase. He'd seen it for himself. However, the case was big, too big for one or two days. Maybe she was packing for storage, or she had loaded stuff to take to her mother's flat.

He stoked the fire while other campers added wood. He smiled and chatted, but his thoughts never strayed from her. He was done waiting for her to choose him, even though they had an undeniable connection.

There was another problem that he was struggling with. Rent was due in three weeks on their flat, and his funds were tapped.

He'd put everything on his credit cards to outfit the place. He wouldn't take her to a new home filled with shabby seconds. She was used to a certain level of wealth.

Once they were married, her money would become his, and he could pay off the debt. He was beginning to panic because his timeline had been upset twice now. He couldn't afford to wait.

When he got back from the hiking trip, and she was back from her...weekend getaway, he would be waiting.

Watching.

# forty-one

## BÉBHINN

WHY ME? *Why now?* Bébhinn hadn't seen Harold Milton since the day she'd broken things off. She'd blamed it on her father's passing—*sorry, Dad.* The truth was that she'd finally admitted to herself that she felt little to nothing for him.

It still annoyed her that her first sexual partner was a man who was little more than a friend with benefits and very few benefits to boot.

She didn't dare look at Dagr, who was probably smirking over both of them getting cornered by exes not even two hours apart.

"What a surprise," she finally got out, setting her drink on the table to offer her hand in a shake.

Not taking the hint, Harry swooped his arms around her and hugged her to his chest, briefly thank God, but he unfortunately kissed her cheek before he straightened.

"I've been thinking of you for months." He took her hand, asking, "Can I take you for a drink? You can tell me what's been happening in your life since I've graduated and moved from town."

She barely managed not to roll her eyes. He'd only graduated the year before for the love of God, yet he acted like he was an old working man, used to the grind. "Feck off," as her great-gran, Nan, would say.

"Not much to tell, I'm afraid." *Take the bloody hint, bro.* No catchups required.

"I have so much to tell you too."

He clearly took her hint like an ostrich with its head buried in the sand. When he slid his arm around her waist and she felt his hot fingers splaying across her bare skin, she was about to tell her ex to take a hike when another voice joined the conversation.

"I'm afraid, young man, that Bébhinn and I are here together. *Very* much together," Dagr added as he forcibly removed Harry's hand from her waist and pulled her into his side.

She was amused at his antics, not so dissimilar to her own with Lauren. She played along and smiled, kissing the edge of his mouth. She smelled the whiskey on his breath when his lips parted in surprise. Despite the venue and the audience, she wanted to move the kiss to his lips. Desperately.

Their eyes met as she pulled back. It was intense and knowing, lust soared through her middle at the feel of his hand tightening on her waist.

Returning to the conversation, she cleared her throat and looked back at Harry, who was clearly unhappy with what he saw.

"I suppose that's the biggest and only news worth sharing, Harry. Dagr and I are very happy." Not a lie. She was very happy standing next to him. "I hope you have a special someone that I can meet someday. It was great seeing you. Maybe Dag and I can meet up with you again. We meet here or Dublin all the time." *God, please, hear me out. I'm usually not such a big liar.*

Harry's face pinkened, but finally, he stepped back an appropriate distance, nodding his head in agreement. She would have felt bad about Harry's obvious discomfort, but they'd been broken up for nine months. He should have known better than to think they would step back into a relationship after one chance encounter.

Despite Dagr staking his claim, Harry was brave enough to say, "I'm glad I got to see you. I've missed you, Bébhinn." He flicked his eyes once to Dagr before adding, "Call me. Anytime."

She was thankful Lee was still with them and broke the tense silence Harry's parting words had left them in.

"The past can be so inconvenient to our present, can't it?" he asked, chuckling.

At the same time, she and Dagr answered, "Very," and "Yes." A moment later, Lee said his goodbyes and moved on to another group of acquaintances, leaving them alone.

She held up her glass of Jameson and proposed a toast. "Here's to not seeing another ex tonight."

"To not seeing another ex, ever. Cheers," Dagr countered, clinking their glasses.

"Quite an evening." She smiled and bumped his side with her elbow. Despite the interruptions, she was enjoying the evening. She was here with Dagr, and he had yet to loosen the arm wrapped around her waist.

When he didn't come back with an amusing retort, she glanced up at his profile. He appeared to be watching someone across the room, and when she followed his line of sight, she found Harry deep in conversation with a group of men and women.

"How long were you two together?"

His tone was serious. Could he be jealous? "Oh, umm, less than a year. It wasn't serious or at least not as serious as it should have been," she corrected.

"What happened?" He finally pulled his gaze from Harry and let his hand slide across her back until they faced one another. He looked embarrassed for asking, and added, "You don't have to say. I'm being incredibly rude and nosy."

"I told him I couldn't handle a relationship while I was dealing with my feelings about my father's passing."

"And was that the real reason?"

"Am I speaking to Solicitor Griffiths?" she asked, but grinned to let him know she was teasing.

He winced at the playful reprimand. "Sorry," he shook his head and chuckled, "you're right. Forget I asked. It's just the way you worded why you broke up sounded like it wasn't the real reason."

"It wasn't," she tapped the top of his hand that now rested on the table by their drinks, "which makes you correct. As heartless as this might make me sound, he just wasn't it for me, and I knew it. I did as Dad always advised, and 'cut my losses.'"

"Sound."

"Finish your drink, Mr. Griffiths, and take me to the dance floor. I didn't get all dressed up to be hidden in a corner," she teased—and yes, flirted.

He threw back the remainder of his shot and held his hand out for her to grasp. "I despise any other man looking at you, but I won't deny you a dance, Miss O'Faolain."

She was thrilled that he admitted that he didn't want anyone else to look at her and was more than delighted when he bent to kiss the side of her mouth as she had his.

She wanted more than that, and after tonight, she believed he did too.

The dance turned out to be just another gathering place for business talk, but she hardly minded. She was held tightly to Dagr's body, moving to a slow beat. She had her hands resting on his chest, and his hands were both flattened against the naked skin of her back.

In between the mini, impromptu dance floor meetings, Dagr leaned down and whispered, "I'm glad you're here."

"I'm glad I'm here." He'd kept his ear close to her head, and she was able to whisper back. "Could I talk you into leaving, grabbing some greasy takeout, and going back to your place?"

"Easily."

---

Changed into sweatshorts and a loose t-shirt, Bébhinn finished the last bite of possibly the most decadent burger she'd ever been treated to. "Mmm," she said for the tenth time, wiping the last of the over-easy egg yolk from her chin.

Leaning back, she patted her satisfied belly. Thank goodness she worked out regularly because tonight's caloric intake had to be astronomical.

She and Dagr were comfortably sprawled on the living room couch, happily watching Gordon Ramsay lose his shit and slam his hand down in the middle of a stone-cold halibut.

Once all the takeout trash was set aside, Dagr and she reclined side-by-side. She felt ridiculously juvenile, hoping his hand would find her hand. If she were honest, she hoped his lower bits would find hers, too, but she would take the glancing brush of a finger at this point.

She told herself not to, but she shifted just that little bit more so that their arms were completely touching. A breath later, he covered her hand with his, where it lay between their legs. She suppressed a sigh at the contact.

She kept her eyes trained on the screen even when he flipped her hand over and began rubbing circles in her palm. She could have moaned it felt so good.

"Bébhinn."

He only said her name, but he had her full attention.

# forty-two

## ROWAN

ROWAN WALKED through the front door after a hellish Saturday. She'd flown to Paris to meet with an estate manager selling off a home's antiques, from furniture, linens, paintings, and sculptures to crystal, china, and silver.

She'd made the trek for an eighteenth-century Limoges china serving platter. One of her clients had been searching for the last few pieces to complete her set for years.

Rowan had hired an expert in antiquities to meet her at the estate situated several miles outside Paris to authenticate the platter.

It was a replica.

She was still pissed at the missed opportunity to relax and read a book. The minute the heavy door closed behind her and before she'd even had a chance to set her satchel and keys down, her sisters came flying down the staircase to intercept her.

"Thank God, you're home!" Raven said breathlessly.

"You'll wish you weren't in a minute," River wheezed, as out of breath as her older sister.

"Give her the short-short version," Raven said, elbowing River.

"Right. You didn't tell us, which we understand. Well, Raven understands. I think you're a bitch." River frowned.

"Hurry up, Riv!" Raven moaned.

By this point, Rowan's head was spinning, which was not an unusual occurrence when she and her sisters were in a state of excitement.

"The boys found out that Bébhinn didn't go on the weekend hike with her hiking club and is instead spending the weekend with a man. I'll save you how Bran and Pat got hold of the news," River dumped the information on fast forward.

"We've made them wait to call Jo's man to track her until you got home," Raven finished right as her brothers-in-law—or sons-in-law, as the case may be—pounded down the stairs to join them in the first floor's main room.

Rowan felt her headache from the achingly long day ratchet from a pinch to pounding. This scenario was exactly why her daughter had asked for a moment to figure out her feelings before being bombarded with the two towheaded, scowling men currently standing in front of her.

Used to their antics after over twenty years, she knew it was essential to take an offensive position first.

Holding her hands up, palms facing the men to stop them from speaking, Rowan started with, "I know exactly where my daughter is and who she is with. I gave Bébhinn hugs, kisses, and my blessing as she left my flat yesterday morning. I appreciate that you guys have always loved and protected her, but I want to be very clear here. Raising a daughter is a wholly different experience from raising a son. Sisters?" She glanced at Raven and River for confirmation.

"Completely different," Raven affirmed.

"You guys dodged a hormonal ticking time bomb," River agreed.

"I love you, Bran. I love you, Patrick. You're my sisters' heart. You were Hugh's heart. Bébhinn asked for time. Just a bit of it. She entrusted me with her feelings, and I will guard them.

"She is my daughter, and I will always have the final say in her care. Will you let her feel out this new relationship before sending in the troops? For her? For me?"

Bran and Patrick each took deep breaths, looking at each other, their wives, and finally back to her.

"We were afraid she hadn't told you either," Bran admitted.

"Our sister has never done something so grownup, or mature, or...I don't know...not like a young girl," Patrick's cheeks pinkened in embarrassment, still uncomfortable with his baby sister dating.

Rowan had to remind herself that Hugh would have been worse. So much worse. Hugh trusted her, though. He may have created a hundred obstacles, but he would have relented in the end if Rowan or his daughter asked him to.

"I know it's hard to see her as a grown woman, but she is. Are we agreed, then? You'll step back until she comes to you herself?" Rowan looked at the two men with her sternest mom face.

"Fine," Bran spat out sullenly.

"For the moment, Row, but she'd better come to us sooner than later," Patrick finished.

Rowan moved to the first floor's lovely full-sized drink bar, suddenly needing two fingers of Slane whiskey more than air. As she moved behind the bar, she noticed Bran and Patrick kissing their wives goodbye as they slipped out the front door.

"Drink?" she asked her sisters.

"A double of anything dark and at least eighty proof," River answered.

"Three Wolves." Raven raised her finger to order.

"How long do you think our husbands will wait before they enlist Daniel and Jonathan to stalk Bébhinn?" River asked Raven.

"I bet they're meeting our sons now," Raven sighed, reaching for her whiskey.

Rowan leaned her elbows on the smooth wood of the bar, moving her glass across the surface with her pointer finger.

"She came to me. She opened up, really opened up, for the first time since…since Hugh." Rowan pressed her lips tight, willing the tears that wanted to spill a swift retreat.

"You are an amazing mother," Raven said solemnly, touching her sister's hand in solidarity.

"I love you, Row," River whispered.

# *forty-three*

## DAGR

EVERY TALK he'd given himself drained from his brain and straight to his dick, apparently, because the second Dagr thought about moving beyond friendship with Bébhinn, his body and mind were in complete alignment.

"Bébhinn."

Her name leaving his mouth, her eyes finding his, their game of skirting around their attraction—over.

She twisted her body on the couch until she was on her knees, and with his help, he slipped her body over his lap until her knees rested against the side of his thighs.

She leaned forward and held her lips shy of touching his. "Dagr," she murmured, mingling their breaths and dragging a moan from him.

His fingers went from her hips to her ass, pulling their centers even tighter before he closed the distance between their mouths.

Their breaths mingled, warm and unsteady, as Bébhinn's fingers traced the line of his jaw. He met her gaze, his eyes searching, before pressing his lips to hers—soft at first, then deepening as the moment charged. Her hands slid over his shoulders, anchoring herself to him, while his arms encircled her waist, holding her close. The world faded, leaving only the hush of their movement and the shared electricity in the space between them.

As his sex grew hard, her hips began to glide up and down his length. He despised himself for not having a conversation with her before they changed their status, but now that she was in his lap, and he was sucking her tongue down his throat, there was no room for heartfelt discussions.

She broke the kiss and leaned back while tugging the hem of his shirt until he crossed his arms and grasped it to tear it over his head. She gasped as she took in his chest, having never seen his tattoos. He wondered whether she would like them.

Her hands were instantly on his bare skin, tracing the Welsh dragons that were surrounded by knotwork and spirals. Feeling her delicate fingers lightly skimming across his chest, shoulders, arms, and abs set his skin on fire.

"You've been holding out, Dagr," she grinned. "I don't know whether to stare at your muscles or ink."

"As long as you keep touching me, I don't care what you look at." He leaned forward and retook her mouth. Their lips and tongues warred, unable to get close enough or deep enough to give them relief.

Her fingers barely skimmed the top of his joggers, but his stomach clenched tightly in anticipation. He rubbed his thumbs over her sides under the bottom of her t-shirt, moving the fabric up inch by slow inch.

She glanced to the side when her phone began vibrating with text notifications. She ignored them, thank God.

"When did you know you wanted more than friendship with me?" she asked after turning back.

"The cave."

Her eyes shot up in surprise.

"Me too. For you, that is. So why haven't you ever...I don't know, said anything, tried something?"

"There are a few reasons," he began, knowing it was too soon to share that he was ready to settle down with one woman. He didn't want to scare her off. He could tell her the biggest reason, though. "Our age difference." He expected her to say something like, "Oh, I don't mind," or "You don't look old." Her laughter took him by surprise.

"What's so funny?" he asked.

"You worrying about age." She sighed out the last of her mirth, leaning forward to kiss him again before adding, "My parents were much further apart."

Her lips found his again, and within seconds, they were both panting. He dragged her t-shirt off, his mouth watering at the sight of her high, round breasts. She was wearing a soft, nude bra that was sheer enough to see her dark, puckered nipples.

"Christ, you're stunning." He slipped one narrow strap off her shoulder, wanting to slow down the pace and unwrap her leisurely. She moaned when he licked her nipple through the bra and moaned louder when he uncovered one breast and sucked her deep into his mouth.

"Dagr," she whimpered. She cupped his head, encouraging him to stay right where he was. He pulled the second strap down, freeing her breasts completely, and started sucking and kneading and pinching and pulling until her breath became frantic.

He loved that she was so sensitive. She was close to falling apart from breast play alone. Without breaking contact, he rotated their bodies until her back was on the couch, and he was covering her with his body.

"I want to—" He was interrupted by her phone ringing and vibrating its way across the table.

"Noooo," she wailed when he sat up to grab it. He handed her the phone as she readjusted her bra. "My friends and mom know where I'm at. They wouldn't bother me on a Saturday night if it weren't important. Sorry." She grimaced, unlocking her phone.

"I'll live. Barely," he added, earning a smile from her. He watched her read messages from where he sat at her feet, massaging her calves. "Is everything okay?"

"It's Mags. Lord, save me," she sounded more exasperated than upset. "This is embarrassing."

Doubly curious now, he asked, "What did she say?"

Shaking her head, she told him, "Apparently, my brothers found out I'm staying with you this weekend, well, not with you," she corrected, "but with a stranger."

"Are they coming here?" The thought was even embarrassing to him, but it was no less than he deserved for not formally meeting them prior to laying his hands on Bébhinn.

"According to Mags, she sought out Jonathan, who was on a date, and forced him to tell her what Bran and Pat know. He'd been trying to get a date with that chick for months, and Mags knew it.

"Jon was pissed, but he told her that his dad and Bran visited him and Daniel and said that as soon as I got back to town, he wanted them to shadow me until they could figure out who I was seeing.

"Don't worry, though, I'll handle the assholes when I get home. Good news. Mom approves and didn't tell them anything. That's all I care about."

When she reached behind her back and unclasped her bra, dropping it on the table next to her phone, he suddenly gave zero shits about her brothers.

"I hope that didn't crush the mood," she said right before his mouth met hers in a hungry rush.

"I think you can feel that it didn't," emphasizing his meaning by pressing his hard shaft between her legs. He lay on top of her with only his thin pants and her shorts separating them. Holding her hands above her head, he kissed his way down her neck and licked between her bare breasts. He sucked above her nipple, wanting to leave his mark before moving lower.

He licked and nipped his way down her stomach, finally letting go of her hands so he could hook his fingers in her shorts and panties. She was already writhing beneath him. He planned on making her scream his name as soon as he got his tongue—

At the exact moment he heard the door open to his flat, he heard his father's booming voice. "Son, Christ, but you better be home. I've worn my fingers to the bone trying to reach you."

Bébhinn yelped and tried to scramble out from underneath him. He gripped each of her arms. "Be still. It's my damn father." He dragged his t-shirt off the back of the couch and quickly shoved it toward her before standing up and going to the kitchen, where his dad was rummaging through the fridge.

When he noticed his son, he slammed the door and rounded on Dagr. "You are here, you bast—" he stopped mid-curse before saying, "Have you been at the porn? At least put your fucking hard-on away. My poor eyes, boy," he growled at the same time stifled laughter from the living room could be heard.

His dad's incredulous look would have been comical if Bébhinn hadn't heard the asshole discussing his dick. He didn't blame his dad for assuming he was alone. He knew Dagr had been taking a break from dating.

He felt his whole body flush and heat prickle his face when Bébhinn joined them. She was completely dressed in her clothes and, without batting an eyelash, handed Dagr his t-shirt.

"For your modesty, Dagr," she grinned before sticking her hand out to his dad. "I'm Bébhinn O'Faolain from Dublin. You must be Mr. Griffiths."

His dad's handshake had never looked weaker as he stared at the beautiful, barefoot woman standing before him.

Clearing his throat—twice—his father strengthened his grip. "Ulf. Hugh O'Faolain?" he asked, having no idea of his passing. "I've met your father. Well," he corrected, "not in person, but he and I were on a few conference calls dealing with some land that Trinity owns. The land held numerous minerals and flora that they wished to preserve for their students to use for study. How is Hugh? I appreciated his zero-bullshit way of problem solving."

The brief, wide-eyed glance she threw Dagr's way broke his heart. "Dad—" he started.

Bébhinn spoke over him. "He passed at the end of last year." She cleared her throat. "I'm happy to know you knew him, even briefly. I've told Dagr more than once that you two seem to have a few similar qualities." She smiled, trying to lessen the uncomfortable news.

His dad instantly sobered. "Forgive me. I didn't know. You'll never stop missing him if he was half the man I thought he was."

She blinked several times, her lips twisting briefly as she regulated her emotions. "He was that and more. Thank you, Ulf." And then she shared, "You know, your son spent the night in a cave with me during a snowstorm on one of Snowdonia's peaks?"

He gave his son a sharp look. "I didn't know. It seems my son is full of secrets these days."

Dagr decided to end the exploration for more information, saying, "I didn't expect to see you until Monday."

His dad's face turned ruddy with anger. "That old bastard Williams is trying to buy the land near the reserve that he bloody well knows I want. I was only holding off until things were settled with the reserve."

"Are you kidding me? Williams is a prick. Jesus, that man couldn't care less about the countryside. He just hates you."

"I'm aware," his dad replied. "I want that property to build a family cabin for us. Can you block his offer?"

Dagr looked at Bébhinn, seeing his romantic evening slipping away. She looked back at him and shrugged, smiling. If anyone could understand family, it was her.

"I have a million messages to return before bed anyway. Please," she said, briefly touching his hand, which his dad caught if the smirk was any indication, "get your dad that property. Be a pirate, not a pussy." She laughed, and so did his dad. "That's one of my brother Patrick's favorite sayings."

He stopped her as she turned to leave and gripped her hand despite his father's presence. When she looked up at him, he pressed a brief kiss to her lips and said, "Thank you for understanding. I'll make it up to you."

"I know." It was all she said before walking out.

"You've been holding out, Dag," his father growled.

He and his father were as close as brothers and shared almost everything. Dagr wasn't sure why he hadn't spoken of Bébhinn.

"Aren't the O'Faolains the family Lee wants you to help on a case?"

"Among other things," he replied, purposefully being vague. He knew Lee wanted him to take over his firm so he could retire, which would be a hell of a lot more than helping on a case.

"Get me my fucking property, son, and then tell me why I found you humping O'Faolain's only daughter on the couch."

*forty-four*

## BÉBHINN

BÉBHINN HAD BEEN HOME for a few hours, having left London early. Dagr's father had spent the night, which meant there had been no more sexcapades.

Still, she'd had an amazing day and evening with Dagr and enjoyed meeting Ulf. His gruff no-nonsense reminded her of her father, and she'd felt instantly comfortable. She'd also been thrilled that he had known her father, even if only through conference calls.

Dagr had been waiting outside her bathroom last night after she'd gotten ready for bed. He apologized for his father's unexpected visit and because he had to work.

"Your father is wonderful, and your job is important. Plus, it's not like you could have told him no," she laughed.

"I could have."

"And paid dearly for it later."

"Yes," he admitted with a shrug and grin.

"I'm going to bed." She stepped closer.

Dagr had her lifted and pressed against the wall. Her legs naturally wrapped around his waist.

"A kiss goodnight?" he spoke against her lips.

Her answer was to swipe her tongue between his lips. The goodnight kiss lasted ten minutes and had them as frustrated as they'd been when they left each other earlier.

Sleep did not come easily that night.

The following morning when her car was waiting outside his flat, Dagr was in the middle of a heated conference call with another attorney. She knew he was frustrated that he couldn't properly tell her goodbye, but her feelings were far from hurt. Remembering the look of longing on his face still put a smile on her face hours later.

Dagr Griffiths made her very happy.

She and Gray were finishing the supper dishes after the four housemates decided to cook out so Bébhinn could tell them about the charity gala, especially what was happening between her and Dagr.

"I still can't believe my texts cockblocked you," Mags mumbled through her hands as she covered her face and shook her head in mock pain.

"Technically, his father did that, but my God, you guys, I only got to see and touch him from the waist up; his body is gorgeous."

Blair signed, "I'm glad you didn't take our advice and told your mom before you left."

"Me too. She was great. I should have trusted her from the beginning. I hadn't realized how long it had been since we'd truly shared something that wasn't about Dad."

"I can't believe you were able to put your brothers off a family get-together until tomorrow," Gray said as she handed Bébhinn the last of the dried plates.

"Sending Daniel, Patrick, and Ciar back out the front door

was the best part of this evening. I've never met a bigger bunch of tattletales in my life," Mags griped.

Her nephews and Ciar had waltzed out to their back garden while they were grilling, acting as though they weren't trying to gather intel for her brothers. The girls finally told them to fuck off back to their house. Bébhinn wouldn't lie. She'd taken immense pleasure doing it.

"Even without their dads pushing them to snoop, those three are nosy gossips," Blair signed while making an exasperated growl in her throat.

They'd decided to go to the cinema and were leaving in fifteen minutes when someone knocked on the front door.

"If that's the neighbors," Gray groaned, "tell them we aren't buying Girl Scout cookies." Bébhinn loved that Gray's mom and her mom both grew up in Oklahoma, so they both got the USA references.

Mags threw the door open and spoke to the visitor. The door blocked whoever it was.

When she opened the door wider, Bébhinn gasped while Mags announced, "Bébhinn's boyfriend looks like an O'Faolain. I'm scared. Incest is illegal, right?"

Bébhinn almost choked on her own tongue. Dagr was outside. At her house. Unannounced.

Her legs got the memo to move, and she was shoving Mags out of the way and yanking the heavy wooden door in until Dagr, in all his blue jeans and black tee glory, was within touching distance.

"What are you doing here?" Realizing that sounded like he was unwelcome, she added, "I'm so glad you're here."

He stepped over the threshold without an invitation, probably realizing her surprise voided her manners. "I didn't get to tell you goodbye."

"He chartered a jet to tell you goodbye properly. Keep him, Bébhinn," Gray hollered from the living room.

They stood for what felt like an hour staring at one another while her friends watched them like a zoo spectacle. He looked so serious, so ridiculously handsome, and such a welcome sight that she decided action over words was the better path.

Without warning, she stood on tiptoes and slipped her hands across his broad shoulders until they clasped behind his neck so she could pull his mouth to hers, and the instant he deepened the kiss, it became as explosive as last night. Dagr lifted her against his chest, making it easier for him to devour her mouth. Aware that they had an audience, she stifled her whimper as she slowly forced herself to pull back.

"Blair said she didn't know the romcom we were going to see had a soft porn intro," Mag quipped.

They both snorted in amusement. "Is this a hello or a goodbye?" Bébhinn whispered in his ear.

"Both. I couldn't concentrate worth a damn since I watched you walk out this morning. I didn't like you leaving me without a reminder," Dagr answered.

"A reminder?"

His hesitation had her heart rate spiking. "That you're—"

"That I'm?" Bébhinn lapped at his bottom lip, producing a groan from Dagr.

"Mine."

"I approve," she said softly. She didn't mention that his cheeks were reddened in embarrassment because this was, hands down, the most romantic gesture. She took his hand and led him over to her friends for introductions.

Mags, of course, had to state the obvious. "I'm not saying you look like her brothers, but Jesus, it's creepy as fuck."

"You must be Mags." He held his hand out for her friend to shake.

"Ahh, my perfect personality precedes me," Mags said as she took his hand in a firm grip.

"I'm Gray MacGregor. I'm a fan," she teased Dagr, increasing the blush.

"Nice to meet you. I'm sure I have your father to thank for whatever background check that's been done on me."

"Oh, for sure," Gray laughed. "Her dad would also be responsible." Gray turned toward Blair and pointed.

He turned toward Blair, too, and did something that made her fall for him even harder than she already had.

In BSL, Dagr signed, "Forgive me. I just learn. I am Dagr. Nice to meet you, Blair."

The brilliant smile Blair gifted him, which she usually reserved for close friends and family, brought tears to Bébhinn's eyes.

Slowly, and in the most basic of BSL, she signed back. "You did well. I am glad you are here." She turned to Bébhinn and signed quickly, "Tell him that if he wants, we can all sign everything to give him a crash course. He'll be cursing like a sailor in BSL in no time. Tell him not to get overwhelmed, that I am excellent at reading lips."

When Bébhinn repeated to Dagr what she'd said, he laughed and signed and spoke "Yes" at the same time.

"Seriously, though," Mags began, "can we please do a DNA investigation at least? Just in case..."

"We are not related, weirdo," Bébhinn countered. As introductions went, she was pleased that her friends seemed to genuinely like Dagr. It was nice to have them meet the person who was so important to her.

"How long can you stay?" Bébhinn asked.

"I put in an offer on the land for Dad this morning and put together a report on why my father would be a better candidate to own land so close to a sanctuary than Williams. I dug up some past lawsuits where Williams neglected specific land ordinances that should push the seller our way.

"I don't have to meet Dad until tomorrow evening." He hesitated before continuing, but finally said, "I presumptuously hoped you might put me up for the night."

"Of course." She smiled and nodded her head when what she really wanted to do was giggle and clap like a child who'd been given a pony for her birthday.

"No worries, Bébhinn, we'll all keep our music loud tonight," Mags announced as she stood.

Gray and Blair stood as well. "It was nice to meet you, Dagr, but we'd better get going if we don't want to miss the movie," Gray said before snagging her purse off the table.

She and Dagr followed them to the door. "Okay. You guys have fun." Bébhinn was still reeling that Dagr stood at her back —and was staying the night.

Mags had stopped on the front steps and was looking at them strangely, shaking her head slowly like she was confused. "It's like I'm looking at Bran and Raven or Patrick and River."

"Totally a mind bender," Gray agreed.

"It's the hair for crying out loud! Quit making it sound like he looks like my brothers. Gross."

"I assume I'll find out tomorrow at lunch. You did tell me you were having a family lunch."

"Oh God," she whisper-moaned. "I can skip." The thought of taking Dagr to meet all of them made sweat break out on the back of her neck.

"I need to meet them if you and I are going to—"
Mags interrupted, "Screw like rabbits."

"Date," Dagr said firmly.

Blair signed quickly, smirking at Bébhinn. "I missed that. Damn it," Dagr cursed, "I've been working on sign for six weeks and I only got two words."

Blair looked chagrined. Very slowly, she signed, "Sorry, Dagr. I will slow down."

"Thank you."

The girls' Uber pulled up, and they piled in. Bébhinn shut the door as Dagr grabbed his duffel.

"What did Blair say that I didn't catch?"

Her blush was instant. "She said not to worry about making noise on her account." She chuckled as Dagr's eyes widened in understanding. "Don't let Blair's precious pixie look fool you. Her wit is deadly."

"You have great friends. I can't wait for you to meet some of mine."

"I'd love to. Are you hungry?" She stopped in the kitchen. He didn't stop when she did, dropping his bag on the floor before stepping close enough to crowd her between his body and the counter.

She watched in wonder as he ducked his head and spoke against her lips. "Not for food."

Like most of their kisses, raw passion and need exploded. She ripped her mouth away, gasping and asked, "Bed?"

"Now."

Bébhinn took his hand and practically ran to her bedroom, kicking the door closed. Whatever was between them was the very thing that had been missing with Harry. She'd never felt so frantic to be intimate with someone.

He took over the moment her bedroom door slammed behind them, pulling her shirt off and then his. They kicked their shoes off and ripped their pants down. Breathless, they stood only in their underwear.

He closed the gap and ran his hands up her bare sides, stopping at her bra. "Are you sure this isn't too soon for you?"

She appreciated the question, but it was unnecessary. "The cave would have been too soon. Now, not so much."

It was all he needed to hear. He unhooked her bra and slid her panties down, where she could kick them off. He was on her as soon as she'd toed off the last remaining barrier. He had her in his arms, her legs around his waist, his mouth and hands touching her everywhere.

Her hands weren't idle either. Since the moment they were interrupted on his couch, she'd thought of nothing but getting him naked. She leaned back in his arms to give him better access to her breasts.

"Feels so good, Dag," she moaned. She tightened her legs, rubbing her slickened sex up and down the bulge stretching his boxers, causing him to groan around her nipple.

He watched her face as he let one of her nipples slip from his wet mouth and guided her body to slide down his until her feet touched. "Lie on the bed."

The huskiness of his voice had her scrambling to obey. She was on her back, elbows propping her upper body. They were both watching and waiting.

"Bend your knees and let them fall apart. I want to see all of you." He was slowly stroking himself through his black boxer briefs.

She complied, whimpering at how aroused she was having him see her like that. Finally, he shed the last barrier to the part of him that she wanted most. When his sex sprang free, saliva flooded her mouth.

He was thick and long with protruding veins and a leaking, swollen head. "Dagr. Please." She wanted him so badly. Her hips began to slowly thrust up and down, her body's way of enticing him closer.

"You want this?" he asked as he stroked his length.

"I want everything."

He kneeled on the bed and crawled slowly over her body,

kissing and licking as he went. He kissed her core as he passed, causing her to fist the sheets.

"Later, baby. I need inside you. Now."

He stayed on his knees and grasped her hips to lift her high enough to align their bodies. He slid his sex along her wetness twice, hissing at the ecstasy the friction caused.

"Ready for me?"

"More than," she groaned, lifting her ass even higher. Dagr looked like an ice-cold villain set on mayhem, with his white hair and almost clear eyes—he looked vicious in the best way.

There was no easing her into the invasion. He slid into her body in one go, causing them both to gasp at the surge of heat and tightness.

He stayed as deep as he could get while he fused their mouths, their warring tongues and teeth clashing until she had to turn her head to breathe.

He began to pump in and out, slow at first and then faster, frantic, hitting her G-spot over and over until a high-pitched whine erupted from her throat. The pleasure was too much and not enough.

"Dagr. Dagr. Dagr." She repeated his name like a spell she wished would bewitch her forever.

His movements became less smooth, faster, and out of sync. "I'm close," he practically roared. "Come for me again, baby. Now!"

Her body obeyed, as her back bowed and her thighs quivered. Dagr Griffiths marked her body inside and out.

She knew there was no going back for either of them after this.

# forty-five

## THE WATCHER

HE WAS NUMB. Shattered.

That man stayed with her all night. Slept next to her all night.

Fucked her over and over again all night.

That man had taken her every way a man can take a woman, and she wanted it. Wanted him in her body, her mouth, her bed, her life.

He hated that man. He almost hated Bébhinn.

He hated himself the most. Had he talked to Bébhinn months ago, before Wales, maybe even before her father died, she would have never met that man.

What did he have left? How would he move past that? Would it matter if he finally told her what had been in his heart for so long now?

They'd had breakfast in bed, laughing and talking to each other like they'd been together for years. He had thought she'd only ever seen him the once after the hike.

He'd been wrong. This was clearly a relationship, not a one-off.

He closed his eyes and swallowed the pained scream that needed release. He couldn't stand to look at her bed in its current state of disarray, but his eyes were glued to it, nonetheless.

Bébhinn and that man were in the shower.

Together.

They must have left the door open because he could hear muffled moaning and groaning. They were at it again.

Without her...without the hope of having her someday...

He should just lie down and die. Would she miss him? Would she cry at his funeral? Would she regret not choosing him?

*forty-six*

## DAGR

DAGR WAS SATISFIED BEYOND MEASURE. After weeks of mooning over her like a teenager, Bébhinn was his.

He hoped. They hadn't discussed the future. They'd been busy having more sex than he'd ever managed in one go. He'd never felt such a burning need for another woman. She'd probably run if she knew he was looking at her as his lifetime partner. He at least needed to know if this relationship was, in fact, a relationship.

Bébhinn was young. She might be thinking he was a bit of a good time.

Dagr was sitting on her bed when she emerged from the bathroom, dressed in baggy blue jeans and a fitted white tee. The white Hermès tennis shoes made the whole look seem effortless but chic.

Her long black hair was pulled over one shoulder. He remembered how the sleek, straight strands felt when they dragged over his naked body. He had to adjust himself quickly, forcing his mind to the family lunch—a perfect boner killer.

"You're looking awfully serious." She stepped between his spread legs, bending to give him a peck on the cheek. "I hope you're not worried about lunch. Everyone will love you, and I admit, I really want you to meet my mother."

He hesitated for only a moment before deciding he just needed to come out with it. Beating about the bush had never been a part of his nature.

"What are we? I mean, what are we telling your family?" He felt her stiffen and, in return, felt his body tense.

She looked at him solemnly before answering. "I've known what I want us to be for a while. I need to know what you think."

Fair enough. "I want something serious. Permanent. I'm not interested in dating or sleeping with other women or you sleeping with other men."

"If you did, you wouldn't be adding me to the rotation. I don't sleep around. I don't want to sleep around. You're only the second man I've ever slept with, and I'm not interested in adding to my body count."

"Good."

"Fine."

"So, we're dating?" He wanted clarification.

"Yes. Exclusively."

"Exclusively," he agreed. "Now that we've settled that—your family lunch?"

She groaned, burying her face in the crease of his neck. She kissed him beneath his shirt collar. "There are only so many hours in a day. It can't last forever. Let's go."

"Enough hours to get the shit beat out of me." That was what he wanted to say, but didn't.

At thirty-nine, he never thought he'd find himself squirming at a girlfriend's parents' front door, but here he was, gripping Bébhinn's hand in what must be an uncomfortably tight clasp.

"Ready?" Bébhinn asked.

"Of course." *Not at all.*

Apparently, when she said her family owned a building of flats, they really did. The O'Faolain monolith was a four-story monstrosity of old-world glory—gray stone and a few steps from the men's wives' business, Triskelion Design. He couldn't wait to see the inside.

Lunch today was on the fourth floor. Her mother's floor. He could handle her brothers' posturing, but Rowan... Her opinion meant everything to Bébhinn, which meant it was everything to him.

Bébhinn entered the door code and shoved the heavy door open, and he was greeted with three women who looked like his girlfriend standing fanned out before the entrance. Beyond, leaning against an impressive pub-style bar were four white-haired men, arms crossed, their stares like loaded weapons aimed his way.

It was silent for no more than half a second, until...

"I'm so glad you're here."

"Why do you look like Patrick?"

And finally, the one introduction he needed to ace. "I'm Rowan, Bébhinn's mother. Come in. Please."

He might have squeezed Bébhinn's hand harder than intended, but between his girlfriend's doppelgangers surrounding him and his own, well, doppelgangers sneering at him, the coming lunch was proving to be a worse nightmare than he'd imagined.

When Rowan, ignoring the men flanking the bar, waved a

hand in front of the large display of liquor, clearly asking his preference, he said, "Glenmorangie."

"Year?" Rowan asked.

"18. If you have it."

"I do. Good choice, it's one of my favorites."

Raven and River—he wasn't sure who was who—went to their husbands and sons. "Dagr, this is my husband Bran, his brother Patrick, my son, Daniel, and Patrick and River's son, Jonathan."

So that was Raven. Then River, which he would have guessed eventually since Bébhinn said she had the sharpest tongue of the three sisters, faced the men, clearly annoyed.

"This is Dagr Griffiths, our Bébhinn's boyfriend. Shake hands before I lose my shit."

One of the sons mumbled loud enough for the group to hear. "Bébhinn's old man friend, more like."

Several things happened at once. Bébhinn's head whipped toward her nephew-cousin, and she took a step forward as if she meant violence. He gripped her hand tighter and pulled her back to his side. Rowan sucked in breath, her eyes instantly glassy. As a woman who had loved a man many years her senior, her nephew's comment would have hit her harder.

The eldest brother, Bran, saw Rowan's reaction and slammed down his own glass of whiskey, rounding on his son who briefly closed his eyes in...regret, maybe.

"Do not ever disparage age in this house, son. No two people loved each other more than your grandfather and your Aunt Rowan."

Daniel looked at his aunt first. "I'm sorry, Row. I shouldn't have said that. I never once thought it of you and Grandpa." Then he turned to Bébhinn. "I'm sorry, Bébhinn. I was being a dick. Apologies, Griffiths."

He felt the tension ease out of her fingers where they still held hands. She only nodded in acknowledgement of his words. It wasn't necessarily forgiveness.

Christ, the shock of being in a roomful of men who had his exact shade of hair was still a mind fuck. Jonathan, the younger white-haired nephew-cousin, spoke up then.

"In Daniel's defense, we've known you've been keeping something from us for weeks. It hasn't sat well with either of us. We've always been closer than that, Bébhinn."

Bébhinn shifted by his side, clearly feeling guilty. She was very close to her whole family. He let go of her hand and wrapped a supportive arm around her back. She looked up at him and graced him with a soft smile.

"Sorry, Jon. Daniel." She nodded to them both, acknowledging that she'd hurt their feelings, though unintentionally.

Patrick stepped up then and stuck his hand out. "Can we start this awkward fucking meet and greet over? I'm Patrick O'Faolain."

Dagr took the offered hand immediately. "Dagr Griffiths. Thank you for having me."

Bran stepped forward then, hand offered. "That was our wives and stepmother's doing. Don't get too comfortable." His smirk softened his words, and Dagr shook his hand.

Jonathan shook his hand but had no words of encouragement or discouragement. Daniel was the last to shake his hand.

"Where did you sleep last night?" Daniel asked, dropping Dagr's hand and stepping back to stand by his cousin.

"What the hell, Daniel. Screw off. You don't want to start a war with me, boyo. I have too much on you, and it begins and ends with—"

Daniel quickly cut her off by holding his palms up in surrender. "Peace." The look he gave Dagr didn't have a bit of amity couched in the five-letter word.

Dagr was pleased to see Daniel walk to Rowan, where she

hovered just outside the group. "I love you, Aunt Row. Please tell me you truly forgive me. I would never—"

"I know," Rowan patted her nephew's back. "You will show the same respect to my daughter and her boyfriend." It wasn't a question.

"Yes," Daniel agreed. Hesitantly.

---

Lunch had not been so much a pleasure as it had been a practice of endurance. Not to say that there weren't some good moments. The sisters were hysterical even when they didn't mean to be. He did notice that even though Rowan participated she held some of herself back.

Perhaps the highlight of the meal was when River asked Dagr if he liked sourdough bread.

"I do. My mother used to make it for me and Dad."

"Raven makes it for us. She has her own starter."

"River," Bran growled.

That got Dagr's attention. Bran's face was turning a brilliant shade of crimson. River was definitely trying to start some shit.

"I do." Raven smiled tenderly at her husband. "Bran is the one who started it for me before we were married as a present. Besides having our son, it's always been my favorite gift."

Dagr couldn't help himself. "Bran sounds like he must be incredibly romantic."

"Yes. Always," Raven sighed as River and Rowan chuckled behind their napkins.

For his part, Bran glared daggers across the table. It had been challenging for Dagr to keep his smile contained. Bébhinn didn't bother hiding hers.

Now that lunch was over, they were back downstairs,

everyone saying their goodbyes, when River asked, "Does your father have white hair?"

"Christ, babe," Patrick grumbled. "Leave it already. We aren't flipping related."

Dagr agreed with Patrick, but he answered anyway. "He does. We look very similar."

"And his parents?" Now, Raven was playing inspector.

Bébhinn looked at him with wide eyes and a barely contained smirk. She knew what he was about to admit would only encourage her aunts.

"No. They adopted Dad when he was an infant." Gasps and an "Oh my," and an "I knew it" from River followed that announcement.

"Come on, guys," Bébhinn chided. "Surely you don't believe that I went on a hike and met the son of Bran and Pat's long-lost brother!"

Rowan shocked everyone when she added her voice to the conversation. "Well," she hesitated as everyone stopped speaking and turned to her, "I watched all the men during lunch, and they do have certain...similar mannerisms."

In an embarrassing display of synchronicity, the five men crossed their arms over their chests and scowled at the giggling women, who thought the men's discomfort was hilarious. All men and women crossed their arms. It was just that their timing was terrible.

Phones were out, and pictures were snapped before Dagr could blink. Then, before he could leave the tow-headed huddle, Bébhinn said she wanted a family picture. She set her phone on the bar and put a timer on it. When Rowan tried to opt out, her daughter wrapped an arm around Rowan's waist and one around Dagr's.

When she grinned up at him, clearly enjoying the moaning

and groaning coming from the men, he couldn't help but kiss her upturned lips.

*forty-seven*

## BÉBHINN

BÉBHINN COULDN'T HELP the snorts of amusement on the ride home to her house. She and Dagr had flipped through the burst of pictures she'd set her phone to take of the group once they'd left the O'Faolain building, and while they sat in her Jeep, she had already sent them to her mom and aunts.

In one of them, Bran, Patrick, and Dagr had all leaned down to kiss their women. That one was getting framed.

Seeing Dagr's face turn red when he saw all the twinning was hysterical. Bébhinn knew they were all having fun with the "long lost brother thing," but it was just too amusing to let slide.

Another bonus of the teasing was that her family finally relaxed around Dagr. The men were able to interact in a comfortable camaraderie.

Being able to claim Dagr as hers in front of her family—euphoria.

River made Dagr promise to ask his dad if he'd ever heard of a "bitch" named Helen Lowell. She was my father's first wife and, from all accounts, a horrible excuse for a human being. The story of when her mom had verbally kicked Helen's ass had been a favorite one to retell over family meals. Bébhinn could always tell that it moved her father.

Things had gotten more serious when Dagr dropped a bomb by admitting his father had mentioned his birth mother was American and had been very young.

"Are you really going to ask your dad about his birth mom?" she asked as they pulled up to her house.

"Absolutely. I'd do just about anything to get your aunts off my tail."

He leaned over the console and kissed her until they were both breathless before stating, "None of us believes I'm really a long-lost family member, but it sure broke the ice faster than a silent luncheon. Your mom and sisters are very clever."

"Oh, they are," she assured. Bébhinn knew what they'd been up to and completely approved. "It helps that my brothers love their wives more than anything else in the world and would do anything to make them happy."

"Including family photos with their sister's new boyfriend, who happens to be much older."

"And that," she admitted. "What did you think of Mom?" she asked as they exited the Jeep.

"I really liked her. Your aunts too." He hesitated like he wasn't quite sure if he should say whatever it was he was thinking.

They paused on the steps leading to the front door. "What is it?"

"I sensed that your family might be treating your mom more carefully than maybe she would like. When they did that, I could see her withdraw even more."

She sighed, knowing what he witnessed was true. The

house was empty when they walked inside. Mags and Gray were at a yoga class, and Blair was surely in the back garden tending her plants. "It's getting better, but yeah, I probably need to say something to my aunts. It's not been a year yet, we're all still trying to find our new normal."

"I understand. I do." He sat on a kitchen chair and pulled her between his legs. "It took years before I stopped looking for Mom when I walked into our house."

She placed her hands on his shoulders and felt his muscles ripple beneath her palms. "You were so young. I can't imagine."

He started at her thighs, moving his hands along her sides to her ribs and back down again, bringing her a little closer to his body with every pass. When his fingers began to drag over the side of her ass to the undersides of her breasts, her breaths increased in rhythm.

"When do you have to leave?"

"In an hour. I've a car scheduled to pick me up."

"Do you want to spend the next fifty-nine minutes in my bed?"

"God, yes." He surged to his feet and brought her along, lifting her easily and carrying her to her bedroom. "I was afraid you might be too tender after last night."

They kissed down the hall, bumping into tables and pictures. "Tender, but not too terribly." She bit his lip.

"Fuck, I can't wait to be inside you. I've wanted back in the moment I pulled out this morning."

Her head spun as he wheeled on his heel, slammed her door, and had her pressed against the wall in a heartbeat. He set her on her feet only as long as it took to yank everything off below the waist, and then she was back in his arms.

Gripping her ass, he aligned their sexes. They watched him slide into her. She was utterly mesmerized seeing his length disappear into her body.

Once he was as deep as he could go, he told her, "I'm sorry, baby, but I—"

His voice faltered into a deep groan as he pulled out and slammed home again. He was all furious passion, frantically taking her mouth as he took her body. She could only hold on and take it. She loved that he was out of control in his need for her. She felt pretty out of control herself.

"Don't stop, Dag. So close," she begged. She was in the eye of an orgasmic storm, and when it hit, she couldn't hold back the scream that ripped from her throat.

"Christ!" he shouted, pumping twice more before stilling. His body pulsing and jerking in tandem with her own.

Her orgasm kept going as she felt the rush of heat released in her body. She stayed wrapped in his arms while he walked them to her bed. Good on him, her body was in a squishy marshmallow stage.

He laid her down gently, with a care that had her heart pounding furiously at the thought of him leaving her soon. As he finished undressing her and lay his big body over hers, she only wished they could stay like that forever.

He was propped on his elbows, gently stroking his fingers through her hair. "I don't want to leave you," he admitted before kissing her gently.

"I don't want you to leave, either." The truth was that her stomach ached knowing he was leaving in less than an hour. "We'll figure it out. It won't be easy once school begins, but we can take turns visiting each other on the weekends."

"Not enough," he growled.

Sitting up, he bracketed her thighs with his knees with enough pressure that she couldn't move easily. He took her hands and stretched her arms above her head, which had her back arching and her breasts lifting like an offering.

"It's not enough," he repeated.

He changed his grip until only one of his hands held hers, using his other to trail his fingers down her arm, her cheek, neck, shoulder, and between her breasts. Full body shivers racked her already-sensitized flesh.

She stayed silent, watching him watch her. She looked down her body, from her pointy nipples, down her stomach, finally resting on his quickly hardening sex.

Her eyes skipped to his face. He was still just watching her. Waiting.

"No. Not enough," she finally said.

He let her hands go then, shifting his palms to her ass and lifting her until they were aligned, and he could slip inside her. Even though she was wet from before, his size still took adjusting to. She whimpered, trying to move her hips, but he held her firm, exactly where he wanted.

Except instead of moving, he stilled. His expression was solemn when he said, "Bébhinn." His grip tightened, and she felt him swell even fuller deep inside her. "This might be too soon. You might not... You might think..." He winced before saying, "I love you."

She felt tears prick her eyes. To think that if she hadn't gone forward with her and her dad's Wales trip, she would have missed meeting him. She had known her feelings for a while and had wanted to tell him. "I love you too. So much, Dagr."

A shuddering breath of what must have been relief was released from his mouth. He stretched out above her, moving in and out of her slowly. Kissing her slowly. Making love to her.

"God, baby, I've dreamed about hearing you say those words to me."

He continued the slow, sweet assault until they both reached their peak, swallowing each other's moans and gasps and *I love yous.*

She and Dagr stood kissing goodbye in the doorway while his car patiently waited at the curb. When they'd emerged from her bedroom, it was to walk by a smirking Gray and a wide-eyed Ciar. Their walk of postcoital bliss couldn't have gone smoother.

"I have a plan." Dagr spoke quietly in hopes that their audience wasn't hanging on every word. Fat chance.

"Do you?"

"Jesus Christ, Gray," Ciar groused, "does it not freak you out to see Bébhinn sticking her tongue down a man's throat when he looks like her fucking brother?"

"Don't ruin the moment, dickhead." Gray must have elbowed his side if Ciar's "Oof" was anything to go by.

"I do," Dagr continued, ignoring her friends. "I have to go, damn it. I love you, but when I say I have a plan, I swear on it."

"I trust you, and I love you too. Now go."

# forty-eight

## THE WATCHER

SHE LOVES ANOTHER MAN.
I hate her so much.
I love her more.

*forty-nine*



Dad,

The family met Dagr today. It went how I dreaded—in the beginning. All four of the boys didn't try as hard as I hoped, yet they didn't throw him out... Silver linings? Things got better once Mom and the aunts got involved in torturing them.

I'm not under any false illusions that you would have behaved any better, but I do believe you would have enjoyed meeting him. Dagr took all their nonsense in stride. Being only ten or so years younger than Bran and Patrick probably evened the odds.

He spent the night last night—probably one of the things that you're glad to have not lived through. He flew to Dublin only to see me. He got to know Gray, Mags, and Blair. They love him, by the way.

He's it for me, Dad. I wish you could yell at me or

shake me or hug me. I need your advice. I need you to tell me not to jump the gun (America has the best sayings).

We said I love you to each other, and oh my God, I'm so gone for him. You're the first person I've told. I think he's my person, like Mom was for you, and you were for her.

Before leaving for Wales, he said he had a plan for us to be together, maybe even before I graduate. Whatever it is, I'll do it. The "boys" won't be happy. You probably wouldn't be happy either (though I believe Mom and I could talk you around).

I wish you were here to give me a hard time about it. I wish we could have argued about Dagr's age or that I'm sleeping with him or anything really.

I just need you. It's getting easier, though. I don't cry anymore, or rarely anyway. I always remember that you wanted me to be happy, and Dagr makes me more than that.

I think Mom likes him.

River thinks he's some long-lost relative of Bran and Pat's. I'm gagging. I'll keep you updated on that saga.

When I find out Dagr's plans for our future, I'll let you know first.

Thanks for listening, Dad.

I love you,

Bébhinn

"So, he's like inviting all of us to his house in Colorado?" Mags clapped her hands in excitement. "I've always wanted to visit."

"Are the two turds invited?" Blair signed.

"They are," Bébhinn laughed. "He even invited Ciar."

"I hope Dagr told them they aren't allowed to bring any of their trashy dates with them." Gray clearly hadn't forgiven the boys completely for what their dates had said to Blair months ago.

"He didn't tell them, but I did. Not that I can stop my nephews from trolling the local bars for willing women. I'm just excited about the trip. We leave in three weeks, which will leave us six weeks before school starts once we're home.

"Bran and Patrick said they would cover Daniel and Jonathan's work commitments. I think that Mom, Raven, and River must have 'encouraged,'" Bébhinn air-quoted, "the guys to do whatever it took to get Daniel and Jon to go. I'm hoping the trip will solidify, at least to some of my family, that Dagr is perfect for me."

"Clearly, the man knows how to give orgasms if the noises coming from your bedroom earlier are anything to go by," Gray teased.

Bébhinn felt her face heat, but she was too pleased with her life right now to be embarrassed. "Jesus," she heard Mags mutter and followed her friend's line of sight to see that Daniel, Jonathan, and Ciar were approaching the bar where she and her friends were seated. Bébhinn was about to wave to them when her phone rang.

"Dagr's calling me. I'm going to step away for a sec. Be nice to the boys, will you?" Eye-rolls were all she got. "Oh, hey, guys. Be back in a sec," Bébhinn told the guys as she walked by them.

Rounding the corner near the restrooms where the music was muted, she answered. "Hey, how are things in Carmarthenshire?"

"Productive. Dad will get his land. I only called because," Dagr hesitated, "I miss you."

She leaned against the wall between the male and female restrooms, her legs suddenly feeling less than stable. His admission made her feel faint with happiness.

"I'm out with the girls, but God, Dagr, I miss you too."

"Good, because I'm closer to a solution to our problem of long-distance dating."

She could hear the grin in his voice. "Tell me!" she demanded.

"No can do. I'll be back in Dublin in two days. We have a lot to discuss, which reminds me, I asked Dad about his birth mother. He said Grandma had a small box of items somewhere with a bit of information. Dad never looked. He never wanted to, but to prove he isn't a long-lost brother, he'll try to find it. The birth mother made it clear that she never wanted to be contacted, but it wasn't a closed adoption for all that."

"I can't wait. Should I plan another family get-together for the big reveal?"

"Actually, yes. I have some business to discuss with your brothers. It's not confidential, so everyone can hear. If Dad digs up Gram's information on the mother, I'll bring that too. Dad said he had amazing parents and isn't interested in looking into his past."

"I understand that. I hope he isn't offended that we asked. We don't need to see anything. Honestly, Dagr, we don't."

"Oh no, he found it all amusing, especially that your friends think I look like your brothers. He simply isn't interested. Listen, you'd better get back to your friends. Text me when you get home."

"I will. Love you." Before he hung up, he said an "I love you" that was heartfelt and final and had her confidence in their relationship soaring.

Bébhinn made her way back to the bar and found her friends and family discussing the Colorado trip. She aimed her words at her eldest nephew, Daniel. "Thank you for rearranging your schedule to go." She looked toward Jonathan and Ciar next. "I appreciate you two also making the effort."

Daniel only nodded, but Patrick said, "He seems fine, B, but Christ, he's old as balls."

To which she replied, "Mom seemed to like your grandpa's balls just fine, dickhead." Ciar sprayed whiskey over Mags and Blair, earning him glares.

"Christ, Bébhinn, you're more like Aunt River every day. Stop," Daniel complained.

"Honestly," Ciar started, "none of us has ever been to Colorado. I'm stoked. Plus, it will give me and Gray a chance to discuss the new Murphy's nightclub."

Bébhinn was as excited for his new club as Gray was. She would be working on the hospitality side, while Bébhinn would be working on the interior design side. It would be her biggest solo job yet for Triskelion Design.

"I appreciate that Dagr's trying to make an effort to know us, Bébhinn, but Jesus, don't you think you two could have gotten to know each other a little better before fuc—" Jonathan cut himself off, going with "—sleeping with each other?"

"It does seem like you jumped right into it," Daniel chimed in.

"Trust me, guys, from the noises coming out of Bébhinn's bedroom, there was no sleeping going on."

Mags elbowed Ciar at the same moment Bébhinn told him to "Shut up, dickhead. I didn't know you were in *my* house."

Blair had been quiet up until now. She usually was when the guys were around, even though the group was close. So it was a surprise when she signed, "At least one of us is getting some action." That coming from Blair was shocking enough, but then she doubled down with, "But everyone knows, I'm very good with my hands."

She, Mags, and Gray all burst out laughing, high-fiving the little redheaded imp. They laughed harder when they saw that Daniel, Jonathan, and even tough-as-nails Ciar were all staring in horror at Blair with their jaws on the floor and a bit of pink in their cheeks.

"I approve of three-drink Blair over two-drink Blair," Mags chortled.

They had all had a few more drinks than their regular casual evenings out, but it kind of became a celebration for her and Dagr, making it official. She couldn't wait to see him again. She really couldn't wait to hear what his plan was to keep them from living apart.

Speaking to Daniel and Jonathan, Bébhinn said, "Dagr's coming back to town in a couple of days. He said he needs to go over some business stuff with your dads, and if his dad, Ulf, can find the information on his birth mother, he'll bring that too."

"Jesus, don't get Mom started again," Jonathan complained. River did enjoy teasing the guys.

They stayed another hour. The guys said their goodbyes and headed off to some back-room poker game that Ciar had been invited to. At home, the girls decided to put on pajamas, make popcorn, and settle in the living room to watch the newest episode of Amazing Race UK. The show had to be in its hundredth season.

She had been texting Dagr since she'd gotten in the Uber, and they were still texting. Unfortunately, she'd also had a few strange messages from Justin.

Gray glanced at Bébhinn's phone when she sighed and read the latest message, where Justin said he'd missed her at the Club's indoor rock climbing that evening. He also wondered if she had any plans for the weekend.

"You're going to have to be blunt. No one likes to hurt someone's feelings, but in this case, where you've never encouraged his feelings and he still keeps on, you're going to have to."

"Here," Mags said, holding her hand out, "give me your phone. I'll do it." She held up her other hand to stop Bébhinn's instant protest. "I promise not to hit send until you've approved it." Bébhinn shrugged and handed it over. Thirty seconds later, she heard her phone ping while Mags was texting.

Mags touched Blair's leg to make sure she was still lip-reading the conversation. "Dagr just texted, by the way, and said his dick got hard during a video conference because he thought about you coming on his tong—argh!" She squealed when Bébhinn snatched her phone back.

"You're such an asshole, Mags." Gray practically fell out of her chair laughing, and Blair's soft chuckles further kicked Bébhinn's blush up to fire mode. "You're all assholes, come to think of it."

Mags threw a handful of popcorn at Bébhinn, still chuckling. "At least read my message to Justin."

Bébhinn read the message out loud. "'Hope you guys enjoyed the rock climbing. I saw the pics on Facebook. It looked like everyone had a great time. I've been swamped with work, and this weekend my boyfriend and I are going house hunting.' And then Mags put a house, diamond ring, three hearts, and five aubergine emojis. Christ, I'm at least taking the purple dicks off. The rest isn't bad though. Thanks." She pressed send and prayed Justin finally got the hint.

Gray was on her phone again, which she'd been on since they'd started watching the movie. Since voyeurism amongst friends clearly wasn't out in this group, Bébhinn gave a meaningful glance toward Blair and Mags before leaning into Gray's side and asking, "So who've you been texting, Miss MacGregor?"

Gray flipped her phone over so fast, Bébhinn could have sworn her hair ruffled from the resulting breeze. She, Blair, and Mags all had similar faces of raised brow suspicion as they observed the normally unflusterable Gray become very, very flustered.

Finally, Gray found her voice. "A difficult client."

The responses were "Hmm," "Ahh," and from Mags, "Bullshit."

Gray stayed silent. Bébhinn took mercy on her, knowing well there were times that the truth wasn't an option. "No matter, Gray. We all need to keep a few things secret." She bumped Gray's shoulder to let her know that she genuinely meant what she'd said. She held up her glass of green tea. "To best friends," she cheered.

"Best friends," Mags repeated.

Blair nodded in agreement and held her glass of Diet Pepsi up.

Gray shrugged off her unease and raised her glass of wine. "Cheers."

# THE WATCHER

HE KEPT WAFFLING on what to do. He heard her tell that man that she loved him. He said it back. However, she had been sleeping alone for two nights now.

It didn't matter. Not really. She spoke to him on the phone while she lay in bed. She touched herself and let him watch. He tried to pretend she was putting on a show for him, but she kept saying that man's name. It ruined the moment.

His life was in ruins. His finances were critical. He had no money, debt collectors hounded him every moment of the day and night, and he'd lost the will to try to fix them. He had no way to fix them.

He couldn't continue this way.

He sat now in the dark and quiet of his apartment, days from being evicted, simply staring at Bébhinn's empty bedroom and wondering if he could let her go...thinking about all the opportunities he'd let slip away.

His life had shrunk down to one video feed.

He should have been bolder. Braver.

His life was in shambles, and he was to blame. He tried to hate her, but his conscience wouldn't let him. She had no idea the lengths he'd gone through to make her happy. The hours of studying her videos, learning her habits, her favorite position to sleep in, her favorite colors, and even how she liked men to touch her body. That had been the hardest, but it was still a lesson on how to please her.

Could he wait through another boyfriend? Could he go on hiking excursions with The Ramblers and see her smiling face and know that another man had put it there?

No. He didn't think he could.

Her bedroom door opened, the light shining through her fabric blinds haloing the dark crown of her head. She looked over her shoulder, and that's when he realized that she wasn't alone.

That man was back and kissing her the moment he entered the sanctuary of her bedroom. Their hands touched everywhere.

He heard their moaning and panting, and as tears ran down his cheeks, he heard them exchange words of love.

Still, if he told her how he felt...

# fifty-one

## DAGR

DAGR WAS nervous about how Bran and Patrick O'Faolain would receive his news. And Bébhinn, of course. He glanced down at the woman walking by his side. She must have felt his hesitation as they neared her family's front door because she paused her stride and met his eyes.

Her cheeks were still rosy from having sex right before they got into the car that brought them to her family. He'd gone straight to her house from the airport, and the moment they'd laid eyes on one another, clothes had been ripped off.

He'd been out of his mind to have her after she'd teased him with her body over video the night before. As soon as her bedroom door had closed and they were naked, she'd told him to lie on his back before climbing on top of him. Remembering that moment had blood rushing to his already throbbing dick.

Watching himself disappear as she'd slowly slid down his length... "Christ, babe, I've got to stop thinking about you naked. I really don't want to eat supper with a hard-on."

"Yeah, try not to do that," a man's voice said behind him. Daniel O'Faolain.

Jonathan stepped up beside his cousin, where Dagr and Bébhinn had turned to greet them. "While you're at it, never speak about seeing Bébhinn naked in front of me again. I might not be able to eat."

"Shut up, assholes," Bébhinn practically growled before looking at Dagr. "I have to have the nosiest family in the world."

"Don't be mad at us. Your boyfriend is the one standing in the middle of the walk talking about his dick." Daniel shrugged and lifted his hands in peace.

The fact that he was trying not to laugh made Dagr want to poke the man back. "You're right, Daniel. It's just that your aunt loves it when I talk dirty."

"You should have heard us over video chat last night," Bébhinn teased. She gave Dagr a wicked smile. "Right, babe?"

"Still thinking about it, baby," he replied before leading Bébhinn the rest of the way to the entrance. He heard Jonathan mutter, "And there went my appetite."

The meal and the company were easy and pleasant. The men seemed to have thawed toward the idea of him being in Bébhinn's life, which he assumed the women had some influence over. When they retired to the bar downstairs for drinks, he knew it was time to discuss what he'd come for.

Shaking off the nerves and putting on his confident solicitor mien, he began with, "I know your solicitor, Lee Whiten, well."

He had everyone's attention with the unexpected segue. "We've worked several environmental cases over the years. He always spoke highly of Hugh," he nodded solemnly toward Rowan and Hugh's sons.

"Not necessarily related to what I want to speak about, Rowan, but my father was on a few different committees over the years with your husband. They never met in person, but Dad enjoyed their calls."

Rowan blinked rapidly momentarily, and the whole table held its breath. Dagr was kicking himself for bringing that up when Rowan finally said, "That makes me so happy that your father knew, at least a little bit, of Bébhinn's father. Thank you for telling us."

"I'm sure you know that Lee brought me in as a consultant on the conservation guidelines for your new property acquisition." The four men nodded in confirmation. Bébhinn gave Dagr a quick side eye at the news but didn't interrupt.

"That case isn't what I wanted to discuss today. Lee wants to retire. He's asked me for two years now if I want to take over his firm. He doesn't have any children or family in the business. If I agreed, Lee's clients would agree to be integrated into Griffiths & Wallace or find a new firm.

"I told Lee yesterday that I would accept his offer to buy him out. For two reasons. First, I want the challenge, and I want my firm to diversify. The second, and most important reason, is because of Bébhinn." He turned and briefly gave the woman at his side a look that he hoped showed how much she meant to him.

"Lee has an office in London, which will be integrated with mine, but there is also an office here in Dublin. I plan to take over the Dublin office and leave my partner to head the London division.

"Bébhinn is here. Her family is here. She has a year left at uni and plans to work at Triskelion. I want that for her, and I can make sure that her life goals don't have to change. I only care about having her. With me." And then, because he was already in the deep end, he tacked on, "Always.

"There will be no hard feelings if you choose to find another firm to represent the O'Faolain interests. Business is business.

"In that same vein, personal is personal, and since I know family is as important to me as it is to you, I wanted you to know my intentions with Bébhinn. I plan on finding a place for us to live together. Immediately, if she agrees."

He looked each of the four men listening to his speech in the eye to gauge their reaction. They watched him back with equal intensity.

Bran spoke first. "So basically, what you're telling us is that we can take your representation or fuck off, and that your relationship to my sister is a done deal, and we can fuck off our opinions on that as well."

Dagr hadn't thought he'd been that blunt, but... He clasped Bébhinn's hand and brought it to rest on his thigh. "Yes."

Patrick looked at his brother and their sons before breaking into a wide grin. "Dad would have liked you, Dagr, which means so do we."

He was relieved. He didn't have to have their approval, but he'd really wanted it. Bébhinn squeezed his hand before leaning over to whisper, "You did have a plan."

He kissed her cheek softly while running the pad of his thumb over her bottom lip. "Never doubt a Griffiths in love," he said quietly back. As he sat straight again, Rowan watched them with tears in her eyes. He pretended not to notice, understanding that she wouldn't appreciate having attention drawn to her while she was emotional.

"Watching you piss all over my niece like a dog in heat has been amazing, don't get me wrong, but can we get to the good part?" River asked.

"Yeah," Jonathan chuckled, "according to Mom, you might be my long-lost cousin."

Dagr pulled his briefcase closer to his chair and dug out the folder that his dad had found. He'd said there didn't seem to be much information on his birth mother.

"Dad warned me there wasn't much. My grandmother kept bits of information from the hospital and notes from the adoption agency. There isn't much, he said. I haven't looked because Bébhinn wanted a grand reveal without me having any prior knowledge."

He opened the folder and began reading aloud the notes from his grandmother. "The adoption wasn't closed, which is odd, but the agent in charge of Dad's case said the mother and her family didn't wish to provide any information and never wanted to be contacted."

"How sad," Raven said solemnly.

Rowan dabbed her eyes before saying, "I can't imagine the crushing weight the mother must have been under."

"The family sounds like assholes. Good on your dad, Dagr, for getting out early," River scoffed.

"Okay. So, Dad was born in a fancy birthing center in London," Dagr said as he flipped through the scant notes and hospital papers. "It looks like a nurse told Gram that the mother was a young American on holiday who hooked up with a fisherman when the girl's family traveled through Norway. The notes suggest the family had been in the middle of a European tour for their daughter's fifteenth birthday."

He flipped through more pages, reading the annotations and scribbled thoughts. "The nurse believed that the parents forced their daughter to give up Dad. They extended their holiday so that no one from the States would know she'd ever been pregnant.

"One note says that she had white hair. There is an asterisk with natural by it. The family was from Massachusetts."

He looked up when the table became unusually still. "What?" he asked, unaware of what part had triggered their unease.

Bébhinn patted his arm. "It's fine, babe. Keep looking."

"Okay. Her father was in banking." He dragged his finger down the remaining page, a lined notecard actually, that was partially stuck to the folder from age, and found... "Oh, her name was Helen." *Jesus. No way.*

"No fucking way," Bran said with absolutely no inflection to go along with his words.

"I knew it," River said, slapping the table.

"I think you might want to ask your dad to do a DNA test, Dagr," Rowan said softly.

# fifty-two

BÉBHINN

"THE NAME COULD BE A COINCIDENCE," Dagr said in a tight voice.

It was clear to Bébhinn that where the women were excited at the possibility, the men were quietly staring at one another. None of them was willing to admit their circle might be increasing in circumference.

"So that woman," Patrick began, never calling his mother anything but Helen or that woman, "screwed some Viking fisherman during her posh European tour?"

"Possibly," Bran said grimly. "Humoring this connection, she didn't know Dad yet. Had they been together, our father would have raised your father as his own."

"Your brother, you mean, sweetheart," Raven gently corrected, making Bran wince.

"I'm thankful Hugh didn't know." When everyone looked shocked at Rowan's pronouncement, she explained, "Don't get me wrong, I would have loved to have another stepson." Daniel and Jonathan, and even Bébhinn's brothers, groaned at the

291

reminder of how convoluted their family was. Bran and Patrick preferred Rowan's familial description, sister-in-law.

"Dagr, I'm only glad that your father had a loving mother to raise him. Bran and Pat had that horrible woman, and my Hugh had to call her wife."

Jonathan reached across the table and took his Aunt Rowan's hand. "There's a reason for everything," Jonathan said. "Grandma Nan always told me, Daniel, and Bébhinn that when we were little. It makes sense, right? You ended up marrying Grandpa, and Dagr's dad was adopted by parents who loved him."

Mom tapped Jonathan's hand softly as she pulled her hand free. "You're right, Jon. It's a good thing to remember. This will be just one more interesting twist and turn in our family history if it turns out to be true."

Her mom grinned, actually grinned at the family seated around the table. Bébhinn's dad would be so relieved to see that the woman he loved above all others was trying to smile again.

"You're thirty-nine, right, Dagr?" River asked.

Bébhinn witnessed the telltale heat race across Dagr's fair skin at her aunt's question. She leaned into his side and kissed the underside of his jaw to show her love, which seemed to go a fair way toward alleviating his discomfort.

"Yes," Dagr confirmed.

"So how old is your father? Ulf, right?" Raven asked.

"Ulf," he confirmed. "Dad's fifty-eight."

She saw her family's eyebrows raise in surprise. "How old was Ulf when he and your mom had you?"

"Nineteen," Dagr shrugged and chuckled. "Dad said he knew at sixteen that Mom was the love of his life. My grandparents wished he might have waited until he finished university to have me, but Dad and Mom made it work."

"What happened to your mother? If you don't mind me

asking," her mom asked. The death of a spouse was not something she took lightly for obvious reasons.

"Cancer. I was twelve. Mom told Dad near the end that he would find another woman to love someday. He bellowed at the home nurse to up her meds because she was clearly delirious. If Mom's words were prophetic, they haven't come true yet. He's never so much as looked at another woman twice for twenty-seven years."

When her mother dabbed the tears from her eyes, the family turned their attention to the bottle of Three Wolves sitting in the center of the table.

Daniel gripped the bottle and poured a round of shots before holding his portion high. "To family, the possibility of gaining new members, and Dagr and Bébhinn," he toasted.

Daniel toasting her relationship. Would wonders never cease?

"To the idea of another nephew." Bran brought his glass high.

"To making our complicated family lines even more tangled." Patrick raised his glass.

"To another cousin. Maybe." Jonathan winked at Dagr before raising his whiskey.

"To family," her mom added.

"Family above anything," Raven chimed.

River raised her glass. "To Dagr and Bébhinn waiting longer to have children than both Helen and Ulf!" Her toast caused snorts and shouts of laughter, even from Dagr.

"To my man. I don't give a shit if I have to call you boyfriend, nephew, or cousin as long as I get to call you mine," Bébhinn added her toast to the group.

"Christ have mercy," Dagr murmured, his glass raising last. "To the O'Faolains."

"And the Griffiths," Bran added, looking directly at Dagr and nodding his head.

The chances of them being related surely had to be low even if the woman in question sported natural white hair, was named Helen, and lived in Massachusetts. *Okay, maybe not that low.*

Everyone tossed back their shots and set down the crystal glasses in one.

Bran's phone began to ring, and after looking at the screen, he immediately picked up his phone and answered, "MacGregor."

"That's Gray's father," she whispered to Dagr.

Bébhinn knew that her brothers spoke to her friends' fathers on the regular, so she wasn't surprised by the call until she saw her oldest brother's face turn white. When he stood and knocked over his chair and then grabbed Patrick's arm, a sickening premonition coursed through her veins.

When the call had come informing them of her father's accident, the room had felt similar. One by one, every person at that table stood and waited for Bran to drop another bomb on their heads.

"We're all together. This family doesn't keep secrets from one another. I'm going to put you on speaker and ask you to repeat what you just told me."

The scariest part was that Bran had now grasped Pat's hand until their bones looked close to breaking. Whatever was coming was nothing she wanted to hear. Dagr pulled her in front of him and wrapped his arms protectively across her front, keeping her back tight to his front.

Gray's dad started speaking, and Bébhinn felt her legs turn to withering stocks, forcing her to lean more heavily against Dagr.

"You'll all probably know Mirren was at the girls' house

today visiting." Bébhinn had known and was excited to introduce her to Dagr. Thomas continued. "Mags asked her sister to try to find where Coll and I had placed the security cameras—because she's a wee shit," he grumbled, "and Mirren likes to outsmart me and her Uncle Coll every chance she gets. I'll make this short. Mir said that Bébhinn had told her that she could borrow a purse or whatever. She still had her hidden camera detector on when she went into Bébhinn's room.

"There was a strong reading the moment she walked into the bedroom. Mirren knew that we would never place a device in any of the girls' personal spaces. She played it cool, retrieved the purse quickly, and shut the door behind her.

"Someone has placed a device in Bébhinn's room and her room only. Mirren checked before calling me. Coll and I," there was a hesitation when voices in the background were heard, "without Josephine and Catriona," Thomas growled, "are driving to Inverness airport now, heading your way.

"I've called an inspector that I know well in the Dublin office to meet me as soon as we land. Someone has been videoing Bébhinn. I don't know how they got the camera in there without MacGregor surveillance catching them. I called Ciar to gather up Blair, Gray, and Margaret and take them to his home until this is settled. I will call you when we land. No one is to go to the girls' house until this issue is resolved."

As Thomas gruffly said his goodbye, she looked at her family with the same horror as everyone else at the table. Someone had been watching her while she was in the sanctuary of her bedroom. It was shocking. Sickening. Bébhinn looked toward her mother, who was visibly shaking.

"Thomas," her mom half shouted before he could hang up.

"I'm here, Rowan," he answered.

Her mom hesitated for a moment, fighting the tears leaking

down her cheeks. "Hugh would... He would be... I am..." She stuttered to a halt.

Gray's dad simply said, "Hugh would burn down the world for you and his daughter, and I will too."

In the silence that followed the sickening revelation, Dagr grasped Bébhinn's arms and forced her to look into his eyes.

"Whatever this is, Bébhinn, you've always told me that Gray's dad is the best. This will be resolved. If some sick freak has truly been watching you—"

"Us," she cut in. Bébhinn was sick and so scared. Someone had been in her home, in her room...watching her. The person had possibly seen her and Dagr together. The violation made bile rise in her throat.

"Us," he agreed grimly. "That person will be found, and they will pay. I'm devastated, baby, that this is happening to you."

Bébhinn was a snotty, hiccupping mess, but she simply leaned into his chest and nodded. She believed him. It was just the shock of it all.

"The moment Thomas and Coll can get near the camera, they'll follow the IP address to the person responsible," Bran assured.

Both of her brothers walked over and took turns kissing the top of her head and hugging her, whispering apologies and regrets.

Daniel cleared his throat, clearly as emotional as everyone else. "Jon and I are going to go home and stay with Ciar and the girls. If that's okay with you, Bébhinn."

She meant to say a simple "Yes, please," but all she managed was an affirming nod, before pressing her face against Dagr's chest again.

Her mom and aunts surrounded her next, murmuring love and encouragement, and all the while, she tried to understand how something like this could have happened.

She released her grip on Dagr and caught Daniel and Jonathan before they left. "Hey guys," they immediately stopped and turned, "I've been wracking my brain trying to think if there was ever a stranger at one of our get-togethers. They were always small, and we usually knew them. Did you ever notice a stranger?"

"We'll think about it and have Ciar and the girls do the same, but off the top of my head, no," Daniel answered thoughtfully.

Patrick shook his head negatively. "It had to be someone who was invited in, though. You girls never forget to set the alarm and lock the doors. Barr and MacGregor would know if you didn't and lose their shit."

Bébhinn nodded in agreement. "That's what I was thinking too. Okay, you'd better go. Tell everyone I'll see them soon."

# fifty-three

ROWAN

"MACGREGOR TEXTED and wants all of us to stay home until he calls." Patrick walked behind the bar as he spoke, taking glasses off one of the shelves and setting them on the bar. He looked at his wife as he passed and gave River a soft kiss. "We might as well have another round of drinks."

Rowan felt a horrible spurt of jealousy watching her sisters and husbands touch one another and whisper words of encouragement. Hugh would have known exactly what to say to ease her worries—after he ranted and raved and pounded his fists in fury. Still, he would have been her comfort. He would have been their daughter's comfort.

Now, Bébhinn had Dagr, and she was truly lost. She despised self-pity, and yet here she was, indulging the disgusting emotion.

She was about to back further away from the group when she felt her daughter's arms wrapping around her waist and pressing their cheeks together.

"Mom."

The slight hiccup in her whispered plea gutted her but also gave her purpose. Now was not a time to think about what she didn't have, but a time to fight for what she still held in her arms.

"Thomas and Coll won't sleep until whoever has done this to you is caught. You know that, sweet girl."

"But," she stuttered—trying to find the right words— "but I talk to Dad out loud sometimes, and... Oh God, and Dagr and I."

Rowan knew precisely what she meant. Having her private moments spied on was an abhorrent thought for any person. "I know." She patted her daughter's back and kept her tightly hugged in her arms.

"There is no use jumping to the worst case, my love. Thomas and Coll might not be as fierce as your father when it comes to your protection, but they're close seconds. As are your brothers, cousins, friends, and of course, your Dagr.

"You might have heard some of my and your aunts' horror stories from our pasts, but I can say with certainty that you are strong enough to endure anything thrown your way. The Byrne women seem to draw in the nutters, unfortunately," Rowan said, trying for levity. "Even if this voyeuristic fuck watched your intimate moments, they can't take away the love and joy you felt in those moments. There are sick people in this world, Bébhinn, and they don't deserve an ounce of your life."

Her daughter pulled back with brows raised in surprise. "Damn, Mom. I haven't heard you drop the F-bomb since Dad told you to cut back on your hours at work," she giggled, the sound bringing every eye in the room their way.

"Come on now, daughter. Your brothers are about to go on a destructive rampage if they have to see you cry anymore, and Dagr looks exactly the same. Like, seriously," Rowan whispered, "exactly, weirdly the same. Mr. Griffiths' DNA sample can't come soon enough for me and your aunts."

Rowan was pleased with her daughter's answering grin. "You realize that if they are truly related, how much weirder the O'Faolain family tree will become."

"Oh yes. I know. One of my fondest memories is how pink your dad's ears would burn when someone would ask about the family dynamics."

Rowan led her daughter to the bar and the loving family that waited for them.

Every day was a test in surviving after Hugh, but she would survive.

She was beginning to think her darling husband was somehow behind all the Griffiths shenanigans in his afterlife. He had, after all, insisted on the Wales hike where their daughter met the love of her life. And if Ulf was a long-lost brother to Bran and Patrick, Hugh would have been overjoyed for his sons.

Rowan was sick at heart because of what her daughter was going through, but she also had faith in her family and friends to fix it.

Whoever had done this to her daughter was about to have serious regrets.

# fifty-four

## THE WATCHER

BÉBHINN DIDN'T COME HOME. He knew because he was sitting in his shitty little car on her street. Only her friends and her cousins from next door had shown their faces.

He had been waffling for hours, days, and even weeks on his next course. Praying for a sign. Anything.

He knew she wouldn't pick him now. Perhaps, before Wales, but not now. He'd let the love of his life slip through his fingers. Still, he wanted one more chance. Just one more to finally tell her how he felt. If she chose that other man, he would accept it like a man and move on, but he would regret not trying. For them. For their future.

He stared for two hours at Facebook Messenger, his finger hovering over her name. Finally, his fingers flew over his keyboard, pressing send before he could second-guess himself.

His eyes watered as he watched his phone screen for the receipt that she'd read his message.

This was it.

His last chance. If she saw his message.

He decided he would lay it all out for her. Give her all the reasons he would make the perfect partner for her. He knew her better than anyone else.

From their Rambler meetings and hikes, he knew her favorite food was crab. She despised milk, sunsets made her quiet and introspective, and she despised working out inside. Her eyes were her father's, she hated blueberries and liked to sleep in tank tops with matching panties.

She never wanted to leave Dublin but dreamed of hiking all over the world.

He was hers, and she was his. They were a perfect match if only she would message him back so he could tell her.

# fifty-five

BÉBHINN

THOMAS MESSAGED BRAN TO let him know he was outside Bébhinn's house. She was listening to their conversation since her brother immediately put Gray's dad on speaker.

Her phone pinged, taking her attention away from the conversation. She wasn't going to bother looking, but with everything going on, something made her look at the message. It was from Mr. Todd. He was a professor at another Dublin university, TU.

She'd taken a health and wellness class from Mr. Todd her first year at uni. Trinity and TU had several classes that they shared for different degrees. Before the semester was finished, she'd discovered that Mr. Todd was a member of her hiking club.

He'd never messaged her privately before. The group usually discussed hikes in the group chat. Well, Justin messaged her privately, repeatedly, but they had gone to school together for a few years and had a small connection outside the club.

Mr. Todd's message was odd. Very odd.

> Can you meet me at Darling Café? I need to speak to you about something important. I promise to buy you their famous buckwheat pancakes. Your favorite breakfast food! 😊 Let me know as soon as you see this.

She was getting ready to respond that she was sorry and that things were crazy busy at the moment, when her fingers stilled. Darling Café was where she and her friends always met. How would he know that? And how would he know her favorite order?

Her hands began to shake until her whole body felt like it was one big spasm. This was not right. This was... She didn't know exactly, but Mr. Todd?

With jerky movements, she stiffly placed her phone in front of Dagr. He was on alert instantly. "What is this?"

"He's a TU uni instructor, and a member of The Ramblers Club," she added hesitantly. "The club never ate at Darling's. He shouldn't know I love their buckwheat pancakes." She could hear how shaky her voice was. Everyone standing by her could too.

Dagr shoved the phone toward Bran and Patrick. "Call MacGregor."

Everything happened fast after Patrick called Thomas MacGregor. Blair's dad, Coll, had already noticed a car parked down the street from her townhouse before Patrick warned them about Mr. Todd.

Instead of parking, they circled the block and got the car's registration plate number. Thomas sent the number to his inspector friend.

Bran finished his conversation, his face tight with anger. "The car is registered to the professor, Mr. Todd."

"No," Bébhinn moaned. "Surely, it's a coincidence."

"They are detaining him now while MacGregor tracks the camera. We'll know soon enough."

fifty-six

## DALE TODD

WHY DIDN'T SHE RESPOND? She'd read the message. Dale could see she'd read it. Maybe her new boyfriend told her no.

Maybe he opened her message, and she had no idea that he was waiting to hear from her. Bébhinn would never blow him off. She always smiled brightest for him.

No matter her current relationship status, he and Bébhinn were connected so deeply that she would eventually find her way back to him. He had considered giving up, giving her up, but he wasn't a quitter.

He'd been patient for so long. He was strong enough to endure longer.

Something caught Dale's attention outside his car window. A man looked to be walking straight toward him. He looked in his rearview mirror, about to start his car and leave, when he spotted more people surrounding his car.

"Oh, God," he whimpered. It was the police. They shouted at him to roll his window down and put his hands up.

He closed his eyes in pain, realizing that he'd been right. Bébhinn never saw his message, and her shitty boyfriend had called Dale in under false pretenses.

Bébhinn probably admitted to that white-haired fuck that she had feelings for Dale, and he couldn't stand the competition.

He smiled, then, as he manually rolled down his window. This was precisely the type of move that would push Bébhinn into his arms. She would never stay with a bully.

Except...the officer who leaned down to speak to him said something about a camera, stalking...under arrest.

*fifty-seven*

## BÉBHINN

MR. TODD CRIED and begged authorities to please let him speak to Bébhinn. If he could only talk to her, she wouldn't press charges. He believed that she would not only forgive him but would want to spend the rest of her life with him. Todd believed that Dagr had set him up.

Thomas, Coll, and her friends had only gotten to the O'Faolain residence minutes ago, Bébhinn's stomach a tight ball of anxiety. She sat on the couch downstairs with her friends, mom, and aunts sitting next to her, surrounding her in support. Mirren called earlier to tell her how sorry she was. Once she knew the man was caught, Mirren left town to meet one of her artist clients and would call Bébhinn later for an update.

Dagr, Bran, Patrick, Daniel, Jonathan, and Ciar stood with their arms crossed as they all listened to Coll and Thomas give their report.

"I'm sorry to tell you, Bébhinn," Coll began, "but Dale Todd admitted that he fell in love with you—his words—when you took one of his classes two years ago. He's spent all the months since planning some fake life with you.

"He went into debt renting a flat well over his budget. He planned for you two to live there together. The officers went through the flat and found that almost every wall was covered with pictures of you and several of you and Todd."

"Wait," Bébhinn interrupted, "he and I might have been in a few hiking group photos, but I never took a picture with just him."

"He pasted himself next to you. The man was so mentally compromised, his delusions must have become all he lived for."

Thomas took over. "Once they got him to the station, he started telling the officers all the ways he'd stalked you. Todd didn't use the word stalk, obviously," he shook his head in disgust. "He didn't care that he was further incriminating himself, only believed that if they let him explain his level of devotion, they would understand he'd done nothing wrong.

"He followed behind you on your hiking trip in Wales. He believed you secretly knew he was there and enjoyed his little gifts. He even slept in one of the bunkhouses with you. He knew your schedule because of the Ramblers meetings."

"Oh my God, I would find flower bouquets in my bag, things would go missing, and for a couple of days, my journal to Dad was gone. He...he...slept... Jesus, I can't wrap my mind around all of this."

"He planned on surprising you on the last night of your hike and professing his feelings. The snowstorm stopped him from finding you. When he finally caught up with you, he saw you with Dagr."

She looked at Dagr, shocked at how close she'd come to being alone with that man. He walked over and held his hand out. She scooted off the couch, her friends patting her back as she stood, and sighed in relief when he wrapped his arms around her and held her close.

She tilted her head back so he could hear her. "I truly believe Dad sent you," she said quietly.

"He did." He kissed her forehead. "You are safe."

Bébhinn didn't want to ask, but she forced herself to twist in Dagr's arms so that she could face Thomas and Coll. She needed to know. "Do you know how long he's been watching me?" She felt Dagr stiffen behind her.

Thomas scanned the room before he focused on her. It was clear that Gray's dad didn't want to discuss the camera. She saw his deep barrel chest inflate before he exhaled on a rough breath. "They haven't finished looking at the time stamps, but at least for a year. I'm sorry."

She felt tears prick her eyes. It wasn't just the horror of a stranger seeing her naked or watching her have sex. It was the nights she'd cried herself to sleep after her father died.

"The Gardaí have notified TU," Thomas continued. "The administration will be handing over all electronic devices Todd used. I'm sorry, Bébhinn. I made sure that none of your videos would be viewed, only the timestamps. After he is charged in court, all of the content he saved will be permanently destroyed."

Coll crossed his arms over his broad chest, glancing at Thomas, who nodded his head to finish.

"Before we arrived here tonight, Thomas and I were informed that they believe Bébhinn wasn't the only woman Todd stalked. They have evidence of at least two others. They will be contacted. Once this all goes to court, and the judge sees that Todd is a serial stalker, he should go to prison for a very long time.

"Tom and I are sick that something like this happened

under our watch. We've people coming in tomorrow to install a whole new security system."

Hearing Mag's moan coming from the couch was the only thing that brought a smile to her face that night. She'd wanted less security, not more.

She turned back into Dagr's arms and let him carry some of her weight. A numbness had been stealing over her limbs as she'd heard just how sick that man had been. A man she'd allowed into her home. She shivered thinking about him following her all those days on the trail. Worse, maybe, than the camera.

At the end of it, Mr. Todd was a thirty-six-year-old man who preferred to live in fantasy rather than reality, and hurt people as a consequence. She wouldn't let a coward like Mr. Todd alter the trajectory of her life.

Was she sickened over the violation? Yes. Would it take her a while before she was ready for another solo hike? Yes. Would she go to sleep tonight knowing that she was surrounded by family and friends who love her? Yes.

Dagr squeezed her tighter while he gently kneaded the back of her neck. "Bébhinn is exhausted. I booked a room at Fitzwilliam. Would it be okay for us to run into her house to pick up a few things?"

"Yes," Thomas answered. "Coll and I are staying here tonight." He looked at his daughter, Gray, then Mags, and Blair. "Our team is starting before sunup to make sure they'll be done by tomorrow evening. Everyone can stay at the house, but it would be easier if the girls stayed next door tonight."

Blair signed, "Fine," knowing her dad, Coll, would insist, and that it was not worth fighting him over.

"Yay," Mags deadpanned.

Gray broke the evening's tension, making everyone chuckle when she said, "A sleepover at the fart house. Thanks, Dad."

The guys all grinned, like she'd given them a compliment. Bébhinn kissed her mom goodbye and filed out the door with the rest of the group.

Dagr ordered a car, and as they waited, he chatted with the guys while her girlfriends stood quietly by her side. At their concerned looks, she told them, "I'm fine. Truly. It's just…you know, nothing to do about it but move on. I feel terrible that I had that man in our house, you guys. I'm sick over it."

"That's the dumbest thing I've heard today," Mags chided instantly. "We can't read a person's mind, Bébhinn. You couldn't have known. He violated your privacy. The piece of shit trailed you in Wales. Never say you're sorry for that."

Tears were already welling in her eyes when Blair quickly signed, "Fuck that piece of shit. Never think about him again."

Those words of wisdom dried Bébhinn's tears before they could fall. When Gray added, "Go have sex with your boyfriend. Let him comfort you and then leave this Todd fuck in the past, write your dad, and put paid to this…this single chapter in your life, and move the hell on. Leave the fart bros to us."

A laugh burst from Bébhinn's throat, drawing everyone's attention. "Fine. All three of you bitches have a point. Thank you for being my friends," she said as her and Dagr's car pulled up.

"Always."

"Always."

"Always."

---

*Dad,*
*There are two things I need to tell you.*
*The first one, which you won't be happy about, is*

that I found out today that I've had a stalker for the past couple of years. His name is Mr. Todd, a TU professor. He was caught and is in custody, so don't worry.

He never physically harmed me.

I took some generic health class from him almost two years ago that Trinity didn't offer. He joined the Ramblers Club soon after I did. I guess that makes sense now. He started following me after the health class ended.

I'm sitting in a Fitzwilliam suite. Dagr's taking a shower. It's midnight, but I couldn't sleep without telling you everything that happened today.

He put a camera in my bedroom, Dad! He's been watching me, well, he's been watching me do everything that a person does in their bedroom.

He admitted to the inspectors that he used the hiking club meetings that I hosted to place the first camera and then, later, an upgraded model.

I don't want what he did to me to make me scared of having people in my own home, but seriously, how can it not? I want to trust that I'm safe. I don't want to look over my shoulder.

I suppose that means I won't, and that's the end.

Anyway, he bought a flat and decorated the damn thing with pictures of me. He planned on us living there together. He decorated it in my favorite colors. Crazy.

Though the worst thing, even over knowing he was watching me in my room—that was at least done from a distance—was when he told one inspector that he actually trailed me for ten days during my Wales hike.

Christ! I thought I was being a child, afraid of my own shadow, without my father there to protect me. But it wasn't my imagination. He admitted to putting those flowers in my bag. He is the one who took my journal to see if I was writing to a man.

He watched me sleep!

He had planned to confront me on the last day. Thank God for the snow and an even bigger thanks for putting Dagr Griffiths on my path.

I told Dagr today that I believed it was you who sent him to me. I believe that with everything that I am. You knew he would become my person.

I love him beyond measure. You gave me that.

Sidenote: (but of great interest to you) Mom has smiled a few times. She even giggled.

Second sidenote: Lee is bringing me the gift you left. Whatever it is, I'm sure it will become something precious to me.

Also, plot twist...Dagr's father, Ulf, might be Helen's first-born son! I know. The shock of it all. Mom told Dagr that if it was true, she knew you would have loved him as much as your own children. I know she's right.

Do you think the world could seriously be that small? Blair, Mags, and Gray keep teasing me about dating someone from "the family." Too bad it's probably true.

Which brings me to the second thing I need to tell you.

I'm hesitating because I don't want to think it, let

*alone say it, but here goes.*

*I'm going to take a break from writing to you. Even to tell you Ulf's DNA results. It's not that I don't want you to know, it's just that I know you <u>already</u> know.*

*These letters were all about me. I do know that. They were all <u>for</u> me.*

*They were to help me accept your loss. Come to terms with your passing. To drive home the fact that you aren't here anymore, and you never will be again. And I guess they did do that.*

*I don't wish you back. I no longer pray that when I wake up, your horrible helicopter crash will have been only a nightmare.*

*Life happened. I hate that it did. But you're nothing but a pragmatic man. You would be so pissed if I kept using these letters instead of fully living in the present.*

*Which is a world where you no longer exist. You'll always exist in my heart, in the very being of my soul.*

*I will never forget you. I will never forget your face, your hugs, and especially your love.*

*I will think of you always and look forward to seeing you again.*

*Watch me live my life, Dad, and be proud of me.*

*Your beloved and most devoted daughter—*

*Bébhinn*

Putting her pen down, Bébhinn sat for a moment and felt the quiet wrap around her. She felt good, less burdened, and despite the shocking revelations of the day, very hopeful.

Standing, she gave the closed journal one final caress before moving toward the en suite bathroom, shedding her clothes as she went. She slipped in unnoticed since Dagr leaned against the warm stone wall inside the steaming shower. Hot water cascaded over every muscle and ridge of his body, making her mouth water, thinking about following the droplets with her tongue.

His eyes snapped open when she pushed the glass door in and stepped into the steam. "I thought I might join you." His flaccid sex began filling the closer she came, until she stood before him, blocking some of the soft spray. The heat felt amazing on her back.

He wrapped his hands around her arms and pulled her close, diminishing any space between their bodies. "I was just thinking of you. Of today." He kissed her softly as he slid his arms around her back and lifted her to stand on a raised shelf, which made them almost the same height. "I'm sorry you had to go through something like that."

"It's sad to think that a person I barely knew was able to walk around and talk, go hiking and hold a job, but live in an alternate reality of their own delusions," she said quietly before trailing her tongue up the side of his neck. His moan made her smile. "You're mine, you know."

"I know, thank fuck," he growled, "and you're mine."

She ran one of her hands up and over his chest until she could clasp the back of his neck, tugging until he kissed her again, this time taking it deeper. Breaking the kiss after a moment, she leaned far enough back to slide her other hand between them to wrap her fingers around his thickened shaft, slowly pumping up and down.

"Christ," he hissed, his almost clear eyes watching her work him over with an intensity that left her panting.

Though he was enthralled with the show, his hands were

busy slipping over her slick skin, pinching her nipples until she whimpered, running over her sides and stomach, to her back, and massaging her ass.

Her rhythm faltered when he slipped his fingers between her thighs, caressing her everywhere but where she needed it.

"Dagr," she pleaded, rotating her hips in the hopes of making him touch her.

"What do you need, baby?" She was glad to hear how hoarse he sounded and feel that his hips weren't immobile either.

"Stop teasing me," she growled.

He chuckled but complied, pressing two fingers deep inside her, keeping the same excruciatingly slow pace that she'd been subjecting him to.

"That's right, Dag, yes," she hissed. She picked her pace up as his own increased. She wished that all the mirrors weren't covered in steam so she could see how they looked together.

He grunted when he removed his fingers, as if it pained him to leave her body, and though she hated the loss, he wasn't done playing with her yet. He ran his hands down her slick sides until he could clasp one of her thighs to lift her leg to the position they both needed. "Dag," she moaned as he slid all the way in. As he rocked into her, pressure built until she was screaming his name. Two more strokes and her name ripped from his mouth as her release forced his own.

Misty heat still sprayed their lax bodies as they held on to each other. They rested their foreheads together while dragging in ragged breaths.

Dagr chuckled against her mouth, saying, "Life moves on, I guess."

Bébhinn pecked his cheek, chuckling in return. "It does, and thank God for that. I love you."

"I love you. Let's go to bed. We have the rest of our lives to plan when we wake up."

*fifty-eight*

## DAGR

IT HAD BEEN ALMOST two weeks since Todd had been arrested, and one day since Bran, Patrick, and his dad's DNA results arrived. His dad was to arrive momentarily to open the results, though he wasn't happy about it.

"Your dad still throwing a mantrum at having to be social?" Bébhinn asked him, while they all loitered by the downstairs bar.

"Dad's life is one long miniseries of mantrums," he sighed before grinning at his girlfriend. Soon to be something more if he had his way.

He'd been working on finalizing the turnover of Lee's law firm. There was a long way to go before it was sealed and delivered. Lee had leased a historic four-story building for his firm. Dagr was thrilled that the owner was open to selling. He wasn't interested in anything that wasn't permanent.

He and Bébhinn decided that remodeling the top two floors would work perfectly for their new home. There was a separate, private entry in the back to reach the upper floors, private parking, and a small back garden for entertaining or for children to play in.

Bébhinn said the last with a twinkle in her eye that just about took his legs out. It also made him want to drag her into the nearest dark closet and have his way with her.

The whole crew had met at O'Faolain's because they were flying out as soon as breakfast ended. Their Colorado trip was about to commence, and even he admitted excitement about the holiday.

His dad had a meeting with investors in London, which would probably end up in an argument without Dagr's mediation, and then his father would resort to funneling his own money into the reserve.

MacGregor called that morning to let them know that Mr. Todd's hearing wouldn't be for at least three months as the Gardaí went through the years of tapes. They believed there were three women besides Bébhinn. Two of them wanted to press charges as well. The first was a woman Todd had gone to high school with. He had mainly taken pictures of her and stolen things from her bedroom, which he still had in a box with her name on it.

To their knowledge, he'd never physically assaulted anyone, but the possible intent was present. They would not be charging him as mentally insane. He would be forced to attend trial as any other criminal.

Bébhinn's presence at the trial would hopefully be little to none. Dagr'd thought she might be more upset by the whole thing, but she was more relieved for herself and any other women he might have eventually set his sights on.

"Ready to meet big brother?" Mags loudly asked Bran and Patrick, much to everyone's amusement.

The thunderclouds riding her brothers' shoulders for days since they'd been strong-armed into taking DNA tests were testing all the women's patience. She thought it would be amazing to find a missing brother.

Rowan had explained to her daughter that she believed they were being shitheads because if Dagr's dad were their brother, it would be a massive shift in the family. A change that their father, Hugh, wasn't there to guide them through. Bébhinn was immediately contrite for not understanding where their antics had stemmed from.

Dagr wasn't worried. The O'Faolains might be fierce, but they were also fair, and his father wasn't a man easily cowed.

He grinned when he saw Blair take a step forward to gain the group's attention. She signed, "Please promise, Bébhinn, that you'll not call your boyfriend's dad 'Brother.'"

That comment had everyone breaking out in guffaws. Bébhinn signed back, and it didn't need interpretation since it was only her middle finger saluting her friend.

At the sound of the bell and brief knock, silence descended. Patrick nodded to Dagr to answer, anticipating that his father would be more comfortable with his son opening things up.

Bébhinn patted his butt and whispered loud enough for the room to hear. "Life's too short for normal. I always wanted another brother. Older and better than the other two."

Dagr grinned at Bébhinn stirring the pot.

# fifty-nine

## BÉBHINN

"WATCH IT, SIS," Bran warned.

"Behave, brat," Patrick growled.

Bébhinn watched as Dagr opened the door for Ulf Griffiths. She'd met Dagr's father before, so his appearance wasn't a shock to her, but for the family... The collective inhalation of disbelief was hilarious. She had to admit, she'd blown off the similarities to her brothers, but watching an older version walk through the door was breath-stealing.

Ulf was big, good-looking, with a permanent sneer on his full lips. The man could still be a model if he could speak to anyone without pissing them off first.

Where her brothers had golden skin like their father and dark to amber eyes, Ulf had pale skin and paler eyes. Matched with their signature white hair, it was damn eerie. Then add Daniel and Jonathan, who were their father's mini-mes, and Dagr, who was Ulf's younger doppelganger. It was a lot.

If the DNA proved a match, she'd have to give it to Helen

Lowell. The woman clearly carried a Titan's strength of DNA sharing.

She stepped forward and shook Ulf's hand. "I'm so glad you could make it."

"As if I had a choice," was his response, earning snickers from the crowd.

Dagr thankfully took over. "Dad, let me introduce everyone."

Bébhinn thought she heard the older Griffiths mumble, "If you must."

The introductions took an inordinate amount of time, what with the side explanations of family connections, including those of her friends.

At the end, his only response was, "Christ, okay then."

Ulf laid a large manilla envelope he'd brought on the bar top, at a loss as to how to proceed. Thankfully, Bran took mercy on the man. Clearing his throat, he asked, "A drink before we find out if we're family?"

"We're family regardless, what with Dagr and Bébhinn," Raven said, smiling at Rowan and River, who both smiled back. Well, River did. Bébhinn's mom stayed stoically blank-faced through it all. She probably was missing her husband something fierce.

"Absolut, ice, and lime," Ulf practically growled, his patience for family niceties hitting its limit.

Once everyone had drinks, an uncomfortable silence spread across the room like the plague. Dagr looked at Bébhinn with wide eyes, and she knew she needed to do something. "Let's get to the result then, Mr. Griffiths."

"Ulf," he corrected. "You've made my son happy. I think that deserves first names."

She nodded, fighting a sudden surge of emotion. She looked

to her mother, who was blinking rapidly herself. She only nodded.

"We'll either be celebrating a new member of the family or making toasts to having an amazing holiday in Colorado." Bébhinn took a sip of her Three Wolves in the hopes that she might stop rambling.

Bran and Patrick moved around to stand on either side of Ulf—which was mind-blowing to look at—and waited for Ulf to open the large envelope.

Ulf took a gorgeously ornate pocketknife from his jeans pocket and slit the envelope's top. When he pulled the results out and laid them flat for him, Bran, and Patrick to view, Bébhinn swore no one breathed.

The three men didn't speak. Ulf turned and looked from Bran to Patrick and back again. Her brothers looked at Ulf.

"There are three of us, then," Patrick finally broke the silence, his voice reflecting the wonder in his statement.

"You're our older brother," Bran finally choked out.

Ulf's face didn't give anything away. Their audience was shocked when he placed one hand on Bran's forearm and the other on Patrick's.

"Oldest and best. Nice to meet you, brothers. I hear our mum's a right bitch."

_sixty_

CIAR

THEY WERE all on the jet Dagr had chartered, headed to Colorado. They were also on their way to a congratulatory drunk in honor of the O'Faolain's newest family members, which was a total mind fuck.

Ulf had agreed to stay with his new-found brothers and their wives, and Rowan, of course, while the younger crowd started their trip across the ocean.

Ciar wanted to relax like everyone else seemed able to do, but the tension in his neck held the premonition of a migraine.

His boss sent him a text before boarding. He was to go to London the moment he stepped foot back in Europe. His boss, Anders, wasn't one for dramatics, so Ciar's head was spinning over possibilities.

Ciar got paid an extraordinary salary to put out fires in the real estate world, not start them. He could think of nothing. _Damn it._ He huffed, ignoring the animated conversations around him, concentrating on sipping his iced vodka instead of everyone else's preferred whiskey. He blamed his Russian mother. May she not rest in peace.

He felt eyes on him. Gray eyes.

He glanced up and met Gray MacGregor's steady gaze. She had been avoiding Ciar since he'd managed to screw things up so royally between them. She wouldn't listen to him. She wouldn't forgive him.

With good reason.

His stare didn't waver until Mags said something to her friend, ending their standoff.

He shouldn't even allow his thoughts to stray toward that woman, and yet his every thought starred the leggy blonde.

He squeezed the back of his neck in frustration, their gazes clashing once again. When she raised her brow in haughty question, he couldn't help the smirk that twisted his top lip.

She rolled her eyes and went back to looking at pictures of Dagr's cabin. Ciar tipped his head back and forced his muscles to release one by one.

Gray had always gotten under his skin.

Always.

**Irish Wolves Legacy**

Irish Goodbye

Irish Breath

**The Scottish Lions**

Josephine

Catriona

Mirren

**The Irish Wolves Trilogy**

Raven

River

Rowan

# *about the author*

Anne Gregor has a Master of Arts in History with a Civil War emphasis. For her thesis, she focused on Irish immigrants working the transcontinental railroad across America, specifically those who settled in Oklahoma amongst Native Americans. A love for research turned into a love for fictional writing, and soon, every old document Anne studied became the premise for a novel. Though Oklahoma remains near and dear to her heart as she lives on Grand Lake O' the Cherokees, she enjoys traveling the world with her characters. **Anne is the author of three contemporary romance series, The Irish Wolves, The Scottish Lions, and Irish Wolves Legacy.**

A small press bound by the belief that every voice matters.

Sign up for our newsletter to learn about new releases and more.
https://oliver-heberbooks.com/subscribe/

Follow us on social media:

facebook.com/oliverheberbooks
instagram.com/oliverheberbooks
amazon.com/oliverheberbooks
youtube.com/@OliverHeberBooksPublisher

www.ingramcontent.com/pod-product-compliance
Lightning Source LLC
Chambersburg PA
CBHW020244010826
48973CB00006B/1643